A VERY MERRY MURDER

KATE WELLS

Boldwood

First published in Great Britain in 2025 by Boldwood Books Ltd.

Copyright © Kate Wells, 2025

Cover Design by Head Design Ltd

Cover Images: Alamy and iStock

The moral right of Kate Wells to be identified as the author of this work has been asserted in accordance with the Copyright, Designs and Patents Act 1988.

All rights reserved. No part of this book may be reproduced in any form or by any electronic or mechanical means, including information storage and retrieval systems, without written permission from the author, except for the use of brief quotations in a book review. This book is a work of fiction and, except in the case of historical fact, any resemblance to actual persons, living or dead, is purely coincidental.

Every effort has been made to obtain the necessary permissions with reference to copyright material, both illustrative and quoted. We apologise for any omissions in this respect and will be pleased to make the appropriate acknowledgements in any future edition.

A CIP catalogue record for this book is available from the British Library.

Paperback ISBN 978-1-83678-147-9

Large Print ISBN 978-1-83678-146-2

Hardback ISBN 978-1-83678-145-5

Trade Paperback ISBN 978-1-80635-307-1

Ebook ISBN 978-1-83678-148-6

Kindle ISBN 978-1-83678-149-3

Audio CD ISBN 978-1-83678-140-0

MP3 CD ISBN 978-1-83678-141-7

Digital audio download ISBN 978-1-83678-144-8

This book is printed on certified sustainable paper. Boldwood Books is dedicated to putting sustainability at the heart of our business. For more information please visit https://www.boldwoodbooks.com/about-us/sustainability/

Boldwood Books Ltd, 23 Bowerdean Street, London, SW6 3TN

www.boldwoodbooks.com

*For Fi, who gave me the idea and loves Christmas as much as I do.
And for the choir of St Andrew's, Caversham, whom I will miss more
than they know.*

1

The quiet of the early morning, when a large part of the world outside was still sleeping, was the best part of the day for Jude Gray. She liked making a head start before everything became too cluttered and her time and attention were demanded from all directions.

It was the first day of December and bitterly cold as Jude crossed the dark yard with her two loyal collies, Pip and Alfie. Jude had a fleece headband on under her hat and extra thermals below her winter outer layers but she still felt the chill. By the light of her head torch, she began to pull bales of hay from the stack in the barn and throw them into the quad bike's trailer, feeling the physicality of the job start to warm her up. The early hour gave her time to think and there was plenty to think about with only twenty-four days left until Christmas and only twenty-seven until the wedding of her sister, Lucy.

Both occasions were something to celebrate and look forward to, yet both still needed an awful lot of planning and preparation. And, as if that wasn't enough to be getting on with, she'd somehow agreed to play host to an entire filming crew for the next three weeks.

'It'll all be fine,' she said aloud, filling the air with a thick cloud of warm breath. 'Just take one step at a time.'

This had always been her coping mechanism when things got tough.

Left foot, right foot. One after the other. Just keep going.

It had helped enormously when her husband had died, leaving her to run the farm as a young widow. And in the years since, Jude had relied on her gumption and ability to push onwards when tackling the challenges, big and small, that life had thrown her way.

Once the trailer was loaded, she jumped onto the seat of the quad and set off across the yard with Pip and Alfie running beside her. It was still dark but the sky held the first promise of a new day as she stopped to open the gate into the bottom field. Jude's boots crunched through the thick frost and she could feel the solidity of the frozen mud below.

The sheep didn't mind the cold. Malvern Farm had a large flock of Cheviots, which were a hardy hill breed that had adapted well to colder, more exposed climates. They also had a field of Suffolks, lowland sheep with shorter fleeces who weren't quite as happy when the temperatures dipped too far below freezing but who found shelter under the trees and against the hedges.

Being December, the ewes were a couple of months into their pregnancies, which meant it was even more important to keep them well fed. They were all very happy to see Jude as she pulled up at the first row of hayracks.

Pip and Alfie knew what their job was and they kept the greedy animals away whilst Jude filled the troughs with sheep nuts and put fresh hay out for them. Once breakfast had been served, she called the dogs to her and the sheep surged forward to get their share of the food. For them it was first come, first served until you got pushed out of the way by another hungry customer and had to reclaim your place at the buffet.

The water trough had frozen over so Jude used a mallet to break the ice before moving on. She went from field to field, the headlights of the quad guiding her to the troughs until the new sun, still hidden by the hills, began to light the sky above the peaks with a spectacular display of pinks and lavenders.

'Red sky at night, shepherds' delight,' Jude said to the dogs. 'Red sky in the morning, shepherds take warning.'

The ancient country rhyme was a reminder that a beautiful, early winter sky such as this meant they were in for a cold day.

In the last field, Jude found she wasn't the only person to be out and about with the sunrise. A woman wrapped in an enormous white coat that made her look like a marshmallow and wearing a striped woolly hat with tasselled ear flaps was standing next to a camera on a tripod. She waved and Jude pointed the quad her way and went to meet her.

'Morning, Mary. I see it's not only farmers who like to make an early mark on the day.' Jude stepped down from the quad and nodded at the tripod. 'I bet you're getting some beautiful footage for the show.'

Mary Taper had been the first of the television crew to arrive and had been staying in one of the shepherd's huts on the farm's campsite for a few days already. Jude had given her free run of the farm and seen her out and about, filling her camera with all sorts of scenes to use as fillers for the show once it started.

'It's so beautiful,' Mary said in her soft Irish accent. 'I've taken maybe eight to ten hours' worth since I arrived here. Daft to think that probably only fifteen minutes total of that will make the cut.' She dug her hands deep into the pockets of her coat. 'Big day today. Are you regretting having us here yet?' She grinned at Jude.

'Not at all.' Jude was thinking of the money as she said this.

Three weeks of live broadcasts from her paddock every evening and days with a full crew roaming the farm wasn't exactly her idea of fun. When she'd been contacted earlier in the year by a production company responsible for the television hit *Countryside Live* to ask if they could use Malvern Farm as the base for their very first Christmas series, she'd almost said no. But, as well as the extra layer of stress and busyness, it also brought with it a much-needed cash injection for the farm's permanently wobbling coffers. The sum they disclosed was roughly the same as she'd make from the entire lambing season, once she'd taken into account the costs of rearing them, so she had no choice but to jump at it.

'It's going to be fun,' she said.

'Very diplomatic of you,' said Mary. 'I have to say, we really lucked out coming here though. It's wonderfully peaceful and, with the hills just behind, there are so many angles we can use for filming.'

Jude had lived in Malvern all her life and felt herself smile with pride at the praise being bestowed on her home. She'd grown up on the east side of the hills, which was more built up, with the two centres of Great Malvern and Malvern Link. Moving to the rural west when she'd married Adam had been a completely new way of life for her but she'd adapted quickly and now wouldn't choose any other.

'Your director didn't seem quite so enthusiastic when I took him for a look around yesterday,' said Jude.

Mary rolled her eyes. 'So, you've met Dean then.'

'Oh, yes,' said Jude. She'd taken an instant and rather out-of-character dislike to Dean Dickens, the director of *Countryside*

Live. During the tour she'd given him of the farm – her in her ancient, muck-coated farm gear and him in a pristine pair of leather yard boots and a brand-new Barbour jacket – he'd bombarded her with demands and ridiculous questions. He was the sort of man who clearly believed himself to be on a higher plane to everyone around him.

Jude had not appreciated the lascivious way he'd looked at her, nor the misogynistic quips that fell all too easily from his lips.

'Bit of advice from me...' Mary pulled a face as though someone had stuck a wheel of Stinking Bishop cheese under her nose. 'If he asks you to check facts or run through a video with him in his caravan – just say no.'

'Gotcha,' said Jude. 'I'll bear that in mind.'

'Right then, well, I'm wanting to get a little more film fodder whilst the lighting and mood of the place is so good. So I'll see you around, Jude.'

Whilst Mary went back to the tripod and her filming, Jude drove on to the empty hayracks.

Once all the sheep had been fed and she'd cast a seasoned eye over the flock to make sure there were no problems, she returned to the farmhouse to warm up with a mug of tea and a bowl of porridge.

'Happy Advent, Jude.' Noah, her soon-to-be brother-in-law, joined her in the kitchen.

Like Jude, Noah was an early riser and had already been out doing jobs around the farm. He had worked there as a teenager and risen through the ranks of farmhand to take over from his father as shepherd. When Adam had died, it was Noah who'd supported Jude and helped her make sure the farm survived. He had been her lifeline and close friend for years and when he'd fallen in love with Jude's sister it had been one of life's true happinesses.

'Morning, Noah,' Jude replied. 'Cup of coffee? I've just put the kettle on.'

Noah nodded and went to fetch a mug from the cupboard.

'When's the rest of this film crew of yours arriving then?' he asked.

Generally speaking, when anything happened on the farm, Jude and Noah took shared responsibility for it. However, when it involved something that Noah wasn't entirely convinced by, then he labelled it firmly as Jude's.

'I don't know.' Jude poured water from the old Aga kettle onto the coffee grains in Noah's mug. 'Some time this morning.'

Some of the team had arrived, Mary, Dean Dickens – the odious director – and a couple of others, but the bulk of them, including the two stars of the show, were due that day in preparation for the live filming of the first episode that evening.

'And they're here for three weeks?' Noah asked as he stirred a good glug of milk into his coffee.

'Don't worry, they'll be out of our hair by Christmas,' said Jude. 'By the time you and Lucy are walking down the aisle, you'll have forgotten they were even here.'

'Hmph.' Noah looked doubtful as he took his first sip of caffeine for the day. 'Right then, well, I'd best get on. Dad and I are moving the sheep in the far field over to the stubble turnips this morning. You all right to take a look at that hedge that needs patching?'

That was how it worked at Malvern Farm. A divvying up of jobs and something new happening every day. Never boring and always busy.

* * *

The kitchen was warm and Jude was prolonging her time in the cosiness of the family nest with another cup of tea when Sebbie, Jude's whirlwind of a nephew, ran into the room. His dressing gown was flying out behind him like a superhero cape as he whipped the collies into a frenzy of excitement. Jude's sister was a few steps behind, carrying a hairbrush.

'Whoa, slow down there, Sebbie,' said Jude as he rushed past.

'You almost knocked Aunty Judy's hot tea from her hand,' Lucy scolded.

'It's nearly Christmas!' Sebbie shouted at the top of his lungs as he picked up the Advent calendar waiting on the dresser for him.

Jude dropped a kiss on the top of his tangled curls. 'Have you seen where Clarence is hiding this morning?'

Sebbie looked around for the little toy elf dressed in red clothes with a mischievous smile painted on his face. Lucy had hidden him in the crockery cupboard the night before with just his face and hands poking around the door.

'There he is.' Sebbie dragged one of the kitchen chairs across the flagstoned floor so he could stand on it and reach the cupboard.

When he opened the door, a banner dropped down that read *HAPPY ADVENT SEBBIE*.

'He left me chocolate coins,' said Sebbie excitedly.

Lucy beamed at the response to her efforts. 'Look,' she said. 'The naughty pickle has already had a nibble of one of them.'

Jude caught her sister's eye. 'What a busy little elf,' she said. 'I wonder what other elaborate tricks he's going to get up to every single day from now until Christmas.'

Lucy crossed her eyes theatrically as they both knew her enthusiasm for Clarence would no doubt dwindle before the week was out.

'Hey, Aunty Judy,' said Sebbie. 'If we stuck Alfie the dog on a shelf do you know what he'd be?'

'No,' said Jude as she put the slices of bread she'd just cut into the Aga's toasting rack. 'Tell me.'

'He'd be Alf on a Shelf. You know, because elf and Alf only have one sound swapped.'

'That's a really good joke,' Jude said. 'Remember it to tell Noah, only you don't need to add the explanation, I think the joke does that on its own.'

2

Later that morning, with the bulk of her daily farm jobs done, Jude went up into the attic to bring down the Christmas lights. She'd leave Lucy and Sebbie to put up the inside decorations but she took a big box out into the yard. The lights were in a jumble and she cursed her January self for being so slapdash about putting them away properly. It took a while to untangle them and lay the strings of tiny bulbs out before she could start pinning them up.

Jude was up a ladder, hammering cable clips into the beams of the black and white farmhouse when Dean, the loathsome director, strolled up, causing her heart to drop.

'Morning, Jude. Are you busy?'

It was a daft question considering she had a loop of fairy lights around her neck, a hammer in her hand and two cable clips wedged between her lips, which she had to remove to answer him.

'Just getting the lights up whilst I have a rare moment of quietness.' She hoped her hint would be enough to make him go away.

It wasn't.

'Brilliant.' He took his hands out of the pockets of his jacket and banged them together to warm them up. 'It's going to be another cold one, which is great for the show. They're predicting a bit of snow too later in the week, which will look fantastic and give the programme a really festive feel. Folk do like snow at Christmas.'

'Hmm,' said Jude, thinking about the impact of a snowfall on the farm.

'Anyway, I'm here to talk to you about the horse in the field where we're filming.'

'Rodney Trotter?' Jude hadn't been best pleased when Dean had chosen her animal paddock as the best location to film live episodes of the show every evening until Christmas Eve. It was home to a lively assortment of pet animals and she wasn't entirely sure how'd they react to a film crew in their territory. So many cables and expensive bits of equipment made her edgy.

Still, it was only three weeks and the money would mean she could invest in a new quad bike which would be a godsend as the other had broken down far too many times for her liking.

'What's the problem with Rodney?' she asked.

'I've just been in there with some of the team to set up for this evening and we thought he'd make a great addition to the set, only he won't come anywhere near us. I need you to sort it.'

'Sort it?' Jude tried not to snort with laughter. 'Um, in what way would you like me to sort it?'

'Do whatever it takes to make him more... compliant.'

'I wish I could. If I had the Dr Dolittle gift of animal compliancy then I'd be the richest farmer in the world, but sadly not. They all tend to do their own thing but he might come over if you offer a piece of apple or carrot.'

'That's your job, not mine.' Dean looked at Jude as though he thought she was being deliberately difficult. 'What about the other animals?'

Jude bristled at the way he was talking to her in her own yard but she bit her anger back and thought of the new quad.

'You shouldn't have any trouble getting the Valais Blacknoses to come over – those are the sheep that look like giant teddy bears. They behave more like dogs and love human company. And there's a sheep called Pancake and a goat called Gertie who we've had for years. They're both more than happy to be petted.'

Dean looked at her thoughtfully. 'I think we can keep Gertie but the name Pancake is all wrong. We'll call him Archie.'

Jude frowned. 'She's a girl.'

'Gretel perhaps then. It goes well with Gertie.'

'She's called Pancake because she was rolled flat by her mother when she was a newborn,' Jude explained. 'It was why she ended up being petted. Perhaps that would be an interesting story for the show?'

'Good God, no.' Dean was aghast. 'I don't think our viewers would like that very much. They prefer fluffy lambs, happy stories and tiny horses. So that's what I want to give them.'

'Ah, well, in that case I'll let you get back to what you do best,' Jude said. 'I hope the animals behave for you and please remember to keep the paddock clear of anything they could eat. Gertie in particular will chew through cables if you leave them unattended.'

Jude returned her attention to the lights.

'I'll see you down there shortly,' said Dean. 'There's a good girl.'

Jude was glad she had her back to him as she closed her eyes and counted to five slowly, giving him time to leave. It was only day one and yet she was already counting down until the loathsome man left her farm.

By the time she'd finished with the lights, she was feeling decidedly jittery about her animals in the paddock. Deciding to attack any potential issues head on, she put the ladder away and crossed the yard to go and see what was happening.

Although she hadn't met anyone other than Dean and Mary, Jude had seen vehicles coming and going for the past few days. It seemed as though trailers and caravans had been parked on every spare patch of ground. She passed three next to the lambing shed which was where the wedding party would be taking place just days after the film crew left. More were parked around the pond and three enormous, shiny caravans had been driven into the top end of the campsite. There were a couple of men in boiler suits there fiddling with a large generator and laying cables out.

As Jude walked past the campsite to get to the paddock, the door to one of the caravans opened and out stepped a woman she recognised instantly. It was Annie Bird, one of the husband-and-wife team who had been presenting *Countryside Live*, as well as other popular television shows, for over a decade.

Annie Bird and Simon North were the epitome of wholesome family entertainment. For such a well-known celebrity couple, they had managed to live and work surprisingly scandal free and the nation loved them. *Countryside Live* had begun as a small-budget show on a minor channel and did exactly what the title suggested. It tracked the landscapes, plants, animals and people of rural locations across the British Isles. The format was simple: set up camp somewhere for three weeks at a time and explore everything about that area. Videos were taken during the day and a live show in the evening would talk to guests from the area and discuss any interesting points with experts.

It had become hugely popular and two series per year were aired, moving to a prime channel when viewing numbers proved its viability and success. This was the first time they were doing a Christmas special and it had already received an enormous amount of coverage on radio shows, in magazines and with copious amounts of television trailers.

The country was ready for Annie and Simon to lead them up to Christmas, but Jude was already looking forward to them leaving.

With her white-blonde hair and willowy, tall frame, Annie Bird was incredibly striking to look at and Jude tried not to stare as the presenter walked to the next caravan along and knocked on the door. It was opened by Simon North, who appeared to scowl at his wife before moving to the side to let her in. It did not seem the jovial meeting of a loving couple at all, but then they were off duty and Jude knew that everybody's lives and relationships had glitches. She herself had been blissfully married for ten years before cancer had snatched Adam away. They had been happier than anyone could have deserved to be and yet they'd still had cause to scowl at each other from time to time. Such was the nature of not just sharing a house with someone else but also sharing a job.

'Watch your back,' someone behind her warned and Jude turned to see a woman carrying a stack of boxes towards the paddock.

'Let me get the gate for you,' said Jude.

'Cheers.'

'Do you want a hand with those?' Jude asked once the gate had been opened.

'Thanks, but they're not heavy, just awkward.' The woman tried peering around the pile of boxes so she could see where she was going.

'How about I take the top two from you and then you won't end up tripping over any of the ducks or sheep?' Jude suggested.

'That would be great. I'm Robyn Porter, by the way. Show's researcher, Christmas decoration supplier and general dogsbody.'

'Jude Gray. Farmer, Christmas lights putter upper and fellow dogsbody. Nice to meet you.'

The boxes Jude took were labelled up as 'decs', leaving Robyn with the biggest one that had a picture of an ornamental deer made from little white lights.

'So this is your place,' said Robyn as they walked down through the paddock to the stable block where things were being set up.

'Yep, for better or worse,' said Jude.

'It must be a hard life, being out here every day of the year looking after your animals and the crops.'

'Some days are tougher than others,' Jude admitted. 'Generally, though, I wouldn't want to do anything else.'

Maud and Marlie, the two fluffy-fleeced Valais Blacknose ewes, came over to welcome Jude and Robyn into the paddock and check to see if they'd brought food with them. Running along behind were their two lambs, Mo and Maggie, who had grown at a rate of knots and were catching their mothers up in size. They still looked young though with softer, whiter fleeces and rangy limbs that would need another year of fattening up before they took on the sturdy appearance of the adults of the breed.

'They're adorable,' said Robyn. 'I know the viewers are going to fall for these guys. They almost don't look real.'

'They are pretty cute,' Jude agreed.

'Friendly too,' Robyn noted. 'I bet there's going to be a spike of internet searches by people tempted to get them as pets.'

'Blimey, I hope not,' said Jude. 'We have these two ewes

because someone bought them as pets and didn't know what to do with them.'

They reached the stable block where Dean was fussing over the perfect positioning of a lighting unit.

'It needs to be over to the right,' he said. 'I want to get Annie and Simon in here between the stable and this boat thing. Someone get Christmas lights in those trees behind. It's a festive special and we need to make that bloody obvious.'

'You're on the show tonight, aren't you?' Robyn said.

'Oh, no,' said Jude firmly. 'I was asked but I'm really not the right person to be on camera, especially live.' Even the thought of it made her feel nauseous.

Robyn put the box down on the cobbles and took her phone from the back pocket of her jeans. 'Does Dean know you're not going on?' she asked as she tapped at the screen. 'It's just I'm sure you are on the guest schedule for the opening show. Yes, there you are. Jude Gray, farmer, Saturday the first of December.'

'Definitely not.' Jude shook her head emphatically. 'Trust me, it would ruin your show.'

'What would?' Dean came over to join them.

'Jude was just saying that she hasn't agreed to be on the show this evening and yet you've still got her on the schedule,' Robyn explained.

'Yeah, it's in the contract. Check the details.'

'What?' Jude felt the nausea grow.

'The contract you signed when we booked Malvern Farm.' Dean was distracted by what was happening behind them with the lighting. 'Not there,' he shouted. 'Over there.'

'I didn't see anything about that in the contract.' It had been a lengthy document written with a ridiculous amount of jargon which, in hindsight, Jude wished she'd given more than a cursory skim read.

'Well, it's there,' said Dean. 'You'll be fine. Annie and Simon have been doing this for years, they'll make it easy. Robyn, go and introduce them to Jude. Oh, and see if you can get hold of some haybales for them to sit on. I think it would look nicer than the chairs.'

Dean strode off and Jude turned to Robyn. 'I can't do it,' she said. 'There's no way I'm going on national television, I won't know what to say and I'll just be a stuttering mess. Nobody wants to watch that.'

'I'm sorry, Jude, but Dean's sneaky like that. If it's in your contract then you're going to have to do it or you'll be in breach and you won't get paid.' Robyn was business-like and unsympathetic. 'Right, let's go and find the stars of the show.'

Robyn strode ahead and Jude lagged behind a little, texting her sister as she went.

> Holy shit. It looks like I'm going to be on the telly tonight.

She followed this with emojis of a face blue with fright and another green from nausea.

3

Annie Bird and Simon North were together when Robyn took Jude to meet them at the campsite. Jude saw that each caravan had a name plate on the front, one for Dean Dickens, one for Annie and one for Simon. She wondered why the husband-and-wife team needed separate caravans when each one looked big enough to fit both of her shepherd's huts inside and maybe a bell tent too.

'Come on in,' said Simon once Robyn had tracked them down to his caravan and introduced them. His smile was as welcoming and warm in real life as it appeared on screen.

Jude stepped up into the caravan, which was airy and spacious with a dressing table, a huge television and an L-shaped sofa covered in cushions. There was a chrome and beech kitchenette to one side and two doors that Jude assumed led to the bedroom and bathroom.

'Wow,' she said. 'This is an amazing set-up.'

'We do get treated well when we're on location,' said Annie, who was every bit as smiley as her husband. 'Can I offer you something to drink?' She took a wooden box from a shelf in the kitchen and opened it to reveal an array of little coloured pods which Jude assumed fitted in the funky coffee machine sitting on the worktop.

'Can't stop,' said Robyn. 'It's a busy day for me. Always so much to do for a lowly researcher.'

She looked pointedly at Annie, who held her gaze only for a fraction of second before blinking and turning to Jude.

'You'll have one, won't you, Jude?' Annie asked. 'It would be good to get to know you a little if we're going to be clogging up your farm for the next three weeks or so.'

'That would be lovely,' said Jude. 'Just a coffee, please.'

Robyn left the caravan and closed the door behind her, leaving Jude with the distinct impression that there had been a bristling animosity between the two women.

'It looks like we've got coffee from Italy, Nicaragua, India, Colombia, or some of these have flavours if you want caramel, vanilla, there's even chocolate croissant flavour.'

Jude laughed at the comical expression Annie pulled to show what she thought of a coffee designed to taste like a breakfast pastry. 'I don't know,' she said. 'I'm not used to so much choice. In our kitchen it's instant from a jar except on Sundays when we brew up a pot of real coffee.'

'I sometimes think that life was so much easier before we all got given so many extra decisions to make,' said Simon. 'You look like the kind of person who could be a bit of a daredevil, Jude.' He grinned widely at her and Jude could see why he was so popular with the daytime-telly-watching demographic. 'How about we get spicy and I just throw caution to the wind and pick a random pod?'

It was his turn to make Jude laugh and she nodded. 'That sounds exciting,' she said. 'Thank you.'

'Come and sit with me, Jude,' said Annie. 'Tell me all about you and your beautiful home whilst Simon makes us a coffee.'

Jude followed her to the sizeable sofa and, as she sat down, found it was ridiculously comfortable: a far cry from the baggy old sack of horsehair she was used to in the farmhouse sitting room.

'I saw your little boy earlier,' said Annie. 'He looked a real cutie. Do you have just the one child?'

'Ah, no, he's not mine,' said Jude. 'My sister and her family live with me.'

Annie looked aghast, as though worried she'd just made a terrible faux pas, and Jude was quick to reassure her.

'You're right, he is an absolute cutie. Hard work too though, but I get to be the favourite aunty and then hand him back to his mother.'

'Sometimes the best way,' said Annie. 'Simon and I decided not to have any of our own but I do like borrowing other people's.'

She glanced at Simon and Jude thought she saw the hint of a furrowed brow as he put a pod into the coffee machine. He pushed a button which triggered a whirring sound and a delicious smell soon followed.

'It really is a wonderful spot here,' said Annie. 'Not our first trip to Malvern though, is it, darling?'

'No.' Any trace of a frown was gone as he turned to look at them. 'We did an event at the theatre in Great Malvern when we toured for the book launch a few years ago and stayed a couple of extra days after the show so that we could walk up on the hills.'

Simon brought over three mugs of coffee and passed two of them to Jude and Annie before sitting down with his own. 'I remember being right at the top and watching this enormous rain cloud roll in, then hoping we would make it back down to the car before it broke.'

'Gosh, we were soaked through.' Annie laid her hand on Simon's knee and he put his on top. It was a gesture of such togetherness that Jude knew her initial instinct when she'd seen them outside the caravan had been wrong.

'Luckily the hotel had decent towels.'

The two of them laughed and for a moment it was as though Jude was watching them on the television. Was there the slightest hint of them putting on a show for her? She supposed it didn't really matter.

'I hope you get the chance to go back up whilst you're here,' she said. 'Enjoy the hills in all their glory when the sun is shining.'

'We've got some day-filming up there tomorrow, I think.' Annie looked to Simon for confirmation.

'That's right,' he said. 'And I'm sure it won't be the only time Dean wants to capture the hills. He seems to think there's snow coming and I bet it will look spectacular up there if it does.'

'It is magical,' said Jude. 'Some people say that was where C. S. Lewis got his inspiration from for Narnia. There's an old gas lamp up there which looks as though it came straight out of *The Lion, the Witch and the Wardrobe.*'

Annie sat up and looked at Simon. 'We could use that in the show,' she said. 'Talk about the C. S. Lewis link to the area. I'll ask Dean to get Robyn on the case and see what she can dig out.'

'I love the thought of him walking up there with Tolkien and perhaps bumping into Edward Elgar or George Bernard Shaw on one of the paths,' said Jude.

Annie looked suitably impressed at the rich creative history of the Malverns.

'I think we should sack Robyn and employ Jude as chief

researcher.' Annie laughed to show that she spoke in jest and yet Jude sensed the same dislike she'd noted when Robyn had been so quick to leave the caravan.

'I'm sure she's already got all of this covered,' said Jude. 'You seem to have a really good team around you.'

'We certainly do.' Simon looked adoringly at his wife. 'We've always been lucky.'

'And now we have Jude.' Annie clapped her hands together as though this was the best news she'd had all morning. 'You're our first guest of the series, I hear. That's fantastic.'

Jude set her mug back on the table, deciding that full disclosure was the way to go. 'I'm absolutely terrified. I didn't know I'd signed up for this and... well, I'm really not sure I'm made for television.'

'Nonsense,' said Annie kindly. 'You'll be wonderful. All you have to do is pretend that Mary, that's our camera operator, isn't there. I do it all the time.'

She made it sound so easy but Jude couldn't imagine being able to ignore anyone who was poking a television camera in her face.

Annie and Simon talked through everything that Jude should expect from her debut TV appearance. By the time she left their caravan – with a head full of tips and a promise that she would only be on screen for a few minutes – she felt slightly less nauseous about it.

'All okay?' Robyn asked, joining her as she left the campsite and crossed the driveway to the pond.

'I think so,' said Jude. 'Although I don't really have much of a choice.'

Robyn looked at her disdainfully. 'Not really.'

She made Jude feel rather pathetic. She was a strong and capable woman who had dealt with plenty of real issues in her life so why did the thought of sitting having a chat with two very affable people fill her with so much dread?

Jude's phone pinged then which was a welcome distraction from Robyn's stare. She pulled it from her pocket and saw a text message from Lucy.

> Just bumped into Marco in the village. He says he has plenty of mistletoe in the apple trees at the end of his garden if we want it for the wedding. Said I'd ask you first as I know you were asking around.

At the sight of Marco's name, Jude's temperature rose a couple of degrees in the way it always did when she thought about the man she'd let slip away. Theirs had been a tale of bad-timings and not-quites and now he was happily ensconced in a relationship with his next-door neighbour, Clara. Jude didn't know whether the fact she had always liked Clara and they'd been friends before Marco started dating her made things better or worse. It certainly made them tricky.

JUDE
> Sorry, completely forgot about the mistletoe. If Marco has some then go for it.

LUCY
> OK. He said hi BTW. He's looking forward to tuning in this evening.

The nausea that Annie and Simon had managed to alleviate in Jude rushed back with full force at the thought of Marco Ricci sitting in front of his telly watching her mess things up royally in a live broadcast. Even worse, in Jude's mind, he'd almost certainly be sitting there with Clara, laughing at her or, worse still, cringing in pity as she fluffed every part of her side of the interview.

'Ah, here's the rest of the live team, Mary and Gabe,' said Robyn.

Two people were coming out of the largest trailer, parked between the pond and the shed. Mary had swapped her thick winter clothes for tight jeans and a bomber jacket and, without her woolly hat on, her pale pink hair fluffed out around her face in an elfish cut. Her companion was carrying a rather large furry boom with him.

'You two aren't paid to take so many breaks!' Robyn said with a sternness that Jude thought was a little over-egged. 'I've got a meeting with Dean but I need to find that waste of space work experience prat first. He ballsed up the catering order. Have either of you seen him?'

'Sorry, no,' said Gabe, the soundman.

'Useless,' Robyn muttered as she stalked off towards the paddock.

Gabe and Mary rolled their eyes at each other and Jude sensed that this was usual behaviour from the woman who seemed to be acting as their boss.

'Chris is in the chillout trailer,' Gabe whispered when Robyn was out of earshot. 'But there's no way I'm dobbing him in when Robyn's on the warpath.'

'She gives him way too much to do seeing as he's only here on work experience,' Mary explained to Jude. 'Unpaid too. Anyway, how's it going, Jude? You look anxious.'

Part of the reason for this was definitely down to Lucy planting Marco Ricci in the front of Jude's mind, but she wasn't going to admit this.

'I'm being interviewed on the show tonight and apparently I don't have any choice in the matter,' she said.

'Dean got to you, did he?' the soundman asked. He juggled the equipment he was carrying to free a hand for Jude to shake. 'I'm Gabe, by the way.'

'Hi,' said Jude as she shook his hand. 'Yeah, you could say that. But I've just been chatting to Annie and Simon, who seem very nice.'

'Did they give you any good advice?' Gabe asked.

Jude smiled and looked at Mary. 'Annie said I should just pretend you're not there.'

Mary let out a loud snort of laughter. 'She said that? Well, I suppose she's had a lot of practice.'

Jude had the horrible feeling she may just have inadvertently offended Mary. 'Oh, no, she just meant that I should imagine there's no camera and we're just having an informal chat.'

'I know what she meant.' Mary raised her eyebrows. 'Seriously though, Jude. You'll be fine and it will be over with before you know it.'

* * *

When Jude told Lucy how worried she was about being live on primetime television she was hugely unsympathetic to the point where laughter caused tears to form in the corners of her eyes.

'Thanks for the support,' said Jude as she tried to scrub the mud off the slightly better of her coats in preparation for the event.

'I'm sorry, Judy.' Lucy wiped her eyes on the sleeve of her hoodie. 'It's just that I remember watching you in that Shakespeare thing you did when Dad sent us to that horrendous camp one summer.'

'Oh God, *The Tempest*.' Jude cringed at the memory. She hadn't been given a large part thankfully, but the arty producer had adapted the story to make sure everyone in the group had lines to deliver. 'I hated it so much.'

'Your starring role, or the summer of *ditch-your-kids-at-camp* in general?' Lucy asked.

'Both,' said Jude emphatically. 'I remember feeling so cheated because I didn't get to spend the summer properly with you like usual.'

Jude's father had left her mother when Jude was only five in order to move in with his pregnant girlfriend. Jude couldn't remember being all that bothered when he left but she could remember the total adoration she'd felt when meeting her little baby sister for the first time. Perhaps their relationship had always been so strong because as children, they only saw each other for the odd weekend and when Jude's mother went away every summer for a couple of weeks. Those weeks were short but precious to both girls so when their father decided to book them into different age groups of a holiday club one year, they were furious.

'I remember being so proud when you came on the stage,' Lucy said. 'All dressed up in some weird costume made from rags and rope for some reason. And then you opened your mouth to deliver your first line and...'

'Don't!' Jude felt her cheeks burning at the memory. She'd stood at the front of the stage, staring at the audience with a face like a blobfish, not one single word forming in her mind. 'You're not helping.'

'Sorry, Jude.' Lucy came up behind her and put an arm around her shoulder. 'That was years ago and you had no idea what you were supposed to be doing. I'm sure when they start asking you about farming, they're going to struggle to get you to shut up!'

Jude wasn't sure which was worse and she cringed inwardly at the thought of Marco witnessing the whole sorry thing from the comfort of his cosy sitting room.

'Talking of Dad,' said Jude, quickly changing the subject, 'have you decided whether you want to invite him to the wedding or not?'

'I feel like I probably should.' Lucy wrinkled her nose. Their father was a difficult and often obnoxious man and Jude knew Lucy didn't want him to sour her big day.

Jude put the coat she was still scrubbing down and turned to face her sister. 'It's your wedding, Lou-Lou. Yours, Noah's and Sebbie's. Nobody else gets to say how you do things and who you invite. Okay?'

'Okay.' Lucy hugged her. 'On that note, I have something I want to ask you.'

She pulled away and looked at Jude. 'I know you're already my maid of honour, which is a highly important job.'

'Second only to the bride, I believe,' said Jude.

'Of course. It's just that I wondered if, instead of walking behind me like some sort of lady in waiting or something, could you walk next to me? It might be old-fashioned and not really me at all, I'm not anybody's to give away like a hand-me-down jumper. But just this once I thought I'd nudge towards tradition and I would love it if you could be there to do it. To give me away.'

Both girls had tears in their eyes as they hugged each other and Jude, of course, agreed to her new role with pride.

'Why are you crying?' Sebbie asked when he walked into the kitchen casually wearing a cardboard box decorated with green crayon scribbles on his head.

'We're just happy because Aunty Judy has said she'll give me away at the wedding,' said Lucy.

'Who is she giving you to?' Sebbie sounded confused but his expression was hidden by the box.

'She's not really giving me to anyone,' said Lucy.

'But you just said...'

'It's just a phrase that means she's happy with me marrying Noah.'

'Oh,' said Sebbie. 'Okay. Can I have a snack, please?'

Jude and Lucy grinned at each other and then Lucy went to cut an apple up for Sebbie. Jude held her coat up to check if the stain had been reduced enough to pass as just a shadow, if it was picked up on television at all.

'Haven't you got anything a bit smarter to wear than that?' Lucy asked.

'It's going to be freezing out there,' said Jude. 'Besides, they told me to wear authentic clothing and not dress up.'

'Please tell me you're at least going to brush your hair?'

'Your mummy is so rude to me,' said Jude.

'If you like, you can borrow my Buzz Lightyear helmet,' said Sebbie, taking the box off his head and passing it to Jude.

'That's a very kind thought but I think I'll just go with my new bobble hat with the sheep on it.'

4

If Jude had thought she'd been nervous as she got herself ready, that was nothing to the butterflies, moths and any number of other insects skittering around her stomach as she let Gabe wire a mic to her down in the paddock that evening. At least her family had listened when she forbade them to come and watch filming, so that was one less thing to worry about.

She was standing by the stables where a Christmas tree had been set up behind three haybales. Jude had completely forgotten to bring down some straw but it looked as though someone had helped themselves from her precious supply of animal food instead. Robyn was flapping a clipboard at Pancake and Gertie, who were busy trying to nibble the set, but Jude knew she was fighting a losing battle with those two. Bedding straw would have been fine but the hay that had been set out was like putting Sebbie in front of a Chocolate Orange and telling him not to touch it. On the plus side, Rodney Trotter was also looking interested so might make the starring appearance that Dean had wanted, even if it was just to eat the props.

Jude wasn't sure what her animals were making of the whole

thing. The Indian Runner ducks were certainly confused as they would usually have been locked into their stable for the night before it got dark. Dean had insisted he wanted them to be out, preferably bobbing about peacefully in the old open canoe that Noah had turned into a mini pond for them, something they had no intention of complying with.

It did look pretty though. As well as the Christmas tree, lights had been strung in the winter-stripped sycamores at the edge of the paddock and the electrics team had rigged up subtle spotlights that bathed the haybales where the presenters would sit in golden pools.

A large van emblazoned with the *Countryside Live* logo was parked next to the stable block and through the open door, Jude could see a highly complex set-up of screens, switches and dials. This only served to feed her fear and her heart was beating fast and strong.

Gabe tapped the top of the mic he'd clipped to the collar of Jude's coat and pulled a pair of mighty headphones from around his neck onto his ears. 'Could you say something, Jude?'

'What would you like me to say?'

'That's it.' He gave a thumbs up, which Jude took to mean he was satisfied.

'How are you feeling?' Mary asked. She had dressed for warmth again in her marshmallow coat and the hat with tassels over the ears.

'Nervous as hell,' said Jude.

'Remember that the secret is to forget about Mary,' Annie said as she and Simon came over together. They looked ridiculously chic and gorgeous in their winter wear as though they were about to hit the slopes of some exclusive French resort. 'Lovely as she is, just pretend she isn't there.'

Annie smiled at the camera operator and was rewarded with

what looked very much like Mary had flipped her the bird and then disguised it as an itch to the side of her nose.

'Oh!' Annie had obviously seen it too and looked surprised. She glanced at her husband for support but he was watching Robyn trying to keep Gertie away from the haybales.

He chuckled. 'Do you think we'll have anything left to sit on by the time we're ready to shoot?'

'I'll go over and see if I can help,' said Jude. 'If you've finished with me, Gabe?'

'Hang on,' said the soundman. He fiddled with the box attached to the waist band of Jude's jeans – after what her sister had said, Jude had put on the nicest pair she owned. 'Okay. Good to go.'

Pancake and Gertie had been joined by the four woolly Valais Blacknoses and great chunks of hay were being pulled from the bales now. Jude would have to make sure she took the hay away as soon as filming was over. She sat down next to her animals. Being with them calmed her a little and she tried really hard not to think of Marco, Clara, the rest of Malvern and much further beyond watching her. She dug her fingers into Pancake's warm fleece and felt the movement of the sheep's chewing muscles as the hay was sent down to the first of the four sections of her stomach.

'Is there anything we can do to stop them?' Robyn asked.

'Not much, I'm afraid unless you take the hay away from them,' said Jude. 'I did try telling Dean that my animals are all greedy buggers. All I can suggest is that we throw some apple slices and carrot around before filming starts and that should keep them occupied elsewhere for a bit.'

'We don't have time to swap the set over now.' Robyn cast her gaze around the filming area until it fell on a young-looking, clearly very junior member of the team. 'You, Dev, Div, Dave, whatever your name is. Go and find us some apples and carrots.'

The young man's already anxious face took on the appearance of a cartoon mouse confronted by a tooth-baring wildcat. 'Where from?' he stuttered.

'I haven't got time to think of the details, that's why I've told you to do it,' Robyn barked. 'Go, go, go!'

Jude had already pinned the fierce woman as someone who had a tendency to demand rather than ask and shout rather than listen and she felt instantly sorry for Dev/Dave.

'Go up to the farmhouse,' she said to him kindly. 'I'll text my sister, Lucy, and tell her you're on your way so she has some ready for you. Sorry, what was your name?'

'Bav,' he said with a shrug. 'Thanks for doing that.' He looked ridiculously grateful as he ran off up the paddock.

Jude took out her phone to fire off the promised text and saw one from Marco waiting for her. It was short, intended to be supportive and yet it triggered another unwanted flush of panic.

> Good luck. I'll be watching. M x

Jude sighed deeply, filling her lungs to regain control of her breathing. Then she sent her message to Lucy and switched her phone off to ensure it didn't make any unwanted noises when the camera was rolling.

'Five-minute call.' Dean's voice boomed out of the production van as he stood at the top of the steps to demand attention. 'Annie, Simon and guest on set now, last checks and someone get those bloody animals under control.'

Jude had spent a lot of time – far too much time – in the director's company, showing him around, answering his questions and bending over backwards to accommodate his whims, so was it not a bit rude for him to address her just as *guest*?

'Carrots and apples are on their way,' said Jude.

'We don't mind the animals, do we, Simon?' Annie said as they came to take their places on the haybale buffet.

'They're being very gentle,' he agreed. 'I think they enhance the set, actually. We can work around them.'

'What do you think, Robyn?' Annie asked.

'What does my opinion matter?' Robyn snapped. 'I'm not the director, you need to ask Dean.'

Annie did not seem taken aback by the harshness in Robyn's tone and she didn't seem to notice the look of derision the researcher gave her. Jude did though and wondered why Annie was so unpopular with certain female members of the crew when she seemed so lovely.

'There should be some blankets for you all to put over your knees,' said Robyn. 'Dean thought it would add a festive touch. That work experience boy was supposed to bring them, where the hell is he?'

Robyn stormed off to find the poor unfortunate Chris who, it appeared, was in trouble again. Jude's dislike of Robyn grew and she'd have loved to have spoken up about the way she treated the younger, more junior members of the team. Bav the junior runner, Chris the work experience boy and others too. But at that moment, she was fighting her own battle against her nerves.

The animals stayed close but mostly stopped nibbling when the humans sat on their feast.

'That looks perfect,' said Mary, who was now concentrating on the image on her camera.

'Two minutes,' boomed Dean.

Jude's hands became sweaty and her mouth dry.

Annie fiddled with her earpiece and then leant over to pat

Jude on the knee. 'Couple of deep breaths,' she said. 'Just keep looking at Simon and me, and answer the questions in the same way as you did when we were having that chat in the caravan. You'll be grand. I promise.'

A churlish young man of about eighteen or nineteen came over carrying three sherpa blankets.

'Here you go,' he said as he handed them out.

'That's lovely, thank you, Chris,' said Simon.

Jude was glad to tuck one over her knees, the thinness of her jeans not proving much of a barrier against the cold.

The time ticked down and the nerves ramped up.

'Five – four – three—' Dean shouted and then signalled the two and the one silently before pointing both hands at the presenters to indicate they had gone live.

'Hello and welcome to this, our very first Christmas series of *Countryside Live*,' said Annie, grinning into Mary's camera.

'It's exciting, isn't it?' Simon smiled at his wife, who was looking as if it was Christmas morning and they were both ten years old.

Jude didn't know where to look or how her face should be fixed. Whatever she did felt wrong and she wanted nothing more than to rush off and hide in the tack room until it was all over and she could limp back to the farmhouse.

'It really is,' Annie said. 'We'll be here with you every evening until Christmas Eve and we've got so much lined up.'

'That's right,' said Simon. 'We've set up camp in a beautiful pocket of the countryside on the border of Herefordshire and Worcestershire. Malvern is best known for its stunning hills, the music of Edward Elgar, who lived in these parts, and also for the natural spring water. Over the next three weeks, we'll be talking to local historians, naturalists and people who call this land their home.'

'Today, we've been joined by Jude Gray, owner of these wonderful animals you see around us.' Annie turned her attention to Jude, who felt herself stiffen, grateful for the sheep and goat who were standing in front of her.

'Jude, thank you so much for having us in your beautiful home,' said Annie. 'Although for you, it's much more than just a home as you've been farming this land for years.'

Jude nodded, feeling all words disappear as she'd feared they would. She knew she was expected to talk about the farm here. Annie and Simon had been through this with her. Say something about how many generations of Adam's family had farmed and how she'd come to be the one now holding the reins.

What she actually said was something along the lines of, 'Mmm, yarsh.'

'Tell me who we've got here.' Simon seamlessly pulled the focus back to the animals, giving her a much easier way into the conversation.

Jude looked down into the soft face of her Golden Guernsey goat who was nudging her hand looking for food. 'This is Gertie,' she said, keeping her eyes on the animal and refusing to think about the camera. 'And this is Pancake, our pet Cheviot ewe.' She knew Dean had wanted her to call Pancake something else and it felt like a tiny act of inadvertent rebellion that she'd just dropped the sheep's real name in without thinking.

From that moment, things weren't nearly as bad as Jude had thought they might be. Annie and Simon were utter professionals and talked to her about things that they knew the audience would find interesting. Life on the farm, the need to diversify with the campsite and the petting paddock, being part of a rural community. In answering them, all thoughts of anyone out there who might be watching disappeared and she relaxed into the conversation.

Around five minutes after she'd been introduced, Simon wound the first part of the interview up and introduced a pre-recorded video clip.

'You were brilliant,' said Simon as soon as the live stream had been cut. 'A natural.'

'I'm not sure about that,' said Jude, but she did feel a lot happier now the first chunk was over.

The other live sections after that were much easier and they were soon breaking for the final video clip.

'Weather looks good tomorrow,' said Dean. 'Jude, tell your shepherds we'll record them with their dogs in the morning.'

Jude felt her eyes open wide in surprise. 'You got Noah and Frank to agree to this?'

'Just make it happen, love.' Dean waved his hand dismissively and Jude badly wanted to chuck something at him.

'I met Noah when I was filming a few days ago,' said Mary. 'He's incredibly handsome. It'll be good to get him on camera.'

'Sadly, he's already taken, Mary,' said Annie. 'Jude was telling us earlier that he's marrying her sister straight after Christmas.'

'I wasn't after him or anything,' Mary snapped. 'Jeez, I was only saying he'd look good on the camera.'

'A Christmas wedding.' Dean pushed his glasses onto the top of his head. 'Could be interesting. We'll cover the run-up. Get ready now, we're back on in two minutes. And make it festive, for God's sake. People are switching on for Christmas and we're not giving it to them. Jude, tell us about how you farm sprouts and turkeys or whatever.'

'But I don't,' said Jude.

'You've got chickens and some sort of veggies though, surely you can improvise?'

'No,' said Jude. 'It's not the same thing at all.'

Dean looked as though he was about to argue then looked at his watch and changed his mind.

'I've got gingerbread and hot chocolate for them to close the show with,' said Robyn, carrying a tray of festive snacks. 'And you can talk about what Christmas at Malvern Farm generally looks like. I've got a Christmas tree farmer booked for later this week and a local baker who makes award-winning mince pies. Don't worry, it's all in hand.'

Annie took the tray from Robyn and set it on the table in front of the haybales. 'I've been looking forward to this all evening,' she said. 'Is the gingerbread definitely peanut free?'

'Of course it is,' said Robyn.

'Live in thirty seconds,' Dean shouted. 'And make it shout Christmas, people.'

As soon as his back was turned, Annie rolled her eyes at Jude which made her smile.

'Downhill to the credits,' Annie said as she picked up one of the mugs of hot chocolate and took a sip.

The stream went live for the final section.

'It's getting chilly out here,' said Simon. 'Jude, would you like some gingerbread? I believe it was made by a local baker.'

'Thank you.' Jude leant forward and took a gingerbread man.

'Annie?' Simon looked at his wife who had gone quiet and was staring at the table in front of her with a hand at her throat. He threw the plate down onto the table and jumped to his feet.

Jude stared in horror as she saw Annie's lips and face swelling in front of her and her breathing becoming obviously more laboured. The mug of hot chocolate fell from her hand and spilled across the grass.

'She needs her EpiPen,' Simon yelled. 'Someone fetch her bag. And cut the camera.'

Robyn sprinted on, carrying a bag which she was already

digging around in. 'I can't find it in here,' she said as Simon grabbed the bag from her.

'It should be in the front pocket.' He was clearly shaking as he struggled with the zip on the bag. 'Where the hell is it?'

Jude stood up and moved out of the way to let the others have space to deal with Annie's anaphylaxis.

'She left a spare in the production van,' Gabe yelled, already running in that direction.

'It's here.' Dean waved what looked like a fat marker pen as he came out of the trailer.

Gabe snatched the EpiPen and dashed over to Annie, removing it from the container as he went.

'Someone call an ambulance,' he shouted as he thrust the device into Simon's waiting hand.

Simon slammed it into his wife's thigh.

'Will she be okay?' Gabe asked. 'Will that thing work through clothing?'

'I bloody well hope so,' said Simon.

5

Jude was surprised but hugely relieved to see how quickly the adrenaline in the EpiPen got to work. By the time the ambulance arrived, Annie was already sitting up, wrapped in all three of the sherpa blankets and sipping a glass of water.

'Do you know what triggered your reaction?' one of the paramedics asked after Annie had been given a thorough check over.

'It must have been something in the gingerbread man I ate, either that or the hot chocolate.' She glanced at Robyn.

'I swear I checked the gingerbread.' Robyn was looking understandably flustered. 'And the hot chocolate came from the machine in the chillout trailer which is nut free. I can't understand it.'

'Well, not to worry for now.' The paramedic started packing her equipment away. 'Let's get you to hospital so they can keep an eye on you and make sure there are no repercussions.'

'She won't be there for long, will she?' Dean asked. 'We've got a location shoot booked for eleven tomorrow.'

The paramedic ignored him and directed her answer at

Annie. 'You'll probably be out in a couple of hours, but they might want to keep you in overnight just to be safe.'

Annie looked across at Dean who was observing everything with his arms folded. 'I'll be back in time for the live show tomorrow then. I'm not sure if I'll be up for the day recordings though.'

'Fine,' said Dean. 'Simon will have to do those on his own. We'll also run a piece on your allergy – it might actually fall in our favour. You collapsing live on air will definitely make the headlines which means our ratings should see a big spike tomorrow. Predictions were for 5.5 million tonight, we might make 8 mill or even more tomorrow.'

Jude looked at the man incredulously. Annie would be fine but what had happened to her was frightening and dangerous. If Simon hadn't administered her EpiPen then she could have died and yet all her boss was thinking about was how many people would tune in because of it. Worse still, he was showing no sign of concern for his leading lady, just excitement about what her life-threatening condition could do to boost his ratings.

Jude watched Gabe de-mic Simon so that he could climb into the back of the ambulance and go with his wife to the hospital. The door was about to shut when Dean pushed Mary forward.

'Go with them,' he said. 'Someone get her the location camera. I want this as a feature for tomorrow's show.'

'No.' The paramedic looked at Dean as though she thought him the lowest form of arsehole, a conclusion that Jude could understand.

'What do you mean, no?'

'I mean no filming, and nobody else in the ambulance.'

Jude inwardly cheered as the paramedic slammed the door shut, instantly putting a stop to the ridiculous plan.

Dean looked furious and started bellowing at the film crew,

clearly taking his anger out on them to prove that he was still a force to be reckoned with despite them all having just seen him being dispatched by the paramedic.

As the ambulance drove off, Mary, Gabe and the team busied themselves with clearing the equipment away so it would be safe overnight from the weather and inquisitive animals.

Jude watched Robyn pick up the discarded hot chocolate mugs.

'Wait,' she said a second too late as Robyn poured them out onto the grass.

'What's the matter?' Robyn asked.

'I just thought they might want to test to see if there was anything in there that could have caused Annie's reaction.'

Robyn flicked the last drops out. 'Annie already dropped hers,' she said. 'Besides, it's the same brand we always use. If they're that bothered they can take a fresh pod and test that.'

She picked up Annie's nibbled gingerbread man. 'I'd say it's far more likely to be this.'

Jude hoped feverishly that Mavis, the local baker who'd made the gingerbread, hadn't made a mistake. Something like this could be the end of her.

Robyn exhaled loudly. 'God, this is all we need.'

Jude thought how exhausted the woman already looked and it was only day one of filming. Granted, the evening had taken a disturbing turn but the comment did not seem to fit the moment.

'Is everything okay?' she asked as she picked up the tray for Robyn to set the mugs on.

Robyn held the tip of her tongue to her lips for a second as though gathering her thoughts and preparing for the next trial. 'I'll take that,' she said, holding out her hands for the tray Jude was carrying.

Jude passed it to her and picked up the sherpa blankets. 'Where do you want these?'

'They go in the chillout trailer. Come with me.'

Both women walked out of the paddock to the enormous trailer parked next to the gate.

'It'll be unlocked,' said Robyn. 'Can you get the door?'

Jude bunched the blankets under one arm and pulled the handle of the trailer's door to open it. Then she stepped aside to let Robyn and the tray through first before following and shutting the door behind them.

'Just dump those over on one of those chairs.' Robyn nodded her head to indicate a set of four spongy chairs arranged in a group at the far end of the trailer.

'It's nice in here,' said Jude and she did as Robyn requested.

'It can get claustrophobic when it's busy.' Robyn set the tray down on a draining board next to a little stainless-steel sink. 'We always film for just over three weeks and by the end, I'm so ready to get back home to some peace and quiet.'

'I can imagine,' said Jude.

She walked over to join Robyn in the area of the trailer that had been set up as a mini kitchen.

'Is this the machine where Annie's hot chocolate was made?'

The drinks machine didn't look as fancy as the one in Annie and Simon's caravan. It was bigger and instead of a wooden box of pods, there was a rack full of them in all the colours of the rainbow.

'Yep.' Robyn took a purple pod. 'This is the one we always use. It's the one Annie was given and she's drunk loads of them before.'

'Did you make the drink for her?' Jude asked.

'Actually, no,' said Robyn. 'That would be the work experience boy. He's such a lazy arse – more hindrance than help. He's only here because he's Dean's nephew and I don't think Dean has spent more than five minutes with him since he got here.'

'Could he have used the wrong pod?' Jude asked.

Robyn shook her head. 'I gave him the pods myself when I told him we wanted the drinks ready for the final live section. Besides, we're a peanut-free set-up so even if he had chosen a different one, none of them should have caused Annie to have a reaction.'

Jude glanced down into the bin under the table where the coffee machine sat. There were several pods inside, some purple but others of different colours. Red, green, brown and gold.

Robyn saw her looking and followed her gaze. 'Hang on,' she said. 'I haven't seen a gold one before.' She bent down and picked one of them out of the bin.

'I don't even know what this is.'

Jude looked at the rack where everything was labelled but there were no more gold pods and no space where they might have been.

Robyn took her phone out and ran a quick internet search.

'Holy shit,' she said as she turned the screen to face Jude.

There on the website of the drinks manufacturer was a picture of a matching gold pod labelled *peanut and sesame coffee*.

'That can't have been what Annie drank though,' said Jude. 'She'd have known straight away it was the wrong thing.'

'She wouldn't have had to drink a mug of that though,' said Robyn. 'If someone used the machine to make it and then Annie's hot chocolate was the next one to go through the system it could have picked up enough peanut to cause her to react.'

'You're right,' said Jude. 'But who would have done something so daft?'

'It can only be Chris.' Robyn rubbed her temples. 'Now I'm going to have to talk to Dean about it and he won't be happy.'

'At least we found the cause so it can be avoided going forward,' said Jude, who was also glad that this would keep any finger of blame away from Mavis' gingerbread.

Robyn sighed. 'I suppose so. God, I'll be glad when this series is over and we can all go home to collapse for Christmas Day.'

* * *

Everyone was in the sitting room waiting for Jude when she got back to the farmhouse, still clustered around the television where they'd gathered to watch Jude's performance.

As well as Noah, Lucy and Sebbie – who was up way past his bedtime – Noah's father, Frank, was there along with Jude's best friend, Detective Inspector Binnie Khatri.

'What the hell happened?' Lucy said as soon as Jude joined them. 'One minute we were watching you all on the screen, then it looked like Annie Bird collapsed and a video about adders on the hills came on instead.'

'Did that lady die?' Sebbie asked. 'I heard an ambulance.'

'No, sweetheart.' Jude sat on the floor next to her nephew and put an arm around his shoulder. 'She's absolutely fine. Some people have allergies to things that means if they eat them they can get very ill very quickly and that's what happened to Annie. She had a drink that might have had a tiny bit of peanut in it and she had a nasty reaction.'

'But I love peanut butter.' Sebbie looked terrified. 'Could I get really ill too?'

'It doesn't work like that,' said Noah. 'Most people can eat peanuts with no problem. It's only dangerous for people who are allergic to them.'

'And that's not you.' Jude gave him an extra-big squeeze. 'Besides, people like Annie who know they have an allergy keep special medicine with them called an EpiPen which means if there's a problem they'll be okay.'

'Did Annie have one?' Sebbie asked.

'She did,' said Jude. 'She was already feeling much better when the ambulance got here. They've taken her to hospital just to be safe but she'll be back in her caravan by tomorrow so there's nothing to worry about.'

'Hear that, Seb? Nothing to worry about,' said Lucy. 'So no more reasons for you to still be up. Time to whiz and get ready for bed.'

'Will you come with me?' Sebbie asked as he got to his feet.

'Come on, little man,' said Noah. 'I'll take you up.' He crouched down so that Sebbie could clamber up onto his back and the two of them climbed the rickety stairs to find pyjamas and a toothbrush.

'Is she really okay?' Binnie asked when Sebbie was out of earshot.

'Yeah. It looks like the machine her hot chocolate came from had been used to make a peanut-flavoured coffee so there was probably residue in the system.'

'Blimey,' said Frank, scratching his beard. 'That's all it took?'

'Apparently so. But she'll be fine. In fact, she's still planning on hosting the show tomorrow although whether she will or not, who knows?'

'Good that she's okay,' said Binnie. 'You were great, by the way. Nobody could have told that you were at all nervous.'

'Really?' said Jude. 'I felt like I was going to throw up whilst I was waiting for them to start asking me questions and then I thought I just waffled my way through everything.'

'Not at all,' said Lucy. 'And I'd be the first person to tell you if you did. I was actually really proud of you.'

'Dean, that's the director, wants to film you tomorrow, Frank.' Jude raised her eyebrows at the old shepherd. 'What do you think of that?'

'What's he want to do something like that for?' said Frank, aghast.

'He was impressed with you and Noah moving the flock over to the stubble turnips this morning and he wants a video of you using the dogs to round up the sheep.'

'They don't need rounding up tomorrow.' Frank tugged his beard. 'It's all daft if you ask me.'

'I don't know,' said Binnie with a grin. 'I think you'd be fabulous, Frank. You never know, you might turn into one of those unlikely hits with the public and start getting sacks of fan mail and marriage proposals.'

'Who's getting proposals?' Noah asked, coming back down to retrieve the teddy bear Sebbie had left on the sofa.

'We reckon Frank will after he stars in tomorrow's episode,' said Lucy.

'You're going to be on the telly, Dad?' Noah looked equally surprised and amused.

'I haven't said I'll do it yet.'

'You should,' said Noah. 'It might be fun and it's good to do something a bit different.'

'I'm glad you said that,' Jude chuckled, 'because the director is expecting you both to film a double act in the fields tomorrow morning.'

'What?' Noah looked horrified.

'It'll be fun.' Lucy got up and kissed her fiancé on the cheek. 'And don't forget, it's good to do something a bit different!'

***

The radio was on whilst the inhabitants of Malvern Farm got themselves ready for their Monday mornings.

'Mum, I forgot to tell you I need white trousers, white top, a scarf and a hat for school today,' said Sebbie as he tucked into his Weetabix.

Lucy was in her uniform, gulping down a mug of coffee and some toast to fuel her for a full day shift at the care home.

'And you need this today?'

'Yep. I'm a snowman in the Christmas play and I need to bring my costume in.' He loaded up his spoon with another mouthful of breakfast.

'Tell me exactly how I'm meant to conjure up a pair of white trousers just like that?' said Lucy.

'Kai's wearing his cricket trousers.'

'Sebbie, you don't play cricket,' Noah pointed out.

'What about your England rugby shorts?' Jude suggested. 'Will they do?'

'Maybe.' Sebbie mulled this thought over whilst he finished his cereal.

'Annie Bird is recovering today after collapsing whilst filming the first in a Christmas series of *Countryside Live* last night,' reported the newsreader on the radio.

'Turn it up,' said Lucy.

'The show, which was being watched by almost 5 million people, was broadcast live when Annie was seen to suffer a severe allergic reaction. A statement from the show's spokesperson issued this morning thanks everyone that has sent Annie good wishes and wants to reassure them that the presenter was released from hospital late last night and is doing well. She will not be taking part in the show today whilst she rests but intends to resume her role next to her husband, Simon North, tomorrow.'

'Well, that's good news,' said Jude.

'I bet whoever put that peanut drink through the machine is feeling rubbish now,' said Lucy.

'They reckon it must have been the work experience boy,' said Jude.

'That's one way to make your mark, I suppose,' said Noah. 'Poor guy.'

'Right.' Jude stood up and pushed her chair under the table. 'I need to get on.'

As she went upstairs to finish getting ready for the day ahead, she couldn't help thinking about how someone had ballsed up badly enough to put Annie in hospital like that. Everyone on set had known about the peanut allergy. It was one of the first things Jude had been told when the contract to film at Malvern Farm had been finalised. The message had been loud and clear: no peanuts anywhere near Annie Bird. Surely it was a message that would have been stamped on the psyche of every person working on the show – especially anyone who might have cause to bring her drinks and snacks.

Jude knew that this meant one of three things must have happened. Either nobody had told Chris, which seemed very unlikely. Chris had chosen to ignore the warning, which again seemed unlikely if the consequences had been laid out to him as clearly as they had to Jude. Or it wasn't Chris who had used the peanut coffee in the machine.

And if it wasn't Chris, then that begged the questions who was it, and why, when they must have known what would happen?

Whilst she brushed her teeth, Jude thought about the sequence of events that happened straight after Annie collapsed.

Simon had screamed for someone to fetch Annie's bag, clearly expecting to find her EpiPen in there. But the pocket where she usually kept it was empty. If Dean hadn't brought the spare one out of the production trailer and the adrenaline hadn't been administered before the paramedics arrived, Annie Bird would now almost certainly be dead.

6

Jude and Binnie had fallen into the habit of meeting up at the pub in the village on the first Monday of each month for a catch-up and to give themselves a bit of a break from their busy lives. It was something they'd started back in the summer when Binnie had sustained a head injury that resulted in brain surgery and a lengthy period of rest and recuperation.

Although she'd healed well and had been back at work for nearly two months, Binnie still got very tired and had crushing headaches that took days to shift. Her DCI was very understanding, especially as the injury had occurred whilst on active duty, and Binnie's return was entirely on her own terms. Currently desk based, she was permitted to go in as much or as little as she could manage, with as much time off for medical appointments as needed.

The trouble with Binnie Khatri was that she was not the sort of person who enjoyed taking things easy or working a desk job and, as her health slowly improved, her frustrations grew.

To save Binnie from getting tangled up in all the chaos of the filming team, Jude walked down to the end of the long driveway and waited for Binnie by the old milk churn that marked the entrance to Malvern Farm. She took a box of small bantam eggs from the honesty stall to give her.

It was a perfect wintery day, cold enough for the ice crystals of the night's heavy frost to remain on each blade of grass despite the sun's high appearance in the cloudless sky. Adam had always sworn that he could smell when the snow was coming in and as Jude breathed in icy lungfuls of the country air, she wondered if this was what he meant.

She'd only been there for a couple of minutes when Binnie's familiar hatchback came down the lane and pulled up next to Jude.

'I think this is going to have to be the last Monday lunch,' Binnie said when Jude got into the passenger seat.

'Really?' said Jude. 'Is the DCI putting the pressure on?'

'No.' Binnie set off on the short journey to the village of Malvern End. 'He's being great, actually. It's me, I felt really guilty leaving work to skive off and hit the pub. Besides, I'm feeling much better now and I need to get stuck into some proper work and back to a routine.'

'Just don't push yourself too hard too soon,' said Jude. 'I know what you're like.'

'I hate not being able to pull my weight.'

'You hate not being in the centre of an interesting investigation.'

'That too,' said Binnie.

'In that case we'd better make the most of today if it's going to be the last one.'

Binnie drove past the village shop and post office and pulled into the car park of The Lamb, the old timber-framed pub in the heart of the village. The two friends got out of the car and made their way over to the iron-studded wooden door. It had been built in a time when humans had been significantly shorter and Jude ducked her head as she walked through into the bar.

'Hello there, Jude,' called Barbara, the landlady. 'Afternoon, Binnie. I've put you on your usual table by the fire. A half of Westons and a ginger beer, is it?'

'Thanks, Barbara, you're a star,' said Jude.

It was deliciously warm in the pub and Jude took her winter layers off and hung them on a coat rack before making her way over to the table already set out for them. An open fire crackled invitingly and the Christmas garlands that had been hung across every black beam made the place look even cosier than usual. The scent of warm spices and sweet citrus filled the place and Jude saw that it was coming from an urn that had been set up on the bar with a handwritten sign saying *mulled wine*.

'It looks lovely in here,' said Jude when Barbara brought their drinks over.

'That's all Ted. You should see what he's done in the dining room this year.' Barbara rolled her eyes in mock despair. 'I sent him to the Christmas tree farm over in Leigh Sinton and he came back with the biggest one he could find. It only just fitted in and that's after he lopped the top branch off. I had to send him out again to buy a whole load of new decorations because the ones we had were lost on it.'

Jude and Binnie chuckled.

'I bet it looks amazing now,' Binnie said.

'I have to admit that it does,' said Barbara. 'It's just a squeeze getting all the tables in there too. We've got a full house for Christmas lunch this year.'

Ted himself came out of the kitchen then and waved when he saw Jude and Binnie. 'Afternoon, ladies,' he said. 'Jude, are you still talking to the likes of us now you're a famous star of the telly?'

'Don't be daft.' Jude grinned. 'You saw it though?'

'Of course we did,' said Barbara. 'Had it on in the pub last night. That poor woman gave everyone a scare but they say she's going to be all right.'

'She's back in her caravan at the farm and as far as I know she's resting and planning on being back on the programme tomorrow,' said Jude. 'Granny Margot will be pleased as she's a huge fan and she's been lined up as a guest.'

When Robyn had initially asked for recommendations of local people who would be good to interview, Jude's very good friend had been the first person to spring to mind. Granny Margot had lived in the village all her life and had worked on the farm as a child and adult, seeing over eight decades of change. Several years ago she'd moved into the care home where Lucy now worked and Jude visited her regularly for a chat. Unlike Jude, she had bags of confidence and had been delighted to be asked.

'Well, that's good news then,' said Barbara. 'Margot will be fabulous but I hope these telly people have their ways of getting her to stop talking or the show will go on into next week!'

Everyone chuckled at the thought and then Ted and Barbara went back to work whilst Jude and Binnie turned their attention to the menu. Being the beginning of a new month, it had been changed and the December choices included turkey curry, mushroom and brie wellington and spiced parsnip soup.

'What are you going for?' asked Binnie. 'I'm thinking soup and some bread.'

'I can't come to The Lamb for lunch and not have some of Ted's triple-cooked chips,' said Jude. 'I think I'll have them with a Christmas toasted sandwich.'

Once they'd finalised their choices, Jude went up to the bar to order and returned to the table with two small glasses of mulled wine.

'I couldn't resist the smell,' she said as she set one down in front of Binnie. 'You know Christmas is nearly on us when Barbara gets the mulled wine urn out.'

'How are your Christmas plans going?' Binnie asked. 'Are you sure you really want all of us there when you've got the wedding just a few days later?'

'Of course!' said Jude. 'We'll be cooking the usual giant roast turkey anyway so it doesn't make any difference if it's for four or fourteen really. We'll just throw a load more spuds in and make extra stuffing. Is Sami coming too? He wasn't sure what the rota was looking like at work.'

Sami Abadi was Binnie's colleague and a good friend to Jude too. He had no family locally so it made sense to invite him to join them for Christmas.

'I think he's working during the day but was hoping to come round for a drink when he finished. I'll ask him to let you know.'

'No hurry,' said Jude. 'Call it an open house.'

Jude sipped the warming wine and pushed back into the wooden carver chair. She'd miss her monthly lunches with Binnie. 'Are you sure you can't keep one lunchtime a month clear?' she said.

'I've been off duty too long already,' said Binnie. 'I'm so bored. I need to get back in the saddle.'

'You're not thinking of full duties again, are you?'

'Why not?' Binnie asked. 'In January I will have had over six months to recover and I think it's time to get back out there. The team are stretched covering for me.'

'Just take it steady,' said Jude. 'Promise?'

'Like you promise not to get into any more deadly scrapes and yet somehow you always manage to?' Binnie looked at her over the steaming glass she was holding.

'Touché,' said Jude.

'Talking of which, there was a moment there last night when you were on the telly and I thought we were looking at murder,' said Binnie. 'Live on the screen in front of however many million people.'

'Dean, that's the director, is horrifically delighted that people are still tuning in to watch it on catch-up. It's had over 20 million global views. I think that's what they call going viral.'

'I bet that means a big audience this evening too,' said Binnie.

'That's what he's hoping.' Jude sipped her mulled wine, enjoying the heat as it slid down her throat.

Binnie's comment about murder had brought back her thoughts about the peanut coffee pods and missing EpiPen. 'Binnie,' she said, 'it's funny that you should have brought that up, actually.'

'What, the big audience?'

'No, the fact you thought Annie had been murdered. It's just that there are a couple of things that have been bothering me.'

Binnie looked up and Jude thought she saw a glint of something akin to excitement in her eyes. 'Do tell.'

Jude laid out her misgivings about the coincidence that the EpiPen hadn't been where it should have on the same evening as Annie had been given a drink tainted with the one thing that had the potential to kill her.

'You're in danger of letting your imagination get the better of you again,' said Binnie.

'But what if we do nothing and something else happens?' Jude said.

'Jude, what is it you want to do?' Binnie asked. 'Go marching up to Annie Bird and tell her you think someone deliberately gave her an anaphylactic reaction and hid her medication to try and kill her?'

'Of course, when you put it like that it sounds beyond far-fetched.'

'That's because it is,' said Binnie. 'I know you think there are people around every corner just waiting for an opportunity to commit murder. But sometimes things just happen.'

Ted came along then armed with their lunch and Jude put her misgivings to the back of her mind in order to enjoy her sandwich, which was heaving with turkey, sausage meat, chestnut stuffing and cranberry sauce. Binnie was right. She had to stop looking for murderers around every corner.

The door of the pub opened and Jude looked up to see Marco Ricci walk in. As it had an annoying habit of doing, Jude felt her heart skip a beat at the sight of the man who had so nearly been hers.

'Hello, you two,' said Marco, grinning widely as he came over to their table. 'This is a lovely surprise.'

Jude hated the way he still had the ability to make her heart speed up just a little bit. She missed his constant presence in her life and not just because she had realised too late that what she felt for Marco was more than just friendship. They were still friends, of course, but much less so since Clara had come into the equation.

'Want to join us?' Binnie asked.

'If I'm not interrupting,' said Marco as he took his coat off.

'Of course not,' Jude said. 'I recommend the mulled wine.'

'Shall I bring one over?' Barbara called.

'Why not?' Marco hung his coat up and sat down next to Jude. 'Banger of a show last night. I assume Annie Bird is doing okay?'

He took a chip from Jude's plate and blew on it before biting off the end.

'She's fine,' said Jude. 'Back at camp and planning the rest of the series.'

A thought occurred to Jude then. 'Actually, they're looking for local people to interview. The director and researcher both keep asking me for recommendations. You should do it.'

'What?' Marco looked taken aback. 'Why would they want to interview me?'

'You're a brilliant local artist and it wouldn't do you any harm to have some national coverage. You never know what might get picked up.'

It was Marco's art that had first brought him into Jude's life when he'd stayed at her campsite to paint a series of works showing the Malvern Hills in all their glory. He had a real talent for finding something new in scenes that had been captured a thousand times before and giving them a fresh, bold edge. They were popular too. Marco had sold quite a lot through a gallery in the town centre, and he gained a lot of attention when he was invited to show a collection at a gallery in Devon.

'Jude's right,' said Binnie. 'You could show some of your work and let them have a look at your studio.'

'Or you could take them on one of your sketching walks and show them how you work when you're out in the wild,' Jude added.

'I don't know.' Marco scratched the back of his neck.

'It's really not as bad as it sounds,' said Jude. 'I ended up having fun and if they did a pre-recorded piece you wouldn't even have to worry about cocking up on live television.'

'Are you here for your lunch, Marco?' Barbara asked, coming over with the mulled wine. 'Or are you just going to sit there and eat all of Jude's chips?'

Marco glanced at the menu. 'I'll have a Christmas toastie, please.'

'Same as Jude.' Barbara winked. 'You two always did go well together.'

Jude blushed and tried to hide it behind her almost empty glass of mulled wine.

'I'll have a word with the researcher,' she said. 'I'm sure they'd love to have you on at some point. Granny Margot's doing a feature for it tomorrow.'

Marco chuckled as he helped himself to another chip. 'Now that will definitely be worth tuning in for. How is Margot? I haven't seen her in such a long time.'

'Same as usual. Keeping the other residents on their toes, not to mention the staff. Why don't you come up to the farm tomorrow? Gerwain is bringing her over in the afternoon for the filming session and I've asked them to stay on for something to eat.'

Marco had once been a regular attendee for meals at Malvern Farm and Jude missed him just popping in on a whim.

'Bring Clara with you,' she added. 'The more the merrier.'

'Thanks, Jude,' said Marco. 'That would be really lovely.'

Jude ignored the little toe dig from Binnie and resolutely refused to look at her. Everyone had made it very clear to Jude that she shouldn't just give up on Marco without a fight. But Jude had no intention of deliberately setting out to destroy a relationship. She'd had her chance and she hadn't taken it. Now Marco had found happiness with someone else and Jude had moved on.

So why did he still make her feel like a teenage girl every time she saw him?

* * *

That evening, Jude was very grateful to be with her family in the sitting room, watching the second episode of *Countryside Live* on the television with her pyjamas on and a cup of tea in her hand.

Simon was presenting it on his own and started with a loving tribute to his wife and the happy update that she had recovered well and would be back, well-rested, for the following day's filming.

He went on to thank the quick response of the local ambulance service and exalt the wonderful care Annie had been given at Worcestershire Royal Hospital.

The guest that evening was Mavis, the award-winning baker.

'Look, Aunty Judy,' said Sebbie, pointing at the screen. 'Rodney Trotter is trying to eat the mince pies.'

The haybales from the first episode had been replaced with outdoor seating, which was a huge disappointment to the animals. Now the pull of the baked treats Simon's guest had brought in was proving too much for the little Shetland pony.

'He's so cheeky.' Sebbie giggled.

Simon handled the whole thing expertly, moving the plate out of reach whilst making a joke about Rodney's taste for fame.

Jude found it strange watching her familiar world play out on the small screen, knowing that millions of other people were tuning in at the same time. As the programme ran, she found her mind wandering to the people backstage, pulling together to make the show run smoothly.

Robyn and Mary, who both made no attempt at hiding the fact they didn't think much of Annie Bird, although Jude still had no idea why. Dean the director, who was so invested in achieving high viewing figures that he'd lost any sense of the human touch: he'd clearly thought Annie's live collapse had been good news for the show.

Although Binnie had pointed out that the chances of Annie's nut contamination being anything other than an accident were low, Jude couldn't help thinking that it was still possible.

And the thing that worried her most was, if it had been a calculated attack, would somebody try again?

7

After breakfast the next morning, Jude checked her show stock of Kerry Hill sheep who lived in the orchard with the bantam hens. Once the eggs had been collected, the last port of call was to the animals in the paddock.

The generators that the film crew had brought with them were working hard, keeping the caravans and trailers warm, and Jude tried not to think of the petrol fumes they were spewing out. At least they'd attached long exhaust pipes to keep the toxic gas away from the animals in the paddock. Still, it would be nice when they all packed up and left. Three weeks was nothing, she told herself. They'd be gone before she knew it and then they could get on with celebrating Christmas and the wedding in the knowledge that the bank account was looking much healthier going into the new year.

As Jude got near to the campsite, she could hear two voices coming from around the caravans but the people talking were hidden from sight.

'I'm just saying that he's not listening to me,' said Annie Bird. 'I am well and ready to get back to filming today but I don't think we need to do a whole health section about nut allergies. It's not what people tune into *Countryside Live* for, is it?'

'Dean is the director, not me.' The second voice was Robyn's and she sounded on a short fuse again.

'Yes, but he listens to you,' said Annie.

'Careful there, Annie. It almost sounds as though you're accusing me of being good at my job.'

Jude slowed down just a little, her interest piqued by the argument.

'Stop being so petulant.' Annie had dropped the perpetual warmth of her voice that so enchanted her viewers. It was the first time Jude had heard it and yet she supposed even telly stars were human and snapped now and again.

'Petulant?' Robyn raised her voice. 'In case you've forgotten, it was your petulancy that lost me the directing job. You know I was the best person to take over from Marcia when she retired. She was as good as training me up for the role for six years whilst I was slogging my guts out as her junior on *Countryside* bloody *Live*. It would have been mine if you hadn't been pissed off with me and told the team you would only carry on presenting if they appointed Dean as director.'

Jude felt her eyebrows rise as she put her hand on the gate that led into the paddock.

'That's not strictly true,' said Annie.

'Bullshit,' Robyn countered. 'You didn't like the fact that Simon sided with me, not you, over a couple of features choices. Stupid things that didn't even matter. But enough for you to make sure I was kept in my place as lowly researcher.'

Jude saw Annie come out from between the caravans with Robyn hot on her heels and made herself busy with the catch on the gate. Although they were walking away from her, there was a chance they might turn and she didn't want to be caught deliberately eavesdropping.

'You're being ridiculous,' said Annie. 'Dean got the job because he was the best person for it. That was two years ago, anyway. It's probably time you got over it.'

'You're such a nightmare,' Robyn growled. 'It's no wonder Simon's getting itchy feet.'

Jude knew she had already heard far too much and so pushed the gate open to walk through. She wasn't sure if either woman had noticed her or if they'd been too involved in their spat but she hoped neither would turn around until she was far enough into the paddock.

Pancake, Gertie, Rodney Trotter and the Valais Blacknoses all came trotting over to see her and she felt the usual rush of gratitude that she was guardian of so many incredible animals.

'Come on, gang,' she said. 'Time for breakfast.'

The area outside the stable had almost returned to normal after the previous night's filming. Jude had emphasised the importance of not leaving equipment or rubbish around and the team had been great at making sure everything was cleared away in between the live shows.

In order to stop the hungry animals from pushing their way into the tack room where their food was kept, Jude let herself in and bolted the bottom half of the split stable door behind her.

Whilst she dug in the metal bins for sheep nuts, she thought about the argument she'd just heard. The fact that Robyn blamed Annie for stopping her progression up the promotional ladder certainly made the researcher's reactions to her more understandable. And then there was her comment about Simon getting itchy feet.

Jude had seen Annie and Simon together off camera as well as on it and, aside from a couple of half scowls she thought she'd seen on Simon's face, they seemed as perfect together in real life as they appeared to be on the television. But that didn't mean he wasn't capable of getting itchy feet, whatever that meant. Perhaps Robyn was insinuating he'd had enough of hosting the show with his wife. Or maybe he'd had enough of his wife full stop and the happy marriage was nothing more than an act. A PR front because he knew that Annie Bird and Simon North were far more marketable as a pair than they would be individually.

The animals nudged Jude's arms and legs as she walked out of the tack room carrying buckets of nuts. She tipped them into the long trough for them to pounce on whilst she went back in to fill the hay nets. In order to reduce waste and save money, she'd rescued what was left of the bales that had been used on that first fateful evening of filming.

The Runner ducks weren't all that keen to come out of their cosy stable onto the frozen ground when Jude opened the door. She needed to clean them out and spread a new layer of wood chippings down for them so she threw some food on the ground and chased them out with a broom to many quacks of objection.

Finally, the morning jobs were done, all the animals were fed and happy and Jude was able to grab a couple of sacred hours to plant herself in front of the ancient, ridiculously slow laptop armed with a credit card and a list of gifts she needed to buy. Usually she did try and get as many of her presents as possible from the shops in town and she'd always made a trip into Hereford to finish off her Christmas shopping. But this was the first year she also had a wedding and a film crew to occupy her time.

It took longer than she had expected to find everything she needed and also to dig around for some little things to add to Sebbie's stocking. She'd almost finished when she heard a car pull up outside her office window. Looking outside, she saw

Gerwain, the manager of the care home where Lucy worked and Granny Margot lived, getting out of the driving seat.

Jude added the last of her payment details into the England Rugby website to secure a branded mug, some stationery and socks for Sebbie, before switching the machine off and heading out into the yard.

'Hello, Jude,' said Gerwain as he walked around to open the passenger door. 'Don't you have the red carpet at the ready to roll out for the next star of popular evening television?'

He put his hands out to help Granny Margot to her feet. She was dressed in a pair of bright green corduroy trousers and a knitted jumper with the round face of a jolly snowman on the front. A stripy bobble hat was pulled over her thickly bobbed hair, the slightest hint of raspberry pink tinting the natural silver.

'Oh, do stop teasing me,' she said as she took the walking sticks that Gerwain held out for her.

'Who says he's teasing?' said Jude as she walked over to kiss her old friend. 'I have a feeling you're going to be a huge hit with the public this evening and you'll be asked to make a more regular appearance. Who knows, maybe the director will ask if he can contract you to be a third presenter.'

'Yes, well, I probably wouldn't be able to fit many appearances in between my Scrabble league games, armchair yoga and stitch and bitch sessions.' Granny Margot sounded deadly serious but Jude could see a familiar mischievous sparkle in her eyes. 'We're in the process of making a wall hanging to celebrate the 125th anniversary of the first-ever performance of Elgar's *Enigma Variations*. We've taken a variation each and I'm in charge of *Nimrod* which is, of course, the most important one of all.'

'You're right,' said Jude. 'Without you the entire thing would cease to be.'

'Exactly,' said Granny Margot. 'So you see, this television

malarkey can only ever be a one-off. Now where do you suppose they want me?'

Jude had no idea but she knew that Granny Margot could not go marching around looking for Dean, Robyn or someone else to show her where to go. Whilst she did her best to stay as mobile as possible, her days of off-roading across farmland were over.

'The house is open,' she said. 'Why don't you go and wait in the kitchen whilst I go and track someone down? Make a cup of tea and help yourself to the mince pies on top of the bread bin.'

Granny Margot and Gerwain did as Jude suggested whilst she went to find a member of the *Countryside Live* team.

* * *

Granny Margot came back from her filming session with a huge smile on her face.

'How was it?' Jude asked as she ushered her and Gerwain into the kitchen to warm up.

'Annie and Simon are delightful, aren't they?' Granny Margot needed help to walk through to the table where she sat down. 'Very professional, I thought, but kind too. I had a lovely time.'

'Our Margot was a star,' said Gerwain. 'They asked her to do a live session this evening too but we decided it would be a bit much.'

'I do feel tired,' said Granny Margot.

It was very unlike Granny Margot to show any sign of fatigue or slowing down and this was a stark reminder to Jude that she was ageing fast.

'Do you want to go up and have a lie down before the others get here?' she said. 'You can use my room if you like.'

'Actually, Jude, I think I might.' She pointed at the kettle which was whistling on the Aga. 'After that cuppa though.'

* * *

Later on, a full house were gathered around the dining room table to share the meal that Jude had promised them before they all watched Granny Margot's star performance.

Well used to catering for the masses, Jude had made a huge shepherd's pie with a panful of buttered peas and carrots. Easy food that would hit the spot.

Granny Margot sat at the head of the table, full of stories from her afternoon spent recording with her idol, Annie Bird.

'She's every bit as lovely in real life.' Granny Margot took the plate that had been passed along the row until it got to her. 'Mmm, this smells lovely, Jude.'

'It's good to hear that she's fully recovered after her ordeal with the allergy,' said Clara. She was sitting next to Marco, and Jude tried to ignore the fact that her hand was resting on top of his as they waited for her to serve up. 'It was such a shock, watching her collapse live in the telly like that, wasn't it?'

Clara turned to Marco and the unwanted image of the two of them, snuggled up on the sofa in his cottage, maybe sharing a bottle of wine as they ate his home-cooked food, made Jude's stomach flip.

It would be easier if she hated Clara, perhaps. If there were things about her that gave Jude justification to think Marco would be better off without her and hope that their relationship would come to an end. Jude didn't hate Clara though. Far from it – she had liked her enormously, from the first time they'd met on an organised walk together and they'd become friends well before she'd started to date Marco. That was what made it so hard. Well, that and the fact that Jude knew Marco wouldn't be with Clara if only Jude hadn't ballsed it up so consistently. She'd put up barriers that stopped their wonderful friendship developing into something more, until he'd decided enough was enough and it was time to move on. It had happened at exactly the moment Jude finally realised she was in love with him and now it was too late.

'It sounds like you enjoyed your day, ey, Margot?' Frank said. 'They somehow got me an' Noah to agree to be filmed out with the dogs tomorrow. Not sure I'm going to like it all that much though.'

'Don't be such a codger, Frank,' said Granny Margot. 'If you haven't yet realised that life is all about trying new things then what's left for you at your age?'

Lucy snorted. 'Don't hold back, Margot!'

'I've known Frank since he was a little boy. If I can't tell it like it is then who can?'

The thought of Frank with his old head and heavily greying beard as a child made Jude chuckle. Although he must have been more than twenty years younger than Granny Margot, looking at the two of them side by side, anyone would have been forgiven for thinking that the age gap between them was much smaller.

'Each to their own, Margot,' said Frank. 'Not all of us likes the limelight.'

'But at least you will have given it a try,' said Granny Margot.

Jude spooned the last portion of pie onto her plate and then took the leftovers back to the kitchen to keep warm in the Aga. She remembered to grab the ketchup from the fridge for Sebbie before she returned to her place at the dining table.

'What do you think of Annie and Simon?' Granny Margot asked as Jude sat down.

'Really lovely,' said Jude. 'Almost impossibly so.'

'I meant as a couple. Do you believe it?'

'What, that they're a couple?' Noah asked.

'No!' Granny Margot said it as though Noah's misunderstanding was ridiculously naïve. 'Of course they're a couple. I meant are they a believable couple in a marriage as unbreakable as they want us all to think?'

'Why, do you fancy a shot with Simon North?' Gerwain chuckled as he pushed some mashed potato soaked in gravy onto his fork.

'Don't be ludicrous.' Granny Margot gave him a withering stare. 'I just had the very strong feeling that they were putting rather a lot of it on for the camera.'

'Did you?' Lucy asked. 'What makes you say that?'

'For a start I'm almost certain he's having an affair with the camerawoman.'

'Mary?' said Jude, incredulously.

'That's her. I saw the looks they gave each other when they thought nobody was watching.' Granny Margot raised her eyebrows. 'And when it was just the three of us for a moment – everyone else was busy with a clipboard discussing whether we should move to the village and film something outside my old cottage too – he told her that he was looking forward to seeing her later and he rubbed her hand as he said it.'

'He said that in front of you?' Gerwain asked.

'That's the thing about being as ancient as I am. People forget that I notice things too.'

Jude chewed her food as she thought about what this meant. If Granny Margot was right and they were having an affair then this would explain Robyn's earlier comment about Simon having itchy feet. It also gave weight to the theory Jude had that there was some kind of unrest between Annie and the camera operator.

'Poor Annie,' said Lucy. 'That is, if you're right about them.'

'Unless she is also not quite as committed to a monogamous marriage as she'd have us all believe.'

'You don't think she's up to mischief too?' said Jude.

'I think that lovely sound chappie, Gabe, has a rather big crush on her,' said Granny Margot with a smile. 'And I wouldn't be at all surprised if Annie hasn't been tempted at the very least.'

Sebbie, who had been sitting quietly, tucking into his shepherd's pie, looked up from his food. 'What's mognosomous mean?'

Lucy looked at Noah, who looked at Jude, who looked at Granny Margot.

'It's like only ever having shepherd's pie to eat for the rest of your life,' said Granny Margot. 'Even if it's the best shepherd's pie ever made, it can be tricky if you fancy roast chicken one day instead.'

'But some people love eating shepherd's pie so much they are quite happy to never eat chicken again,' said Lucy quickly.

Granny Margot flushed, perhaps suddenly remembering that two of the assembled were only a few short weeks from promising to only eat shepherd's pie for the rest of their lives.

'Well, I like pizza and chocolate,' said Sebbie. 'If I could only eat pizza and chocolate from now on I would definitely be, what's it again? Monosogous.'

And with that, the conversation was swiftly moved on to the safer topic of what Sebbie had put on his Christmas wish list.

8

Once the supper things had been cleared away, everyone assembled in the sitting room to watch the latest episode of *Countryside Live*.

Annie kicked the show off with her heartfelt thanks for all the messages of support from viewers. She held Simon's hand as she spoke about her gratitude that she had him by her side and her joy at being able to return to the series quickly. Jude watched them closely, mulling over what Granny Margot had said about their possible extra-marital dalliances. Was it all an act? There was a chance that perhaps they had some sort of understanding between them that they would remain united but allow each other to experience other flings outside of the marriage. She wasn't naïve enough to think that these things didn't happen. There were several Hollywood stars who were very open about their arrangements – although Jude had always been a little sceptical about the true happiness of any marriage that required more than two participants.

Granny Margot might, of course, have got the whole thing

wrong and imagined things. Jude was inclined to think that this was unlikely. Despite her well-advanced age, or maybe because of it, Granny Margot had a tendency to see things that others overlooked. And she was almost always right.

'Earlier today we had the pleasure of meeting someone who has lived near this farm for almost nine decades,' said Annie Bird.

'Here we go,' said Lucy.

'Margot Lloyd was born in the village of Malvern End between the two world wars in a cottage she still owns today,' said Simon North. 'She's led an incredible life, working on the farm for many decades whilst raising her daughter and then granddaughter on her own.'

At the mention of the two women who'd both died far too young, Jude reached across and took Granny Margot's hand.

'Never one to avoid the issues close to her heart, she was heavily involved in the progression of women's rights and was an early advocate for the environment.' It was Annie's turn to talk again. 'Simon and I caught up with this incredible lady to ask her about the changes she's seen over the years.'

Jude imagined the scene down in the paddock as the live broadcast was halted to run the video of the interview between the two presenters and Granny Margot.

'There you are!' Sebbie yelled in his excitement at seeing his beloved adopted grandmother on the television. He scrambled across the carpet so that he was sitting at her feet and rested his arm casually against her legs as he watched.

It had been decided that Granny Margot's interview would work best from the orchard in front of the farmhouse. With the apple and pear trees stripped of their leaves for the winter, the views up to the hills were glorious. Granny Margot was sitting on a bench with a blanket tucked around her knees and her coat buttoned up tight, meaning that her festive jumper was not getting its moment in the limelight.

'You've known this farm for the best part of a century,' said Annie, who was sitting next to her on the bench with Simon perched on an upturned oil drum. 'You must have seen a lot of change in that time.'

'I'm not quite that old,' said Granny Margot, who looked remarkably at ease in front of the camera. 'But yes, you're right. I remember coming up here as a tiny dot when my father worked on the land. Back then, of course, there were still horses being used and lots of things were still done by hand. More than half the village worked on the farm during harvest, not like it is now that tractors have got bigger and stronger.'

Jude listened with keen interest and an odd sense of pride as Granny Margot talked about her childhood on the farm and how she'd grown up feeling like she was part of the fabric of the place, as did most of the people who lived in the tight-knit community. Without technology to keep them connected with the wider world, and with cars still being predominantly for the wealthy, the village spirit was clearly defined: something which saw them through the years of producing food to feed a war-torn country.

The shy Kerry Hill show sheep, with their panda-like markings, kept far enough away to not be a nuisance but Jude thought they looked perfect in the background. All in all, it was a beautifully put together piece and her only objection was that they didn't spend longer talking to Granny Margot before they rounded off and the programme returned to the live broadcast.

'You were brilliant,' Jude said. 'Best bit of the show so far.'

'That's just nostalgia,' said Granny Margot with a dismissive flick of her hand. 'Nothing seems as pretty as the past though.'

Everyone chipped in with their praise and although Granny

Margot tried to shrug off their compliments, Jude could tell that she was glowing from the attention.

* * *

In the morning, Jude went down to the paddock as part of her daily checklist. The weather had turned and the blue skies of the past few days had been replaced by dirty yellow clouds that looked ominously full of winter.

Snow was not falling but it was in the air nonetheless and Jude knew that this would make things on the farm more challenging in many ways.

As Jude turned past the pond, she heard a loud hammering coming from the top of the campsite and when she looked over she saw Robyn banging her fists on the door of Annie's caravan. Dean was coming out of his own van next door.

'What's the racket about?' he asked.

'Annie,' said Robyn, as though that was enough of an answer. 'We need you out here,' she shouted into the closed door. 'Filming is due to begin and we have to go through the schedule with you beforehand.'

When there was no answer, Robyn kicked the door and then turned to see Jude watching her. 'Sorry for the noise,' she said.

'Oh, no problem.' Jude waved in what she hoped was a nonchalant manner. 'Perhaps she's still recovering from the other night?'

'She's fine,' said Dean. 'She's a professional. I bet she's already up and about. I'm just heading over to the chillout trailer. She's probably in there.'

'I've looked,' said Robyn through gritted teeth. 'Nobody has seen her and our first guests are due to arrive for interview in half an hour. I need to catch her up to speed before they do.'

Dean raised his hand to remove himself from the conversation as he walked away towards the chillout trailer.

Jude heard a noise at the far end of the campsite and she looked to see Annie, dressed in full winter gear, coming up from the direction of the two shepherd's huts. One of the huts was being used by Mary, and the other by Gabe. Jude remembered Granny Margot's observations about Annie Bird and Simon North perhaps not being quite as monogamous as their onscreen marriage would suggest.

'Morning,' said Annie cheerily. 'Sorry, have you been looking for me?'

'Actually, yes, we have.' Robyn was as frosty as usual and shot her a stare that would have curdled brandy butter. 'We need you for the day's run through and we've got sheep breeders coming in half an hour for you to talk to.'

'Ah, yes, the two sisters. They sound like my sort of people, I'm looking forward to meeting them.'

Annie was looking remarkably perky and Jude couldn't help wondering if it had anything to do with why she was walking up through the campsite from the direction of the shepherd's huts. Surely if she had been, as Granny Margot suspected, tempted to join the handsome soundman in his hut, she wouldn't risk being so brazen about it? It was a very risky thing for the brand if suggestions ever came out that she was having an affair.

'I should probably have let you know that I swapped caravans with Mary,' she said. 'I didn't like sleeping so close to the generator, it was keeping me awake churning away all night. Mary said she sleeps through anything and obviously she didn't mind giving up the little hut for the big caravan so we agreed to swap over last night.'

This fresh piece of information intrigued Jude further and stoked the suspicions that Granny Margot had laid.

Perhaps it was believable that Annie and Simon, the supposedly happy couple, would want separate caravans when filming for several weeks. A bit of space to breathe and the chance to get a good night's sleep during the hectic weeks of a full filming schedule. But now, with the change of caravans, Mary had ended up in the van next to Simon's and Annie in the hut next to Gabe's.

Jude wasn't sure if she entirely believed Annie's story. There was a strong whiff of the clandestine about the whole thing – but it wasn't her business at all how they chose to conduct themselves.

'You'll have fun with Ffion and Caitlin,' said Jude, returning the subject to the sheep farmers. When Robyn had asked her for guest suggestions, Jude had put the sisters forward as she knew they'd come across very well on the television. Together they farmed near Abergavenny on the Welsh border, specialising in breeding Jude's favourite sheep breed, the Kerry Hills. Both women were incredibly knowledgeable and this had made them very successful, the previous September seeing one of their rams sell at the Ludlow sale for a record-breaking breed sum. 'Anyway, I'll leave you to it.'

Jude pushed the gate open and went into the paddock to let the ducks out and make sure there was enough food for everyone. As she stuffed fresh hay into the nets, the first of the fat snowflakes began to fall.

Although snow wasn't the most desirable weather for any farmer, Jude's inner child still appreciated the beauty and felt the excitement as she watched them hit the frozen ground and start to settle.

Having made sure the animals were happy and that there was straw laid in the stable and the lean-to that Jude's neighbour and animal lover, Mike Trout, had built, Jude turned to go. She could feel the snowflakes kiss the cold-reddened skin of her face and see them collect in the folds of her waterproof coat.

As she left the paddock behind and made sure the loop of baling twine was put into place to stop any of the animals escaping, Jude could see that the flakes were falling faster and fatter than before. There was already a dusting of white covering the ground and when this happened, she knew it was here to stay for a while at least.

The door of the chillout trailer slammed open as Jude walked past and Dean stood on the top step with an enormous scarf wrapped several times around his neck.

'Jude,' he hollered to her. 'There you are. I need your thoughts on something.'

There was no please or recognition that Jude might not be able to jump to his beck and call. But then she had already worked out that when she'd rented her land out for filming purposes she'd clearly also inadvertently included herself in the package.

'How can I help?' she asked.

'Come in here out of this godawful weather,' said Dean. 'Although it will look rather good on the telly this evening if it settles. Shame it didn't hold off for the last week when the countdown to Christmas is really underway.'

Jude remembered Mary's warning about being alone with the sleazy director. She walked up the steps into the large caravan but kept her boots on and stayed by the door.

'I'm afraid we had to get rid of the coffee machine but there's a kettle if you want to make yourself a hot drink.'

'I'm okay, thanks,' said Jude who wanted to be as quick as possible so she could get back to her list of jobs. 'What can I do for you?'

'I need a new contingency plan for wet weather. I've just been in to look at the barn we planned on using should it rain – or indeed snow. It's no good. Too dark and gloomy.'

'I'm sorry to hear that,' said Jude. 'Perhaps you could bring in more lighting?'

'No.' He stroked his chin. 'It's not quite right. Too... what's the word I'm looking for? Agricultural.'

'It's an agricultural barn,' Jude pointed out. 'I thought that was the point.'

'Sit,' said Dean as though he was talking to one of the collies.

Jude had no intention of moving away from the safety of the door. 'My coat and boots are wet so I'll just stay here.'

'Take them off then.'

The way he stared at her made Jude wrap her coat a little tighter around herself. She didn't move and he eventually looked away and went to make himself a hot drink.

'I had a look in the barn next door and that's far more suitable. It's more like the stable from the nativity which is what we want to put out there. So we'll be using that one instead, I just wanted to ask if you could get some haybales in there for us? No animals to eat them this time.'

Jude sighed, knowing that the director was not about to listen to what she had to say but saying it anyway. 'That's where we're going to be setting the wedding up. We've got to get the bar in, flooring and all the chairs for the guests.'

'I can't see that will be a problem,' said Dean. 'We can work around each other. Good. So that's sorted then.'

Jude wanted to tell him to sod off but she bit her tongue and thought of the second half of the location fee she would be getting when the film team packed up and left the farm.

The trailer door opened and Gabe leant through, leaving his well-wrapped body outside. 'Anyone seen Mary recently?' he asked. 'Robyn wants to take some footage up with the sheep whilst the snow is falling but we can't find her anywhere.'

'Not here,' said Jude.

'Tell her to call me if you see her,' said Gabe. 'We're expecting our guests soon so will need her to record their piece.'

'Hold the door.' Dean stood up and shrugged on an excessive coat that looked as though it was designed to be worn on the sideline of a rugby match. 'Don't forget those bales for me, Jude. It would be good to film outside in the snow this evening but just in case, we'll need to have that barn set up.'

Dean pushed past Jude, deliberately rubbing up against her in what she knew to be a show of his dominancy. He slammed the door shut after himself and Jude closed her eyes for a moment to calm herself down.

'It's only three weeks,' she whispered to herself. 'Just keep thinking of the bank balance.'

She didn't want to go straight outside so she moved over to perch on the arm of the sofa for a little while, rubbing her forehead to gather her thoughts. After a minute or two, she took a deep breath and stood up. As she did so, her phone slid from the pocket of her coat and fell to the floor where it skittered under the sofa. She bent to pick it up and noticed that there was something else down there. A plastic packet had caught on her phone and was pulled out alongside it.

Thinking it was just rubbish, a half-eaten snack that had been discarded at some point, she picked it up with the intention of throwing it in the bin. But then she realised what she was holding: a packet of chocolate-covered peanuts, opened but sealed shut again with tape.

Peanuts, when every single member of the team knew that Annie had a severe allergy to them. It was possible they'd been left when the trailer had been used for something else, before filming for *Countryside Live* had begun. It was also possible that Chris, the work experience lad who had potentially made the mess-up with the peanut coffee pods, had been snacking on them.

There was something griping Jude though. The packet felt almost full so whoever had opened them would only have taken a few before closing it carefully and pushing or dropping it beneath the sofa. When considered alongside the peanut coffee pod and the missing EpiPen, it was beginning to feel as though there may be something in her theory that Annie's anaphylaxis hadn't been accidental.

Jude pocketed the packet and had just opened the door of the trailer when a scream, piercing and loud enough to reach right down to the village, rang out across the snow-covered farm.

Instantly, her heart sped up and the blood surged around her body as she jumped down from the trailer and followed the sound to the campsite. She arrived as Annie appeared at the door of her caravan, which was now being used by Mary. Jude could see that her eyes were wide and her chin was trembling with fright.

'What is it?' Jude asked as she rushed over to where Annie was propping herself against the frame of the door.

Annie didn't answer, but took Jude's hand and stared at her with haunted eyes. Then she stepped to the side and let Jude into the caravan.

The door to the bedroom was wide open and Jude could see Mary lying on the bed as though she were fast asleep and yet the air around her told Jude that this was more than just a long lie-in. She went over and crouched next to the bed, noticing as she did that the exposed skin of the woman's face, arms and chest was the colour of cherries, as though she had been lying out in the Mediterranean sun for too long.

Jude reached over and moved two fingers across the skin of Mary's throat, searching for a pulse that she felt certain wouldn't be there. No warmth was left in the doughy flesh – cold and clammy beneath Jude's touch.

'What's going on?'

Voices at the door made her look up to see Robyn and Simon talking to Annie.

'She's dead,' Annie sobbed. 'Mary is dead.'

9

Simon pushed past his wife to get into the caravan and Robyn followed, but Jude stood up and tried to bar the way. She didn't yet know what the cause of death was but experience had taught her that she could now be slap bang in the middle of a crime scene and, if foul play had been at work, things needed to be as undisturbed as possible.

'Please,' she said. 'Don't touch anything. The police will want to see things exactly as we found them.'

'Police?' Robyn said. 'You don't think this was done on purpose, do you?'

'I have no idea,' said Jude. 'But a young woman has died in unusual circumstances so there is bound to be an investigation.'

'Have you called them?'

'Not yet. I only arrived a moment before you.'

Robyn took her phone out and made the call whilst Jude turned her attention to Simon. His mouth was slightly open and his forehead creased as though in confusion as he silently stared at the woman on the bed.

'Are you okay?' Jude asked gently, remembering Granny

Margot's deduction that Simon and Mary had been more than just work colleagues.

'What was she doing in here?' His voice, when it came, was croaky and dry.

'I swapped with her,' said Annie, still standing by the door. 'Last night. I couldn't stand the noise of the generator and she was happy to take the bigger caravan.'

'You saw her last night?' Simon turned slowly to look back at his wife. 'Was she unwell? Did she look okay to you?'

'I... I can't remember,' Annie stuttered. 'She seemed normal, I think.'

'Well, she doesn't look normal now. Look at her.' He turned back and Jude saw that his stunned reaction was giving way to pain.

He moved towards Mary but Jude stepped into his path.

'You mustn't go near her,' she said. 'Please. Just wait for the ambulance and police to arrive.'

Jude took his elbow and steered him over to the caravan's door where Robyn was talking on her phone to the emergency services.

'Simon.' Annie reached out to her husband but he looked at her with hollow eyes and walked past, pushing her arm away as he did.

He went silently down the steps of the caravan, out into the snow that was still falling heavily onto the already white carpet coating the land.

'Come on.' Jude put her arm around Annie's shivering shoulders and led her out too.

'I'm going to my caravan,' said Simon.

Annie tried to follow him but as soon as he was inside, he closed the door without a word, leaving his wife out in the snow.

'Why don't we go and sit in the chillout trailer for a bit?' Jude suggested. 'Robyn, you'd better find Dean and tell him what's happened.'

Annie gave Jude the key she still had to the caravan so she could lock Mary's body up safely. She was submissive and allowed herself to be led away from the scene and up into the warmth of the chillout trailer where Jude put the kettle on to boil.

Whilst Jude made a cup of tea, Annie sat on the sofa, staring at a patch of ground directly in front of her feet.

'She looked awful, didn't she?' she said. 'Why was she so red?'

'I don't know,' said Jude as she tossed a teabag into a mug. 'We'll have to be patient and wait for the medical results to find out more but for now, if you can, try not to think about it.'

She knew that was easier said than done. The image of Mary's cherry-red face, eyes closed in their final slumber, would not leave her either. Jude had taken a moment to look around whilst she'd been in there, automatically checking for any obvious sign of something that could explain both the redness of Mary's skin and her sudden death. She'd seen nothing though. No pill packets, no food or drink, nothing to indicate she'd ingested anything before she'd gone to sleep. It didn't look like an allergic reaction and her knowledge of the effects of poisoning was limited so she couldn't say if that was a possibility.

The window above the bed had been open just a crack, letting in fresh, cold air and there had been a paperback book next to her on the bed, open as though she had been reading it when she'd fallen asleep. Nothing strange or out of the ordinary at first glance, but it would take a police search to check the scene properly.

'Here.' Jude passed the mug of tea to Annie. 'Try and drink this. Do you want sugar in it?'

Annie took the mug with both hands, shaking her head to indicate she didn't want the sugar.

Whilst Jude poured another mug for herself, Dean and Robyn joined them in the trailer. She put the kettle on for a second time.

'I've called Holly Kernow,' Dean said as he sat heavily on one of the soft chairs. 'She's coming to take over.'

'Who?' Annie asked.

'You know, pretty girl with rather enormous tits?'

Jude winced at the crassness and noticed Robyn do the same. She was amazed at how quickly Dean had got on to the case of finding Mary's replacement. He must have been straight on the phone as soon as he'd heard the news of her death.

'She's been doing some of the scenery shots for us while Mary was busy with the guests and interviews,' Robyn said as she sat down as far from Dean as was possible.

'She's been staying in Great Malvern but I've offered her the caravan if she wants it as I think it's important to get her on site.' Dean leant back with his hands cradling the back of his head and his knees flopping wide apart.

Robyn inhaled sharply. 'Are you kidding me? You told her that the bed you're offering her is currently inhabited by a dead body, I take it?'

'We'll get new sheets,' said Dean. 'What's the problem?'

'What's the problem?' Robyn stood up. 'You're asking what the problem with this is? Aside from the fact that you didn't even draw a breath after hearing about Mary before you picked up the phone to find her replacement?'

'We have a show to get on with and we can't do that without a camera operator.' Dean clearly wasn't at all fazed by his take on the situation. 'I can't see why Holly would have a problem with sleeping in the caravan – it's not as though Mary will still be there and I will personally make sure that she has fresh bedding. It's no worse than a hotel bed, is it? You don't want to think about what happens in those before you sleep in them.'

'It's not the same!' Robyn was obviously fighting a battle with her composure and was on the verge of losing. 'If you can't see that then perhaps you should sleep in there and give Holly your caravan.'

'Actually...' Jude raised her hand, reluctant to get sucked into the argument. 'I think you'll find the police won't let anyone in there until they've finished their investigation anyway.'

'What investigation?' said Dean. 'They'll come and take the body away, find out she died from a heart attack or sepsis or some ghastly STD, and then we can all get on with life.'

'How can you be so callous?' Jude couldn't help herself. Dean was so awful and seemed to have a complete lack of either empathy or humanity.

'Bloody hell, you women can be so reactive.' Dean threw his hands in the air. 'Fine. If it makes everybody feel better, I'll have someone bring another van for her.'

Jude wondered where the hell they'd fit another van and hoped that it wouldn't be as large as the ones that were already taking up a vast amount of her yard, campsite and the surrounding verges.

Just then there was a knock on the door and Robyn went to answer it.

'Hello there,' said a familiar voice. 'I'm Ffion and this is my sister, Caitlin. We're here to talk to you about our sheep?'

'Come in,' said Robyn. 'I'm sorry, but we're all at sixes and sevens this morning.'

'Heya, Jude.' Ffion's face broke into a warm smile when she saw her friend. 'When there was no sign of you at the house, we wondered if you might be here.'

Jude went over to hug first Ffion and then her younger sister, Caitlin.

'How's things going?' Caitlin asked. 'We've been watching the show, it's great.'

'Dean Dickens.' The director pulled his glasses down onto his nose and strutted over to welcome the two young farmers whom he looked up and down salaciously. 'Yes, good choice, Jude, very nice. You two are going to do well in front of the camera.'

'I'm sorry, but we're not going to be filming today though.' Robyn stood up and moved over to them. 'We've had a rather large upset so we're going to go with footage we've already shot.'

'Nonsense.' Dean shot Robyn a withering stare. 'Perhaps you've forgotten who makes the decisions. I know there's been an upset as you say, but we still have a show to put out. Annie, pull yourself together and go and find Simon. Holly should be here imminently and then we can crack on and get some filming down before this snow stops falling and we've lost our chance.'

Without waiting for a rebuttal, he walked purposefully from the trailer, leaving behind him a sense of discomfort amongst the five women left behind.

'Is everything okay?' Ffion looked at Jude.

It was then that the ambulance arrived, shortly followed by the police.

***

Whilst the emergency services did what they needed to do, Ffion and Caitlin decided to drive back to Abergavenny. Robyn had made the decision to cancel their interview, something that Jude wasn't entirely sure she had the power to do seeing as she was officially the researcher and Dean was the boss. It did feel the right decision though and Ffion and Caitlin were sympathetic and understanding. They hadn't wanted to stay too long anyway. There was no sign of the snow stopping and, even though they'd driven over in a 4x4 pickup, they didn't want to risk getting stuck. The sheep would need tending regardless of the weather.

DS Sami Abadi attended the scene, and Jude knew that Binnie would be twitchy for details as soon as her colleague was able to give them to her. Jude knew she hated being tied to the desk, and a suspicious death on Malvern Farm was definitely not something she would be happy to take a back seat in.

Before he returned to the station, Sami went round to the farmhouse to talk to Jude. They sat together in the kitchen, discussing what had happened that morning.

'I've had a slightly hysterical account from Annie Bird who found the body when she used her key to access the caravan in order to retrieve some personal items. I gather the caravan had originally been allocated to her?'

'Yes,' said Jude. 'She and Mary swapped which is, I assume, why Annie still had a key and had left some of her things in there.'

'We believe you were next on the scene and the first to ascertain that Mary Taper was definitely deceased.'

'I've no idea whether or not Annie checked before me but yes, I found no sign of life and the body was already cold.'

'And then you were joined by—' Sami checked his notes '—Robyn Porter and Simon North.'

'Yep. Robyn phoned for help and I tried to stop Simon from getting too involved in the crime scene.'

Sami looked up. 'Crime scene?' he said. 'You already think this is a crime then before we know the cause of death?'

Before Jude could answer, there was a knock on the door. It was Binnie, looking as poised and elegant as always despite the fact she was bundled into the thickest winter coat Jude had ever seen.

'Binnie!' said Sami in surprise. 'What are you doing here?'

'I couldn't just sit at the station waiting for news,' she said as she walked into the kitchen and shook off her coat. 'I promise not to get under your feet, DS Abadi. This is your case, but I came to see if there was anything I could do.'

Sami grinned. 'I'm not at all surprised,' he said. 'Except for the fact that I expected you to be here sooner.'

'Catch me up,' said Binnie. 'What are we looking at?'

'Initial thoughts from the paramedics is that it looks like a case of carbon monoxide poisoning,' said Sami. 'The redness of the skin and the markings on the body are clear indicators, although obviously the post-mortem will clarify this for certain.'

'Any idea of where the leak came from?' Binnie asked as she took a seat next to Sami at the kitchen table.

Jude thought back to the caravan, trying to remember what she'd seen. 'I noticed the window over the head of the bed was open a little when I went in so there was definitely airflow,' she said. 'I guess whatever has been emitting the carbon monoxide must have been doing so in pretty large amounts.'

Sami tapped his pen on the table. 'On the surface the only possible culprit looks like a small gas hob and oven, but we've got a team of experts coming out to have a proper check of the whole place.'

'What about the generator outside?' Jude asked. 'The noise from it was the reason Annie asked Mary to swap caravans.'

'It's possible,' said Binnie. 'I'd have thought the exhaust would have been carefully measured to make sure the fumes were not being pumped out anywhere near where people were sleeping. Whoever set things up would have had to carry out a risk assessment.'

Jude leant back against the rail of the Aga. 'You're right,' she said. 'They had to keep it far enough from the paddock so it wouldn't interfere with the animals. There must have been just as strict a protocol, probably much more so, for human living space.'

Sami scratched the very centre of his head as though scratching the middle of his brain for inspiration. 'Jude, before Binnie came in, you mentioned something about the caravan being a crime scene. The way you said it made it sound as though you are already doubting the nature of Mary's death.'

'Jude always thinks there's something wicked going on,' said Binnie. 'Only a few days ago you thought there was something suspicious about the trace of peanut in Annie's hot chocolate.'

Jude remembered the packet she'd retrieved from under the sofa in the chillout trailer, forgotten after the terrible turn of events. She took it out of her pocket and put the bag down on the table where Binnie had sat down.

'I found these earlier today,' she said. 'Virtually none missing by the look of it. They'd been hidden in the trailer where the crew go to rest in between filming.'

Binnie took a plastic bag from her pocket, always prepared, and put the packet inside.

'We've all had enough experience to know that coincidences are not to be trusted,' said Jude. 'First Annie's hot chocolate was contaminated by peanut coffee from the machine. Then her EpiPen was missing from her handbag exactly when she most needed it. Put that together with the fact I found these hidden in what should have been a strictly peanut-free zone and I'd say that there's definitely something going on. And now there's been a suspicious death too.'

Binnie rubbed her cheek thoughtfully. 'This could all be about Annie.'

'Exactly!' said Jude. 'Mary was in her caravan when she was killed and, as far as I know, nobody knew that she'd swapped with Annie who was now in the shepherd's hut.'

'Interesting theory,' said Sami. 'She seems so popular and inoffensive though. Any ideas on who might want her dead?'

Jude left the warmth of the Aga and went to join them at the table.

'I think there's a lot of hidden grievances below the surface of the nation's favourite celebrity cosy couple,' said Jude. 'Underneath all the hand holding and loving glances, I think there's a very rocky foundation.'

Binnie raised an eyebrow. 'Kindly expand.'

'It seems that Simon may have been having an affair with Mary Taper,' said Jude.

'Surely that gives Annie the perfect motive to kill her?' said Sami.

Jude was surprised to realise that she hadn't thought of this scenario, as wrapped up as she was with her theory that Annie had been the intended victim. Annie had a key to the caravan and was the person who found Mary's body so she definitely needed more consideration.

'I suppose it does,' she said. 'But it also gives Simon the incentive to want Annie out of the way too.'

'Both equally true,' said Binnie. 'Who else do you have on your radar, Jude? You've been getting to know the team, have you seen or heard anything else noteworthy?'

Jude thought about the production team. 'There are lots of people coming and going who I haven't met properly,' she said. 'Various engineers and members of the crew who aren't staying on site, but they come and go and nothing has stuck out.'

Binnie turned to Sami. 'You'll have got a list of everyone who has been on site since filming started?'

Sami said nothing but gave her a meaningful look.

'Sorry.' Binnie flapped her hand at him. 'Absolutely your case. I'm just here to observe.'

Sami rolled his eyes at Jude. They both knew that Binnie was not capable of merely observing.

'What about the key members of the crew?' He flipped his notebook open again. 'Those staying on site. As well as Annie and Simon, I have the director: Dean Dickens, researcher: Robyn Porter and sound guy: Gabriel King. Anyone else?'

'No, that's it,' said Jude. 'There are others staying at Four Trees B&B in the village and I know some are staying elsewhere too. The replacement camera operator is currently in Great Malvern but Dean's getting another caravan dropped off for her to move on site.'

'He's not wasting any time, is he?' said Binnie.

'It's all about the show for him.' Jude stroked the soft head of Pip, who had come over for a little attention. 'After Annie had the allergic reaction live on television, he didn't seem at all bothered about her health. He just saw it as a fabulous way to boost viewing figures. Even wanted to send a camera into the hospital with her.'

'He sounds like a peach,' said Binnie with a contemptuous look on her face.

'I wondered at the time if he'd been the one to deliberately taint the hot chocolate and hide the EpiPen,' said Jude. 'It was he who came to the rescue with the back-up one from the production trailer. Not sure I can see him going as far as murder though.'

'What about the others?' Sami asked. 'Any of them have reason to poison Annie?'

'Interesting line of questioning,' said Binnie. 'We would all do well to remember two things at this point. Firstly, that Annie is not the person who was killed. Secondly, at the moment we have no evidence that Mary's death was intentional.'

'Thank you, Detective Inspector.' Sami stared at her and Binnie held her hands up.

'Carry on,' she said.

'Jude? Anyone you can think of who would want either Annie *or* Mary dead, if we play with the idea that a freak accident like this might be considered beyond a coincidence so close to Annie's near-fatal brush with her peanut allergy?' He was still staring at Binnie as he spoke.

'Point taken,' said Binnie.

'The only other person I can think of is Robyn,' said Jude, choosing to ignore the tension between the two detectives. 'I heard her arguing with Annie the other day. It seems Robyn went for Dean's position as director of *Countryside Live*. This was several series ago by the sound of it and Robyn thought it was her shot at promotion. Annie put a spanner in the works though and she was overlooked in favour of Dean Dickens. She's clearly still incredibly bitter about it.'

'Interesting,' said Sami. 'But not a lot to go on at the moment. As Binnie says, let's wait for the results of the post-mortem and see if the source of the carbon monoxide can be ascertained.'

'In the meantime, the show is going ahead?' Binnie asked.

Jude nodded. 'Apparently so. Dean reckons there's no reason to cancel, and everyone is contracted until Christmas Eve.'

'I see. Well then, let's hope there are no more off-screen dramas.'

* * *

Jude couldn't let the possibility of murder lie. She had never been one to believe in coincidence and there were far too many things in her mind that pointed firmly at play of the very foulest kind.

When Sami and Binnie left, she found herself wandering down to the paddock to see if there was anything she could do to help. If she was able to carry out a bit of undercover investigating whilst she was there then all the better.

The snow had stopped falling and there was a covering of perhaps three inches everywhere. It softened the edges of everything and made the world seem instantly cleaner and more tranquil.

That was until she got close to the chillout trailer where Dean and Simon were in the middle of an argument, coming to blows over whether the show should continue or not.

'You have no choice,' said Dean coolly. He was standing on the steps of the trailer, which gave him a height advantage over Simon, who was on the grass, his hands balled into fists at his sides and his face full of fury.

Annie was beside him, her hand on his arm as though trying to calm her husband down.

'If you don't do the show you'll be in breach of contract and the network's lawyers will roast you. I suggest you pull your big boy's pants on and get on with it and then you can grieve or whatever this is on Christmas Day when it's all over.'

'Were you always this heartless?' Simon shouted. 'Have you not a single moral or scrap of decency? A member of the crew died today. We should be respecting that, not carrying on as though nothing happened.'

'I tell you what.' Dean was beginning to look bored as he glanced at his phone. 'We'll dedicate today's show to her. How about that?'

'I won't do it,' said Simon. 'I don't care about the money.'

'What about your reputation and your career then?' Dean

said. 'People might start asking why exactly the well-loved and ever so trustworthy Simon North is quite so cut up about the death of a pretty camera-girl. Might also be interesting if they knew about the row you had with her last night. What was it you said to her? Something to do with her getting too demanding? Tell me, Simon. How demanding was she exactly and what would you be prepared to do to get some space?'

'You arsehole,' Simon hissed. He stepped closer to the steps of the trailer and for a moment Jude thought he was going to punch the director in his smug face.

Annie was quick to stop him. She put her arm out and barred the way.

'Simon, don't,' she said. 'I know what she was to you, don't think I've been blinkered all this time. But as much as Dean's an arse, he's right. We have to keep going. You have to do this for me – for us. If you don't then our careers are over. Your affair with... with her will be dragged through the tabloids and that sort of mud sticks. Please. Just three weeks and then you can hibernate for as long as you need. But don't burn everything we've worked so hard for.'

The look on Simon's face as he turned to his pleading wife was hard to read.

He said nothing as he shrugged her arm off, turned and stomped over the snow towards his own trailer. Jude wasn't sure whether that meant he was going to carry on or not. She did know, however, that things between the darling Mr and Mrs of daytime television could never be the same again.

Jude walked past the trailer, trying to pretend that she hadn't been at all interested in the argument that they all knew she'd just heard.

'Just going to empty the bins,' she said as she headed into the campsite and towards the shower block.

Her mind was busy, sorting through the details of the row between the director and his two star presenters. It was clear now that Annie had known exactly what had been going on between her husband and Mary Taper. There was also the argument that Dean had mentioned. Had he been suggesting that Simon had had enough of Mary and might be better off with her and her *demanding* ways out of the picture?

Jude would have to wait to find out the official cause of death but her senses were tingling with the thought that this was no accident.

The showers were housed in an old horsebox at the top of the campsite, just behind the three large trailers and next to the film crew's petrol generator.

It hummed as it ticked over and Jude could see why the noise had irritated Annie enough to ask to swap caravans with Mary. The large machine stood a way from the trailers and there was a long, ridged pipe, attached to the exhaust outlet. It looked like a shower hose, only wider, and it was designed to take the toxic fumes away from the animals in the paddock and the sleeping people in the nearby trailers.

Unless...

Jude stood for a moment, looking at the exhaust pipeline and mentally calculating the distance between the open end and the window of the trailer that Mary had been asleep in. It would definitely have stretched.

She went over to have a look, the heat from the escaping gas enough to melt any flakes that dared to try landing on it. As she stared at the exhaust pipe, she noticed there were a couple of small patches of something magenta stuck a few inches from the end of it. Pulling her scarf over her nose and mouth so as not to breathe in any of the fumes, she bent down for a closer examination. It seemed to be a cluster of very fine fibres, stuck to the pipe with some sort of sticky residue, the kind Jude recognised as being left behind when she used heavy-duty tape for outside jobs.

Jude took out her phone and tried to capture an image but, although the fibres could clearly be seen, the residue wasn't at all visible. She sent it to Sami nonetheless with the caption:

> I think someone may have tampered with the exhaust pipe of the generator.

If Jude was right and someone had used tape on the end of the pipe then it stood to reason that the most likely place for it to have been stuck was through the gap in the window above the bed where Mary had been sleeping.

Jude went over to suss it out and, brushing the snow carefully away from the window frame, found herself wholly unsurprised to discover traces of the same sticky residue. It was easy to see thanks to the scraps of dirt that had been caught on it, perhaps from the mud carried up from the exhaust pipe. Also caught in the grip of the adhesive were the tiniest fuzzy burrs of the same magenta as the fibres stuck to the pipe, bright against the white of the window frame.

There was no doubt whatsoever in Jude's mind: she had confirmation that someone, wearing an item of clothing – gloves, perhaps – the colour of a tropical flower, had deliberately piped deadly gas into the trailer of a sleeping woman.

She'd been right.

This was murder.

10

The forensic team arrived swiftly and Jude was glad to pass over the details of what she'd discovered.

Binnie and Sami also came back to the farm, together this time as any pretence that Binnie hadn't returned to active duty was forgotten. Jude left them to their investigation whilst she went to the chillout trailer to see if there was anyone around for her to chat with.

Now that murder had been very much ruled in, she felt the need to talk to the rest of the *Countryside Live* team and see what she could uncover. It was often surprising what she found out when talking as an informal bystander, things that didn't come to light during official police interviews for one reason or another.

It would also give her the chance to see how everyone was reacting to the news of Mary's death.

Annie and Gabe were the only two in the trailer when Jude went in. They were sitting very close together and pulled away suspiciously when Jude opened the door.

'Ah, Jude,' said Annie, standing up. 'Are you looking for someone?'

'I just came to see if there was anything I could do to help.' She closed the door against the cold and took off her wet boots. 'And to say how sorry I am. You must all be devastated.'

'We are.' Annie wrung her hands together. 'It's just too awful. Poor Mary. Although we've been told they think it was carbon monoxide poisoning and that she would have died painlessly in her sleep, which is a small blessing.'

'It was so avoidable,' said Gabe. 'That's what makes it so terrible. If there had been a working carbon monoxide monitor in the caravan she would have been alerted to the danger.'

'That's what I can't understand,' said Annie. 'I'm sure there was one. I can picture it standing on top of the cupboards by the microwave and hob. It's the sort of thing I notice.'

'Well, if there was then it must have been faulty.' Gabe punched the cushion on the sofa next to him. 'Such a stupid waste.'

Jude knew that the only people who currently had the information that pointed firmly at murder were her and the police. Therefore, to Gabe, a faulty carbon monoxide monitor was a terrible oversight but nothing more suspicious than that. To Jude though, it was another piece of the despicable puzzle of murderous intentions. And if someone had been inside the caravan to tamper with or remove the carbon monoxide monitor then they must have either had the key, or found another way to gain entry. Jude knew that Annie had held on to a key which she'd used to let herself in. Was she the only one other than Mary who had one? If so then this put her firmly in sight as a suspect, especially given that her husband was probably sleeping with the deceased.

'I gather you're still being asked to go ahead with the show today,' said Jude.

'It feels so wrong,' said Gabe. 'Just carrying on as though nothing has happened. I don't know how Holly has the nerve to take the job. I don't think I'd be able to step into a dead woman's shoes quite so readily.'

'That's not entirely fair, Gabe.' Annie sat back down on the sofa next to him.

'Holly's the replacement camera operator, isn't she?' asked Jude, sitting on one of the soft lounging chairs.

'Yes,' said Gabe darkly. 'I bet she was rubbing her hands together at her good fortune when she got the call to say she'd been promoted.'

'Gabe!' Annie admonished. 'She and Mary were friends, she'll be as upset as any one of us, I'm sure, but it wouldn't do anybody any good if she turned the job down. Dean would have just called someone else in to do it.'

'They weren't friends.' Gabe sounded scornful. 'Holly was always resentful of her. You know as well as I do that she accused Mary of only getting the job because she was slee—'

Annie elbowed him sharply in the ribs but Jude knew what he was in the middle of saying. Mary's replacement clearly thought she'd been at a disadvantage when it came to getting the best camera jobs because she wasn't sleeping with the star of the show. This was an interesting snippet that Jude filed away. Quite how interesting it was, she wasn't sure. Would it be enough of a grievance to consider as a possible motive for murder?

'Gabe, can you just stop, please?' said Annie. 'I'm finding this whole thing very difficult and you're really not helping.' She rubbed her hand across her forehead and Gabe moved closer to rest an arm around her shoulder.

'I know,' he said. 'I'm sorry.'

He looked at Jude. 'We're all so aware that Mary was in

Annie's caravan when she died. It's one of those sliding door moments, you know?'

Gabe was absolutely right, of course, and it was something that Jude had already considered at great length.

'Who knew you'd swapped caravans with Mary?' Jude asked.

'I don't know,' said Annie. 'It was late when we agreed and I didn't tell anyone although Mary might have, I suppose.'

Annie looked at Jude and her hand flew to her throat. 'Oh God, do you think someone did this on purpose – because they thought it was me in there?' Her eyes were haunted as she looked at Jude for an answer. 'They must have, mustn't they? First the contaminated hot chocolate and now this. Someone is trying to kill me.'

'It was a horrible accident. A terrible thing that happened but it's over now,' said Gabe as he pulled Annie into an embrace which she allowed for a second or two before she pulled away, smoothing her pale hair with a shaking hand.

Jude tried to give an encouraging smile which she knew would not convey the reassurance that Annie needed, because Jude herself didn't believe it.

This was no accident. A murderer had struck and from where Jude was standing, there was definitely a good chance that someone was indeed targeting Annie Bird.

Jude wasn't sure what to say and was extremely grateful to the trailer door and the woman who chose that moment to open it.

'Guys,' said the woman, her face a picture of deepest sympathy and yet not a wholly believable one. 'Oh, how awful. I'm just so shocked by the whole thing. How's morale in the camp?' She walked over to the sofa where Annie and Gabe were sitting. Her snow-caked winter boots left grey marks on the carpet and she chose to fling her wet coat on the empty lounge chair rather than hang it up to dry on the hooks by the door.

'Hey, Holly.' Gabe nodded weakly at her and Jude realised this was the camera operator called up to replace Mary.

'Morale, as you can imagine, is low,' said Annie as Holly took a seat on the sofa opposite her. 'We're all terribly upset.'

'Sure, sure,' said Holly. 'Totally get that. I'm the same. Couldn't stop crying when Dean called to give me the news.'

'And yet you're here,' said Gabe drily. 'Ready for duty.'

'Yep.' Holly nodded slowly. 'I thought about saying no. Mary and me were so close that it feels really weird. But then I thought that she'd want me to do it. Someone she trusts, who knows her work and her vision. So I'm doing it for her, really.'

Gabe had sat forward, his forearms on his knees and his head and shoulders stretching into the gap between the two sofas. 'And for your career,' he said. 'Let's not forget the boost this opportunity will give it.'

Holly looked completely unperturbed as she crossed her legs and leant her elbow on the arm rest. 'Gabe, I know you and Mary worked together for donkey's years and I'm sure you're missing her loads right now but we can't bring her back and you know I'm bloody good at my job so I do hope we can get along.'

Gabe glowered at her for a moment before snatching his gaze away and up towards the ceiling. Jude could see the watery gleam of tears in his eyes and wasn't sure if this was a symptom of his grief or his anger.

'I don't know about you but I need a bit of a rest.' Annie stood up. 'This is all too much and if we're going to pull a show together this evening, I need to do some meditation and yoga first.'

'Haven't we got an interview to record?' Holly asked. 'Some sheep breeders or something?'

'No,' said Jude. 'They went home ages ago.'

'Oh. Does Dean know?'

'I have no idea.' Jude was in danger of getting embroiled in something that she wanted nothing to do with. If the show was going to go out that evening then it was up to the director to sort it out and she suddenly longed for the relative peace of the farmhouse kitchen.

Jude followed Annie to the door where she put her boots back on. Gabe was hot on her heels and the three of them left together, Jude heading left to the farmhouse whilst Annie and Gabe turned right to go down through the campsite to their huts. They would have to walk past the trailer where police tape now hung across the front door. Jude imagined that would be tough for them both.

As she stomped through the snow, her hands thrust deep into her pockets and her nose reddening from the cold, she heard her name being shouted. Turning back to see Sami and Binnie at the entrance to the campsite, she waited until they'd caught up with her.

'It looks as though your hunch was right,' said Sami as they walked around the edge of the frozen pond.

'Murder?' asked Jude.

'Seems that way,' said Binnie.

'But who was the target? At the moment it seems entirely possible that it could be Annie, although she also has a really good reason to be the killer.'

'I think this is the first time I've ever worked a case when we have that situation. Someone who has equal claim to the title of killer or intended murder victim,' said Sami.

'According to her, nobody knew they had changed vans and the decision was very late in the day, just before they went to bed. Obviously, we can't overlook the possibility that Mary herself told someone though.'

'You say she was having an affair with Simon North,' said

Binnie. 'Could he have known about the new sleeping arrangements?'

'I don't know,' said Jude. 'According to Dean, they'd had an argument earlier that day. He'd accused her of being too demanding. I don't know if this was before the caravan swap or maybe because of it.'

'He has possible motives to kill either way then,' said Binnie. 'With two women on the go at the same time, he might have decided to get rid of one of them.'

'I think Gabe the soundman might have known about the van swap,' said Jude. 'There's a chance he's having an affair with Annie and if that's the case and she moved into Mary's hut to be closer to him then it stands to reason she would have told him.'

'But why would he want to kill Mary?' Sami asked.

They'd walked back into the yard and Jude stopped next to Sami's car. 'That I don't know,' she said. 'Are you coming in for a cuppa?'

'We need to get back to the station,' said Sami. 'Thanks though.'

'One last thing to consider,' said Jude, 'although it might well be on your radar. Whoever taped the exhaust pipe through the window quite possibly also had access to the inside of the caravan. Annie is absolutely sure there was a carbon monoxide monitor in there so if it didn't go off, and I assume these things are checked regularly, then it must have been either removed or tampered with.'

'There wasn't a monitor there,' said Sami. 'It was one of the first things we looked for. But you say Annie is certain there had been one?'

'There seemed no doubt in her mind,' said Jude. 'She'd seen it sitting on top of one of the cupboards above the microwave which seems to suggest someone had been inside to take it.'

'There is a set of keys for all caravans held in the production trailer,' said Binnie.

Jude sighed. 'So anyone could have taken the key and sneaked in.'

'Yep,' said Sami.

'What does this mean for Annie?' Jude asked. 'If she was the real intended victim, who's to say that the killer won't try and strike again now they know they hit the wrong target?'

'It's such a tough one,' Sami replied. 'We have no strong evidence to prove that she was the intended victim but of course it's not something we can rule out, especially after the incident with the hot chocolate. I've called someone from victim support in to talk to her and find out what she wants. If she feels unsafe and we believe the threat to be great enough then we will think about police protection. Otherwise...'

'She'll just have to take her chances,' Jude finished his sentence for him.

'Either way, I think things are going to be interesting round here for as long as those telly people are on the farm,' said Binnie.

'Yes,' said Jude. 'That's what I'm afraid of.'

* * *

Despite the serious misgivings and vocal disapproval of some of the team, the show did air that evening. Simon was there in person but it was painfully obvious that his mind was elsewhere. Whilst Annie put on a good show and tried to jolly things along, Simon remained mute much of the time, grunting his responses and making no attempt at all to hide his feelings. Jude wondered at the ethics of forcing either of them in front of a live camera given what they were both dealing with. There was a far shorter amount of live footage than usual, the programme relying heavily on sections of pre-recorded footage filmed earlier in the week.

When the final credits rolled, there was a note to say that the episode was aired in loving memory of Mary Taper, gifted camera operator and dear friend of the show.

'That was painful to watch,' said Lucy when they switched the television off. 'Poor Annie, she was trying so hard to keep it all together but you could tell she was ready to collapse.'

'Simon looked dreadful,' said Jude. 'Surely Dean is making a huge mistake putting them out on live television every night. It can't be good for the programme.'

'Or Annie and Simon's careers,' said Noah. 'I'd have thought they'd have more than enough money to retire on now. If it were me, I'd cut my losses and live out a quiet life away from all the nonsense of celebrity.'

'There's a reason it isn't you though, my love,' said Lucy as she leant back against his shoulder. 'You'd not have lasted five minutes in the public eye, let alone the fifteen-odd years those two have been doing it.'

'Oi!' Noah looked a little put out by this declaration. 'I'd have lasted.'

Lucy pulled his arm tighter around her. 'No, you wouldn't. And thank goodness for that. I couldn't possibly love you if you did.'

* * *

More snow fell in the night, filling in the footprints from the day before. In the morning, Jude offered to drive Sebbie to school over the fields in the John Deere tractor.

The combined thrill of snow on the ground and a ride in the tractor was enough to turn the small boy into a tornado of excitement and he threw himself around the house, getting in everybody's way.

Once Jude had deposited him safely at the school gate, wellies on his feet, bag in hand containing a pair of slippers as was the way at Malvern End Primary when the weather was wet, she breathed a sigh of relief. She adored her nephew more than any other living soul but on days like this, she was happy to hand him over. Having trained as a primary teacher herself, Jude knew only too well the impact weather had on small charges and she pitied the ever-patient Miss Elgar having to cope with so many of them in one excitement-fuelled class.

Whilst she was down in the village, Jude took a detour to the little shop to pick up some groceries and postage stamps. They'd bought several packs of the Christmas cards Sebbie had designed at school and Jude knew she should find time to write them. Perhaps if she bought the stamps it would be another incentive.

The little bell above the door tinkled a morning welcome as she walked into the shop. Gold tinsel had been taped around the edge of the windows and someone had been up on a ladder to hang twisted crepe paper streamers in swags from the ceiling. Mrs James, who ran the shop and post office, always had a willing stream of locals to do little jobs like that for her.

'Morning, Jude,' Mrs James called. She was dressed in her usual winter uniform of a woollen skirt and polo-neck jumper covered with a floral-print pinny, only now she was also sporting a jaunty pair of the most enormous Christmas baubles in her ears.

'Good morning, Mrs James. It's looking lovely and festive in here.'

'It's my favourite time of the year,' she replied. 'I do love a bit of sparkle.'

'It suits you.'

'And you've got double the excitement up at the farm this Christmas, what with the wedding and everything. How's the bride feeling?'

Jude walked to the fridge near the counter and opened the door to pick out some thick-cut ham and a packet of butter. 'Lucy's fine. You know how organised she is. She's thought of absolutely everything and we all have our lists of things to do.'

'Not long now. And then of course there's that film crew of yours. Janet said she saw an ambulance heading into your campsite yesterday, was it anything serious? We wondered if Annie had had another funny turn?'

The bell tinkled again and Jude looked over to see Marco stamping the snow off his boots at the door.

'Come in and keep the cold out,' said Mrs James.

'Sorry.' Marco pushed the door shut, setting the bell jingling again. 'You know what they say about bells ringing at Christmas?'

'Every time a bell rings, an angel gets its wings,' Jude chirruped in a saccharine American accent, parroting the child from her favourite Christmas film.

'Attaboy, Clarence!' Marco grinned and she laughed back.

'What are you two talking about?' Mrs James asked.

'Don't tell me you've never seen *It's a Wonderful Life*?' said Jude.

'Best film ever made,' said Marco. 'Don't you think, Jude?'

'Absolutely.'

She looked at him and found that he was staring at her with an intensity that she hadn't seen for a while. It ignited her in a way that was not at all helpful and she gave a tiny cough before returning her attention to the yoghurts in the fridge.

'Jude was just about to update me on the film crew,' said Mrs James. 'Did you know they had to call an ambulance yesterday? And I thought it was an odd show yesterday. Simon hardly said a word and Annie looked as though she was only just keeping it together.'

Jude looked across to where the shopkeeper had taken a seat on her stool behind the till and was resting her elbows on the counter. She was a thoughtful soul and infinitely kind but she was still a stalwart of the village gossip vine and Jude knew she had to filter what she said in front of her.

'They had a bereavement and were both in shock, I think.'

'Oh, poor things,' said Mrs James. 'Was it someone close to them?'

'I don't know how close they were.'

'It seems a shame that they weren't given a bit of time off.' Marco joined Jude at the fridges and picked up a block of cheddar.

'They had a live slot on the telly that needed to be filled, I suppose,' said Mrs James. 'If it wasn't a member of the family or a particularly close friend then it must be a case of the show must go on. Although what about the ambulance?'

Jude reached inside the fridge for a tub of custard and Marco chose to take a pot of cream cheese at the same time so the backs of their hands brushed each other. Jude resented the prickles of heat that shot through her skin and pinballed up her arm.

'Ah, at last,' said Mrs James, thankfully distracted by the sound of a van pulling up outside. 'That's the morning newspapers. The snow has made everything late. I was wondering if I'd get them at all today.'

Marco put his butter and cream cheese on the counter and went to open the door for the delivery man who was carrying two bundles of papers bound together with plastic strapping.

'Sorry I'm late today, Mrs J,' he said as he threw the bundles of papers on the floor next to the counter. 'I had to come round the long way. West Malvern Road is a nightmare and I didn't trust my van down Croft Bank anyway, far too steep.'

'Well, you're here now,' said Mrs James. 'Are the lanes clear then?'

'I wouldn't go out unless you have to,' he said. 'It's dicey out there.'

That was one of the pitfalls of living in the country. Snow ploughs and gritters tended to stick to the main roads, although the farmers did their best to clear as many of the lanes as possible to keep people moving.

'I'll just fetch the rest of your papers in.'

He went back out to his van and returned with another two bundles which were unceremoniously dumped on top of the others.

'Will you stay for a cuppa to warm yourself up?' Mrs James asked him.

'Thanks for the offer but I've got a full van still so I'd best get myself away. Hopefully see you tomorrow. Unless there's another dumping overnight.'

'I've checked the forecast and that's our lot,' said Mrs James. 'For now, at least.'

'Good-o. Bye for now, then.' He left the shop and jumped into his van.

Jude carried on with her shopping, picking out a loaf of fresh bread before heading to the furthest part of the shop to find a tin of pineapple rings to make an upside-down pudding.

'I can't find my scissors,' said Mrs James. 'Can you two mind the shop for a moment whilst I nip out back to get the ones from the kitchen?'

'No problem,' Jude called.

'Everything okay?' Marco asked quietly as he came to stand

next to her. 'You don't seem yourself and I know that tinned pineapple and custard can only mean one thing.'

'What are you talking about? I'm fine.'

'So you're not going to go home and make your go-to comfort pineapple upside-down pudding because you need a pick-me-up?'

He was so close to her that she could feel his breath on her cheek. He knew her so well; they'd been the very best of friends for a while. She missed his constant presence in her life so much but she couldn't get that back. Not now he was dating someone else. All Jude wanted to do was beg him to dump Clara and choose her instead.

'I just thought we all needed a bit of stodge to get us through the cold snap,' said Jude.

Mrs James arrived back in the shop then, armed with a substantial pair of scissors to cut the bindings from the piles of newspapers.

'Heavens!' She stood upright, holding a copy of one of the tabloids. 'Jude, look. Those telly folk up at your farm are on the front page.'

'What?' Jude felt her heart sink. Why would Simon and Annie be headline news? Surely this couldn't be about Mary's death. Not even the rags would have picked up on that story so quickly.

'Oh, my.' Mrs James was staring at the paper. 'So it *was* someone from the filming crew.'

'I...' Jude was lost for words as she took a copy of the paper to look at for herself.

TRAGIC COUNTRYSIDE LIVE DEATH

'Jude obviously didn't know that this was supposed to be

common knowledge, until now,' said Marco, reading the article over Jude's shoulder.

> Phenomenally successful television show *Countryside Live*, which is currently running a special festive series in the run-up to Christmas, was hit by tragedy yesterday as one of the long-standing members of the filming crew was discovered dead on the show's location.
>
> The body of Mary Taper (37), who worked as a camera operator on the show for the past six years, was found in her caravan, although the nature of her death has, as yet, not been disclosed.
>
> The programme, which is being filmed in a small Herefordshire village, is known for combining pre-recorded features that address elements of life in the countryside with daily live updates and interviews. It has been hugely popular since it was first aired almost ten years ago but this is the first time that a Christmas special has been commissioned.
>
> Regular viewers of the show noticed out-of-character behaviour from hosts Annie Bird and Simon North during the live sections of last night's episode. Usually well-known for their upbeat banter and the obvious connection between the married hosts, it was unnerving to see Simon North virtually silent and clearly distressed whilst his wife tried her best to keep things going.
>
> A source close to the couple has suggested that there may be more to Simon's grief than merely the loss of a colleague. Simon and Mary Taper have been caught several times in 'close and compromising' situations. Questions are now being asked about their relationship.

'That can't be true,' said Mrs James, who had obviously reached the same part of the article as Jude.

There is also doubt about what this means for the remainder of the show, due to continue running until Christmas Eve.

Jude knew this article was going to be explosive and, like the journalist who'd written it, she wondered if it might be enough to blow what was left of the series apart.

11

Jude loaded her shopping into the tote bags she'd brought with her and added a copy of the paper.

'It's never quiet up at Malvern Farm, is it, Jude?' Mrs James said as she handed her the credit card machine to tap.

'You can say that again.'

'Did you walk?' Marco asked. 'I didn't see the Land Rover outside.'

'No. I brought Sebbie through the fields in the tractor.'

'So you're going back my way then?' said Marco, knowing that the tractor would now be parked in the field close to his cottage. 'Give me a sec and I'll come with you.'

Marco paid for his shopping which he put in his rucksack and then the pair said goodbye to Mrs James and went back out into the snow. The pavement was slippery to walk on as yesterday's footsteps had flattened and partially melted the snow and the night's temperature drop had re-frozen it.

'Woah, steady there.' Marco caught Jude around the waist as she skidded like a cartoon deer on a particularly devilish patch of ice.

The near tumble triggered a rapid increase of Jude's heart rate. At least she told herself that was the cause.

'Are you okay?' Marco asked, still holding her.

'Yes.' Jude stood there for a moment to catch her breath. 'I thought I was going over then.'

'So did I.' Marco smiled and Jude ached at the sight of his familiar dimples and the crows' feet around his eyes. 'But I wasn't worried about you so much as the shopping. God forbid you squashed that tub of custard and had to have dry pineapple upside-down cake.'

'That would have been a proper disaster.' Jude smiled back at him. 'Thank you for saving my custard.'

'Glad to have been of assistance, ma'am.' Marco pretended to doff his bobble hat to her. 'Can I take those bags for you?'

'Thanks, but I can manage.'

Marco nodded at her bare hands which were already starting to turn purple from the cold and the weight pulling down on the thin straps of the loaded totes she was carrying. 'At least borrow my gloves then.'

'You keep them,' said Jude. 'I'm the one daft enough to have come outside without a pair of my own.'

Marco took off his thickly knitted gloves anyway. 'All my shopping is on my back so I can stick my hands in my pockets.' He took Jude's bags so she could put the gloves on.

Pre-warmed by Marco, the cosy wooliness against her skin was a very welcome feeling and the bags were much more comfortable in her hands when she took them back.

'Thank you,' she said. 'What would I have done if I hadn't bumped into you?'

'You'd have had a bruised arse and frozen hands,' said Marco.

'Not to mention the squashed custard.'

The two walked off, away from the shop and towards the edge

of the village where Marco's cottage stood. As they passed the school, Jude could hear excited whoops and laughter and they both looked over to see children outside in the playground, zipped into coats and all wearing wellies. The school was tiny, with less than a hundred children in attendance, but Jude suspected that only those in walking distance would be there when there was snow on the ground. She was pleased to see that the teachers who had made it in were allowing them to enjoy the delights of the winter weather. She would have done the same if she'd still been teaching as they would all have been far too distracted to get anything useful done in the classroom.

'I don't want to pry,' said Marco as they walked on towards the pub, 'but are things really okay? Having the film crew up at the farm and now this death too, it's a lot to be getting on with, never mind having Christmas and a wedding coming up too.'

'Oh, don't worry about me,' said Jude. 'It's like Mrs James said, it's never quiet up at the farm, you know that.'

'But I do worry about you,' said Marco.

'You really don't need to.' Jude adjusted the bags of shopping in her hands.

They stopped just before the pub where there was a small gate through the thick hedge into Jude's field.

Marco pulled the front of his hat away from his forehead so he could itch the skin beneath it. 'You are always so focused on checking that everyone else around you is okay that you forget to do the same for yourself.'

'What are you talking about?' Jude raised her shopping bags. 'I have tinned pineapple and custard in here.'

Marco didn't smile this time. 'Be serious for a moment. I know we don't see each other as much as we used to.'

'You mean since you swapped me for Clara?'

Marco looked hurt and Jude instantly regretted the unnecessary snipe. 'I'm sorry,' she said. 'I didn't mean that. Of course you should be spending more time with her than me, she is your girlfriend, after all.'

'Doesn't mean I haven't got time for you as well. I loved our friendship, Jude. And I miss it. I miss you.'

'We still see each other. You and Clara were up at the farm the other evening.'

Marco looked away and Jude thought she heard him sigh. 'You're right,' he said. 'But if you're ever in need of a quiet night away from everything, just the two of us sharing a bottle of wine and setting the world to rights like we always used to, you know where I am.'

Jude wanted to drop the bags onto the snowy ground and throw her arms around his neck. She longed to tell him that she wanted nothing more than to take him up on the offer and book herself in for that very evening. But how could she when the offer had been one of friendship? It would be a long time before her heart healed and she was okay with that being the limit of their relationship.

'Thanks,' she said. 'Like you said, things are pretty busy at the moment. Maybe sometime in the new year.'

'Sure,' said Marco. 'Well, take care of yourself and I'll see you around then.'

'See you.' Jude turned away and headed for the gate where she paused and looked back to watch Marco disappear along the road past the pub.

'Bugger, bugger, arse, tits and bugger,' she cursed as she screwed her eyes up in frustration. That had not gone well. He'd told her he missed their friendship and she had let him leave thinking that she didn't miss it every bit as much as he did, probably even more so.

Jude exhaled deeply and then opened the gate. The John

Deere was waiting for her and the cab was freezing as she climbed up inside with her bags of shopping. It wasn't until she was sitting in the driving seat that she realised she was still wearing Marco's gloves. Now, at least, she had the perfect excuse to call around later to drop them back. And this time, she'd think carefully about what she was going to say before she got there.

As she drove slowly through the field, Jude cast her eye around the hardy Cheviot ewes. It was a beautiful day and the snow looked even whiter under a blue sky and low winter sun.

Noah had already been out to fill up the hayracks and there were plenty of sheep clustered around, pulling out clumps to chew. Others were snuffling around in the snow, unbothered by the tractor, some bleating in Jude's direction as she drove past. Their thick fleeces acted as a brilliant insulator, keeping the heat in and the cold out. Most of them were pregnant and yet they all seemed completely at home in their snowy field.

At the top of the field, Jude jumped down to open the gate and saw Annie waving at her through the window of the chillout trailer. Jude waved back before returning to the cab to drive the tractor through the gate. Her heart dropped a little as she saw Dean Dickens saunter over towards her. She would have loved to have carried on driving past but she had no choice. If she didn't get out to shut the gate then the yard would be full of sheep escapees in no time.

'Good morning, Jude,' Dean said. He leant forwards and she was surprised to find him landing two continental kisses on her cheeks, the second one lingering for a fraction of a second before she pulled sharply away.

'Sorry, Dean,' she said as she pulled the gate shut and slid the bolt into place, 'I can't stop this morning, I'm afraid.'

'I want you on the show again,' he said with a smile that made bile churn in her stomach. 'The camera loved your face. It's a face that should be seen. I'd definitely like to see more of you.'

He rested a hand on her shoulder and stared at her intently in a way that suggested she should be grateful for the attention and nauseating compliment.

'Why not join me in my van? It's warmer in there and we can have a proper chat.' His mouth twitched lasciviously and Jude thought she'd rather enter a field full of bulls at breeding time than be alone with Dean in his caravan.

'Sorry, no can do,' she said. 'It was most certainly a one-off, I'm afraid.'

'That's a shame.' Dean started to run his hand down her arm but she shook it off roughly. 'You shouldn't be so quick to pull away,' he said. 'I can make things happen for you. I know you need money for the farm and I'm sure we can come to some sort of arrangement that suits us both.'

He stepped towards her and she was quick to step sideways and put her hand on the reassuring solidity of the tractor with its engine still throbbing.

'I'm not that desperate for money.' Jude wasn't entirely sure what he was suggesting she needed to do for the promised funds, but she knew that whatever it was, she wanted nothing to do with it.

Jude got back into the tractor's cab and slammed the door shut, glad to be out of the way of the smarmy man and his wandering hands. As she drove across the yard, she went through every detail of what had just happened with Dean. She replayed it in her head but allowed herself the mental satisfaction of imagining the different ways she could have responded. A knee to the groin perhaps, or maybe a well-executed twist of the arm to show him how much she didn't appreciate the hands-on approach. At least a more impactful vocal response would have been good.

She was bristling as she stowed the tractor safely back in the barn and got out with her shopping. Clever retorts were lining up to taunt her in their tardiness and she wished they'd made themselves known whilst she'd been with Dean. As she walked across the yard towards the house, she saw Annie heading her way and they met by the old stone cider press outside the front door.

'Have you got a moment?' Annie asked and Jude noticed how utterly exhausted the show's leading lady looked.

'Of course,' she replied. 'Do you want to come in?'

'If I'm not putting you out?'

Jude needed a bit of space and some quiet but she ushered Annie towards the porch where they pulled off their boots before heading into the Aga-warmed kitchen.

'Cup of tea?' Jude asked, putting her shopping bags on the side. 'Please, sit down.'

'Thanks,' said Annie, going over to the table.

Jude put the heavily dented, ancient kettle under the tap and filled it with enough water to make a pot of tea. Then she lifted the lid from the hottest of the Aga plates and put the kettle on to boil.

'What can I help you with?' she asked as she took two mugs from the draining board and checked that they were clean.

'I saw you with Dean just now and I actually wanted to check that you were okay. He can be a bit much sometimes.'

'He's definitely got a certain way about him.'

'That's putting it mildly.' Annie took her woollen hat off and ran her fingers through her white-blonde hair.

Jude finished making the pot of tea and took it, along with the mugs, milk and a box of mince pies to the table.

'I'm not sure if these are any good,' she said. 'I don't think there are any peanuts in mince pies but probably best to check the label.'

'I'm fine with the tea, thanks,' said Annie.

Jude sat down opposite her.

'He's an arsehole,' Annie continued, the word sounding out of place coming from her. 'A powerful one who knows he can get away with a lot because of the cards he holds.'

Jude looked at Annie who had her hands in her lap and was staring down at them.

'Annie, has he ever laid a finger on you?'

Annie looked up. 'No. I think I'd be a step too far for him. But I have wondered about other women who've worked here. Not that anyone has ever made an official complaint.'

This revelation didn't surprise Jude in the slightest. She'd heard enough stories about men with authority who used their power to get what they wanted. It happened in all parts of society and would continue to happen until enough women were brave enough to stand up to them and shout about what was happening. The trouble was, people like Dean knew that a lot of the women they tried to seduce would keep quiet because if they rocked the boat, they would be the ones getting wet – not him.

'He's forcing us to carry on with the show, as you know, despite the fact we all think we should pull at least the live sections,' said Annie. 'I spoke to my agent and he basically told me I have no choice. Dean threatened our contracts and he has so much clout in the industry, one wrong move from me and my career could be over.'

'Surely not,' said Jude. 'You and Simon are enormously popular and bring in massive audiences. That has to count for an awful lot.'

'Together, yes. But if I'm ever on my own then I'll need all the industry support I can get. I'm popular as half of a much-loved celebrity couple, Annie and Simon. Who wants rejected, slightly saggy, middle-aged, once-was Annie Bird on her own?'

Jude wondered how much weight there was behind Annie's concerns. Was there really a possibility that the marriage and working partnership were in danger of collapse and if that happened, would she really find it hard to find work on her own? It must be terrible to feel that disposable.

'Gah, I wish I'd not encouraged the network to get him involved with the show.'

'Can I ask why you did?' Jude thought about Robyn and her thwarted attempt to take the job.

'Simple, really,' said Annie. 'Robyn was the network's first choice but she would have been wrong for the job. A good director needs to be a team player, look after the people who work with them. And Robyn? She's a bit too...'

She was a bully, thought Jude. But then wasn't Dean Dickens something even worse than that?

'I didn't know what Dean was really like when I backed him for the job,' said Annie. 'He had a good reputation and he was hungry to progress the show. I thought he had vision.'

Annie's shoulders collapsed and she sighed deeply.

'Annie, I don't really know how to broach this with you but it's inevitable you'll find out at some point,' said Jude, thinking of the newspaper stowed in her shopping bag and hoping that by warning Annie of the content she might be able to prepare her for whatever was coming her way.

'You are sweet,' said Annie with a watery smile. 'I assume you've seen the tabloid headline this morning.'

'I was there when the papers were delivered,' said Jude, as she poured the tea. 'I wasn't sure if you'd have seen it.'

'My agent called me early this morning. It's not the first time they've come for Simon and me. The PR team will issue press statements denying all the rumours, calling it a completely fabricated and highly disrespectful story and requesting privacy whilst we come to terms with the loss of our dear friend.'

Jude wondered how much of that was actually true. The affair had almost certainly been real, and she would not have called Annie and Mary *dear friends* by any stretch of the imagination. But she supposed it wasn't the truth that ever mattered in these celebrity-based stories. It was what the public believed.

'There will also be an official line from the network too about the show, no doubt something along the lines of how devastated we all are but that the entire team have chosen to continue filming as a dedication to Mary and her passion for the show.'

'But that's not the case,' said Jude.

'That's not the case at all. None of us want to carry on. It seems so insensitive.' Annie bit her lip and her brow creased. 'But that's not all, Jude. The more I think about it, the more I think that whoever killed Mary actually meant to kill me. We've been told that someone deliberately fed an exhaust pipe through the window of the caravan, did you know?'

Annie folded her arms across her and rubbed at her elbows as though they were still cold despite the heat of the kitchen.

'I did know,' said Jude.

'I've moved into the B&B in the village as it feels very much safer than sleeping in a shepherd's hut but I still can't stop thinking about who killed Mary and whether they're still going to want me dead.'

'Can you think of why someone might be targeting you?'

'I've had death threats before.' Annie tilted her head and dropped her gaze. 'From someone claiming to be my biggest fan and saying that if I didn't leave Simon and marry him, he'd have to kill me and then kill himself.'

'Bloody hell!' Jude had heard of things like this happening to celebrities but it didn't make the reality any less shocking. 'Did they find out who it was?'

'Yes. Some mentally disturbed man who had been stalking me for ages. It was really creepy, the amount of photos and things the police found at his home when they raided it. I went straight out and booked myself onto a self-defence course.'

'I assume the police have already covered this with you and this man is definitely not back on the scene?' Jude asked.

Annie gave a tiny shake of her head. 'He shot himself before the police could arrest him.'

'Dead?'

'Yes.'

'Blimey.' Jude steepled her fingers together. 'That whole thing must have been terrible for you.'

'It was, but this seems different. Whoever is doing this now is someone who knows me. Someone close who can come and go on the set without anyone batting an eyelid.' Annie put her hands against her cheeks and started to move them in tiny, comforting circles. 'I know not everyone on set loves me. But to go as far as wanting to kill me, that's something very different.'

'You might not have been the intended target,' said Jude. 'I know you said you didn't tell anyone about the caravan swap but you'd both have had to have taken your bags and things all the way across the campsite so really anyone could have seen you. Can you think of why someone might have wanted to kill Mary?'

Annie's hands stopped moving but remained against her face. 'Not really. People generally seemed to like her.'

'What about Holly? Gabe seemed to think there was no love lost between the two of them.'

'I think there was some rivalry between them when they were at university together. They were both hired at the same time on *The Lunch Club*.'

This was the programme that had first launched Annie and Simon's careers. Jude knew it had gone on for years until they decided it had run its course and they wanted to try new things. By that time *Countryside Live* had already taken off and was proving to be an enormous hit.

'I think Mary has had the most opportunities and better jobs since, which must grate somewhat,' Annie continued, 'but I can't imagine it being enough for Holly to kill her. I genuinely can't think of a single good reason why anyone would have wanted to kill either of us.'

'What have the police said to you?'

'With no real proof that I am being targeted, and nobody in mind as a potential threat, they've just told me to report anything of concern. I have to keep my phone with me and to limit the amount of time I'm on my own.' She rubbed her eyes. 'I need to get out of here but I can't be the one to run or I risk my whole career.'

Jude sipped her tea and thought about what Annie had told her. She realised that Annie had had her fill of Dean Dickens and his narcissistic ways. Some things were just not worth the money they came with.

'Do you think it would help if I pulled out of the contract?' Jude asked.

'What?'

'If I took away rights to film on the farm and told Dean he needed to get the crew off site.'

'That's really sweet of you, Jude, but he'd get the network to sue you for breach of contract and even if we did leave, he'd just find somewhere else for us to film.'

Jude sighed. 'There must be a way to knock him off his pedestal.'

'It's my fault,' Annie said. 'It was me who put him forward for the directing job. He put a very convincing pitch to me when our paths crossed at an awards ceremony. He had a real vision for what the show could be and I fell for it. If I'd known then what he was truly like, I'd have fought to keep him away.'

'And you don't have the clout with the network now, enough to get him replaced?'

'He grew the series into something huge. I'm more expendable than he is these days.'

Jude was learning what a fickle world television really was and she felt sorry for Annie, who seemed utterly trapped.

'I bet Dean's fuming about the newspaper article,' Jude said.

'We all are,' said Annie. 'Not just because of what was written but because it tells us that we have a mole amongst us who's making a few pounds selling stories.'

'Do you have any idea who it could have been?' Jude asked. 'The journalist said the information came from a source close to the show.'

Annie shook her head. 'It could be anyone. You've seen how big the wider team is. Any of them could have taken their opportunity to top up their wage packet.' She closed her eyes and took a deep breath. 'Or else they did it to hurt Simon and me. It would fit with the whole spiking my hot chocolate and sticking an exhaust pipe into my caravan. The whole thing just makes me feel sick.'

Jude didn't know what to say. When taken as part of the wider picture, it seemed very possible that the article had been more personal than just a way of making a quick buck.

Annie's phone rang and she dug in the pocket of the coat hanging over the back of her chair to retrieve it.

'It's Gabe,' she said. 'They'll be looking for me to do some filming. We're supposed to be visiting a Christmas tree farm this morning to run an interview. Dean is still expecting us to show up with smiles on our faces and chat about the difference between a Scots pine and Norwegian spruce.'

She pushed her fringe away from her face and answered the phone.

'Hello... No, I'm at the farmhouse talking to Jude... Sorry... I just wanted to pick her brains about something for the show... Yes, I know... I'm heading back now... Sure. See you in five.'

Annie ended the call, stood up and pulled the coat from the back of the chair.

'I'd better get going,' she said. 'They were worried when they couldn't find me.' She put the coat on and zipped herself into the thick padding. 'Thanks for the chat. Sorry, I came to apologise for Dean's behaviour and to check if you were okay and I ended up spilling my heart out to you.'

'Gosh, don't worry at all. Any time. And try not to worry, Annie. I know the police will be doing all they can to get to the bottom of this.'

'I know,' said Annie. 'Thank you.'

Jude let her out of the front door which she closed behind her and leant heavily against.

It was difficult to know what to do about everything she'd just heard. Dean was a predator, that was obvious and she had no doubt that his behaviour had led to many a young woman doing things that she didn't want to. But what could Jude do about it? She had zero proof and he hadn't done anything arrestable to her.

Was Annie telling the truth when she said she didn't have any concrete details either? Jude pondered the idea that the presenter did know more than she was prepared to say. Perhaps she was too frightened to take on a man such as Dean, one of those who probably always managed to slither his way out of trouble whilst leaving a trail of destruction behind him.

What if she had started to make waves though? What if Annie had heard or seen one too many things that didn't sit right with her and she'd confronted him on it? Had he used peanuts as a warning? It seemed highly plausible but Jude wasn't sure if that would then extend to trying to kill Annie with the exhaust from the generator.

The other question that was bothering her was the one Annie had raised about the identity of the person who'd fed sensitive information to the press.

She went over to the shopping bags and unloaded her groceries, stowing the custard, butter and ham in the fridge but leaving the rest on the side to deal with later. Then she took the newspaper and sat with it at the table so that she could read the article again.

Whoever had provided details of Mary's death was clearly very close to the case. They mentioned the fact that it was carbon monoxide poisoning, although thankfully nothing had been said of the murderous nature of its administration.

Was that because whoever it was didn't yet know that Mary had been murdered? Or was it the murderer who'd provided the journalist with the scoop but wanted to spin it to their own advantage?

Jude picked up her phone and called Binnie, who answered after only a couple of rings.

'Jude,' she said, bypassing any pleasantries. 'Have you seen the article?'

'That's what I was calling you about. Well, that and the fact that I've had a busy hour or so. First, I was accosted by that lech of a director and I've just had a terrified Annie Bird sitting at my kitchen table who is convinced that someone is going to kill her.'

'What do you think?' asked Binnie.

'Honestly? I don't know.' Jude picked up the teapot and

poured herself a second cup of well-stewed tea. 'She came here to talk about Dean Dickens, having seen him with me.'

'What happened there, Jude?'

'Nothing that I could report, just his usual level of revulsion. He suggested I needed money for the farm and he wanted me to talk to him about ways he could help me get some, all the time trying to touch me as much as possible.' Jude gave an involuntary shiver at the memory. 'Annie mentioned that he has a predatory reputation but nobody has ever come forward to report him.'

'We've already checked his record as a matter of course and it's clean,' said Binnie. 'Not that this means he hasn't done anything, just that nobody has brought it to our attention.'

'Exactly,' said Jude.

'We'll keep an eye on him and do some subtle probing to see if there's anything else we can draw out of the team. Back to Annie and her worries about being the victim. It seems like a definite possibility.'

'The peanut attack certainly looks deliberate now that we've found not only the coffee pods but the pack of chocolate nuts so I can see why she's so worried,' said Jude.

'But...?'

'But we can't discount the fact that it was Mary, not Annie, who died. Anyone could have seen the caravan swap take place and known that Mary was now sleeping there.'

'Any more idea on who might have wanted to kill her though?'

'Apparently there was some sort of rivalry between her and the other camera operator, Holly. Have you met her?'

'I haven't but I don't know about Sami.'

'Oh God, yes, I keep forgetting you're not leading the case,' said Jude.

'Don't tell him that!' Binnie chuckled. 'What about this Holly? She's not on the list of people staying on the farm.'

'No, she didn't have anything to do with the live parts of the show so she wasn't needed on site. It sounds like she was mainly tasked with providing lots of footage of the area to splice in where needed. She was staying somewhere in Malvern. I don't know how much she was on the set at the farm: I never saw her but that doesn't mean she wasn't there or didn't sneak in.'

'You said *wasn't* needed on site. Past tense.' Binnie had always been quick to pick up the smallest details.

'She's here now,' said Jude. 'Came over this morning to take the lead camera role. Full of confidence, I didn't really take to her all that much.'

'Because she's confident?'

'No. Because she was one of those people who listens without listening, if you know what I mean.' Jude took a swig of tea and grimaced at the strength of the stewed leaves.

'Go on,' said Binnie.

'She said all the right things about being upset by Mary's death and yet I had the very strong feeling that it didn't bother her in the slightest and she was just glad to be able to get her teeth into the new job. I guess you'll have to meet her yourself and make up your own mind.' Jude abandoned the tea and sat back in her chair, stretching her legs out beneath the table.

'Do you know what the rivalry was about?' Binnie asked.

'They went to university together and got work on one of Annie and Simon's other shows years ago. I think Holly feels as though Mary always got the better jobs because she was sleeping with Simon.'

'Something that is yet to be confirmed,' said Binnie. 'Despite today's headline, Simon is very much denying any affair and there is no actual evidence. Although I suspect whoever leaked the information must have something pretty concrete for the newspaper to risk printing the story and getting hit by a libel case of slander and defamation of character.'

'I have a nasty suspicion that the show's sneaky little mole hasn't finished yet,' said Jude.

'I think you are absolutely right. If I were Simon or Annie, I'd be worried about what was coming next.'

'Annie's more worried about what she sees as threats to her life. She wants to pack up and ship out,' said Jude.

'But she doesn't want to risk her job by being the one to walk?' Binnie guessed.

'Exactly that.' Jude wriggled her toes as Alfie came over to lie on her feet.

'Well then, we'd better hurry up and catch the murderer, hadn't we?' said Binnie. 'Look, I'd better get on but keep me posted.'

'Before you go, you didn't get the results back on that magenta fluff caught up in the residue on the exhaust pipe, did you?'

'Oh, yes, that came back this morning and it's a bit of an odd one. It seems to be from a kind of fake fur, the sort that's usually used to make soft toys.'

Jude imagined a giant teddy bear striding through the campsite with a roll of heavy-duty tape and murderous intentions. There was still clearly a lot of work to be done before they cracked this particular case.

12

Noah was nowhere to be seen, nor was he answering his phone, which meant he could well be up in the fields somewhere where there was no signal. Jude knew the paddock animals needed tending and had been hoping to ask Noah to do it so she could avoid the filming team, especially Dean. With Noah otherwise engaged, she had no choice but to pull on her boots and zip herself back into the winter layers. She called Pip and Alfie to her for comfort and possible distraction – or an excuse to leave should it be needed – and headed across the yard.

As she passed the campsite, she noticed that a new caravan had already been delivered, presumably for Holly, and was dwarfed by the three much larger ones that were already in situ for the two stars of the show and their director.

Outside, Dean was having another row with Simon, and Jude put her head down and hurried past, glad to reach the blind spot where she was hidden from them by the caravans.

'I'm not saying I'm quitting the show,' she heard Simon shout. 'I'm telling you to just find a little empathy for all of our sakes.

Unlike you, we're all devastated about what happened to Mary and you need to give us time to deal with it.'

'You can have as much time as you want once we've closed the series,' said Dean. 'Until then, we have a packed schedule and we need to make the most of this. Thanks to you not being able to keep your dick in your pants, we're now less family entertainment show and more primetime soap opera.'

Jude realised that Dean didn't seem upset about that idea. In fact, to the contrary, he seemed jubilant at the sudden change of direction the show was heading in.

'Not that I blame you. She was a good-looking girl.' Dean smirked and Jude felt her insides curl again in disgust. 'But we are now where we are because of you, and it's decision time. You either do things your way and lose the golden career that you and that innocent little wife of yours have built. Or you do things my way and we all come away as part of the biggest fucking telly coup of the year.'

There was silence for a moment before the unmistakable sound of feet could be heard stomping up the metal steps of a caravan.

'See you ready for filming in fifteen minutes,' Dean called as the door of the caravan slammed.

Jude knew that this meant he'd be on the move so she hurried to get the baling twine loosened so she could disappear into the paddock. Annoyingly, someone had tried to make an extra loop and it needed more manipulation than usual. Jude managed to get it undone, but she hadn't been speedy enough.

'Ah, if it isn't Fiery Jude.' Dean's voice made her clench her teeth and close her eyes for a second, her hand on the gate, before she turned round.

'Sorry, Dean, I'm really pushed for time today.'

As soon as she and the dogs had gone through it, Jude went to close the gate.

Dean got there in time to push his way through before she'd looped the twine back in place.

'We'll walk and talk then,' he said. 'I don't feel as though we finished our conversation earlier. I want you on the show, not live again but it would be good to get some shots of you out in the fields whilst we've still got the snow, or I was thinking taking things into your kitchen and you could share your favourite festive recipes with the viewers. I bet you've got an Aga in there, haven't you?'

'Sorry, Dean,' said Jude, slipping the twine into place and setting off to deal with her animals. 'I already told you that I'm not interested in doing any more filming, and sadly for you I don't have to jump when you whistle. I checked the contract and it only mentions one appearance, which I've now done.'

'It's almost as though you're not enjoying having us around.' Dean elbowed her playfully and Jude tensed.

She stopped walking and turned sharply to face him. 'No, I'm not. If I had my way, I'd actually make you all leave right now. This whole thing is toxic and wrong.'

'You really are a feisty one, aren't you, Jude Gray?' The leer returned. 'I admire your spark, but no can do. The show has never pulled such big audiences. A bit of inconvenience to you has turned us into headline news and that means we're making something bigger than all of us. We're here for the duration.'

Jude already knew most of this but it was still nauseating, not least because of the total glee with which Dean had delivered the news.

'Don't you have any empathy at all for what's been happening to your team?' She spoke with an incredulity that was perhaps misplaced considering that she was already very aware of what kind of man Dean Dickens was.

Dean put his hands together and adopted a theatrically fake expression of compassion.

'I am deeply upset by the tragedy that happened within the close-knit *Countryside Live* family. Mary Taper was a highly respected, talented camera operator and friend to us all. She is greatly missed but we, as a team, believe that the best legacy for her is to continue filming the show that she was so passionate about. We know that this is what she would have wanted.'

Jude bristled as he delivered his carefully constructed PR nonsense, both of them knowing it was utter shite.

'Now that I think we understand each other better, I need you to get a list of locations and local experiences to me as soon as possible. I need romantic places for Annie and Simon to visit, things for them to do together. The public want to see where their story is going next.'

He didn't wait for a reply. Having given his latest demand, Dean finally left Jude alone and walked away.

Jude needed to take a few very deep breaths before she felt ready to move and when she did, she was fuming about what had just happened. She was buggered if she was going to waste her time coming up with romantic places for him. There was nothing at all romantic about the situation they were currently in. Dean was delusional if he thought the public would be fooled by a few snippets of Annie and Simon defying the newspaper article and going round Christmas markets or wandering through the light spectacle set up at the Three Counties Showground hand in hand.

'Come on, dogs,' she said. 'Let's go and let those ducks out.'

As she walked with them down to the stables, Jude thought again about the article, which was bound to have an increasing reach now that it was out there. Dean had used it to help turn the show into an attention-grabbing soap opera, and it seemed highly feasible therefore that he could be the one to have leaked the story in the first place.

It had been the same with Annie's nut allergy and collapse which had definitely made for sensational live television. Jude could certainly imagine Dean setting that up for maximum dramatic exposure; he had been very keen to milk all he could from it, no matter how unethical it had been.

Would he have killed to boost ratings though?

If so, had he intended to kill Mary all along? It would help the narrative of the drama. Husband cheats on wife and body of lover is found soon after. But that would work just as well the other way around too. Husband finds new love and tries to remove wife from the picture.

The dogs sat on the cobbles outside the stables whilst Jude fetched a bucket of sheep nuts. She tried to work out if Dean was capable of killing to make it look like either Simon or Annie had done it: Annie to get rid of her love rival, or Simon as a way of achieving a quick, cheap version of divorce. It certainly didn't feel beyond the realms of possibility. It also re-highlighted the fact that both Annie and Simon had very real reasons to kill.

The fact that everything about the murder was so smudgy made finding hard facts difficult. Not only did she not know why murder had taken place or who had blood on their hands, there was the added layer of having two possible intended victims.

And what made it even more complicated was the fact that one of the possible victims was still alive, which could mean that the murderer would now be preparing to strike again and try to finish what they'd started.

'Oh, hi there, it's Julie, isn't it?'

Jude tipped the last of the sheep nuts into the trough next to the stables and stood up to see Holly, the new camera operator, standing there.

'It's Jude,' she corrected.

'Oh, I'm so sorry.' Holly waved her hands chaotically around her head. 'Brain like a marshmallow, especially when it comes to names. Jude, of course. I saw you down here and I thought I'd come and have a quick chat.'

Jude inwardly groaned. Another chat with anyone from the *Countryside Live* team was the last thing she wanted right then.

'How can I help?' Jude didn't stop what she was doing to talk to Holly. As she spoke, she walked past her to the open stable to retrieve the almost empty hay bags that were hanging there.

'I just wanted to get to know the place a little, I suppose,' she said. 'I know Mary was here for a while before filming started and I feel a bit on the back foot, I'm afraid. The rest of the gang aren't all that pleased to see me here which is not fabulously helpful.'

'Mary's death must be hard on everyone,' said Jude as she moved on to the old tack room where the hay was kept.

She let herself in and closed just the bottom half of the split door so she could carry on with her jobs whilst still talking to Holly outside.

'Oh God, yeah. Totally get that.' Holly held a thickly gloved hand to her chest and Jude caught sight of a fluffy magenta sleeve poking out of the arm of her coat. 'I'm devastated too, of course I am. Mary was one of a kind.'

It was impossible to say if the fluff on the exhaust pipe was exactly the same shade of pinky-purple, but it was definitely close enough for Jude to be interested.

'How well did you know her?' she asked.

'Really well. We were so close.' Holly had one of those voices that made everything she said sound less than sincere. 'It was such a terrible shock when I heard what had happened to her.'

'It must have been.' Jude pushed handfuls of hay into one of the nets. 'You've been staying in town, haven't you?'

'That's right. In a darling little guest house.' Holly leant on the half door.

'Did you go back there last night after the show?'

'No. I'd brought all of my things with me so I slept in the chillout trailer, which was absolutely fine, of course. I'm rather glad that they found me a caravan though.'

'How are you finding your way around the farm?' Jude asked. 'I assume yesterday was the first time you'd been here.'

'Yes.' Holly adjusted the furry pillbox-style hat that was pushed down on top of her mane of tightly curled, honey-coloured hair. 'It's such a divine spot.'

'I like to think so.' Jude finished stuffing the first of the hay nets and turned her attention to the second. 'Let me know if you need help finding your way around.'

'That's so sweet, thank you.' Holly pouted and stuck her chin out in what Jude thought was supposed to be a coquettish, appreciative gesture. 'We're heading off soon though to interview some wooden toy carver. Perhaps when we get back, you could give me the tour?'

'Sure,' said Jude. A grand tour wasn't perhaps what she'd planned. She'd been thinking more along the lines of standing in the yard pointing out the way to the various parts of the farm.

'And I'd love to meet these guys properly.' Holly waved her fingers at the animals who were lined up behind her, waiting for their hay.

Jude got another glimpse of the magenta sleeve.

'Anyway, I must dash. So lovely to meet you,' said Holly.

'Bye for now.'

As soon as Holly had left to get ready for the interview, Jude gave Sami a call.

'Hi, Jude. I suppose you already tried Binnie and she didn't pick up?'

Jude assumed this was a dig at the fact that the last time she had something interesting to report, she had bypassed Sami and gone straight to Binnie.

'I just need to get used to it, that's all,' she said.

'Don't worry. She'll be taking over soon enough anyway at this rate. So much for limiting exertion and moving slowly where work is concerned. When I got up today and turned my phone on, there was a message from her sent at ten past two in the morning. She'd been up until then trawling through photos of the crime scene and delving through a heap of records.'

Jude shook her head at the thought. 'Did she find anything?'

'Nothing new in the photos, but when she looked into the details of Mary's bank account she found no record of her paying anything in the way of rent or a mortgage for her flat.'

Rodney Trotter became impatient at the time it was taking for Jude to get the hay nets out to the waiting diners and he started to bang the bottom of the half door with his front hoof.

'Couldn't that just mean she'd managed to pay off her mortgage?' Jude asked as she went outside with the first of the nets held above her head and out of the animals' reach. She closed the door behind her to stop any sneaky food thieves and then went over to the thick iron loop attached to the stable wall.

'Binnie asked me to look into it this morning and I found something rather interesting. The rent for her flat is being paid by a Mr S. J. North.'

'Simon,' said Jude as she struggled to tie the net to the loop whilst still holding her phone to her ear. 'I think it's safe to assume that their affair was a pretty advanced one.'

'It's the most obvious reason,' said Sami. 'But not the only one.'

'You're sounding more and more like Binnie.' Jude grinned as she pulled the end of the rope and stood back to let the animals fight over the hay.

'I'll take that as a compliment.' It sounded like Sami was smiling too.

'Did he have anything to say about the argument Dean heard him having with Mary?'

'He said it was nothing much,' said Sami. 'He said it had been a hard day and he was tired and had a migraine. He just wanted to be on his own and he claims he spent the afternoon in his caravan and went straight there once the evening filming was over.'

'So he didn't know about the caravan swap?'

'Apparently not,' said Sami. 'Anyway, I'd better get on.'

'Haven't you forgotten something?' Jude asked.

'What?'

'I was the one who called you, remember? Don't you want to know why?' Jude went back into the tack room and perched on the wooden bench inside.

'Ah, yes! So you did.'

'I've just been talking to Holly, that's Mary's replacement. She was very effusive about how close she and Mary were and how totally devastated she is.'

'Whilst swooping in to take her job the day the body was discovered?'

'Exactly. Anyway, according to Gabe they were anything but friends. He said they both went for the lead camera operator on *Countryside Live* and Holly believes the only reason the job went to Mary was because she was sleeping with Simon.'

'Yeah, he mentioned that in his interview,' said Sami. 'But a pretty flimsy motive for murder.'

'It depends how deeply the resentment ran, I suppose,' Jude reasoned. 'And the other thing that I think could be very interesting is the jumper or fleece that Holly is wearing today. I couldn't see much of it as it was hidden under her coat, but the cuffs were clearly visible and they were that thick sort of fluffy fabric similar to the stuff they make soft toys out of. Want to guess the colour?'

'Magenta by any chance?' Sami asked.

'Right first time.'

'Now that is *very* interesting,' said Sami. 'Thanks, Jude. Anything else before I really do get on?'

'Nope, that's all. Bye, Sami.'

'See ya, Jude.'

Jude put her phone back in the pocket of her coat and her fingers brushed the warm wool of one of Marco's gloves. She pulled it out and searched her deep pockets for the other. Pulling them on, she imagined him sitting in his front room with paints and a project laid out before him. The wood burner would probably be lit and he might have made a fresh pot of coffee, seeing as it was almost lunchtime.

'Fancy a wander down to see Marco?' Jude asked Pip and Alfie.

The tone of her voice made the dogs stand up and wag their tails in excitement, unsure of what she had just asked but fairly certain it was going to be something good.

'Come on then.'

She gave a sharp whistle and the dogs were instantly at her heel, ready to go.

Tramping through the snowy fields up towards the track that led down to the village, Jude remembered a promise she'd made to take Sebbie sledging before the snow melted away. He only had one day left of school before the weekend and she hoped there might be at least some left by Saturday. It felt so cold that Jude couldn't imagine it ever warming up enough to thaw everything.

The ruts of the track, made when the rain had churned everything to thick clay, were now frozen and hidden by snow, which made walking across the divots and peaks hard on the ankles. When she neared the end of the track, Jude called Pip and Alfie back to heel and they turned out onto the lane that ran through the village. The row of old stone cottages where Marco lived was the first sign of human residency she came to. She opened the gate of the one second to last in the row and walked up to the door. The curtains of the front room were open and she was disappointed to see that Marco was not where she'd expected him to be, at the table in the front room with his paints out.

Before she had the chance to knock, the door of the cottage opened and Marco came out, dressed for the weather with his camera bag hanging across him.

'Oh, Jude!' He stopped in surprise when he saw her. 'I was just heading out to get some pictures of the farm and the hills in the snow.'

The excitement of seeing Marco was too much for Alfie who broke ranks and jammed himself against his leg, demanding attention. Marco bent to stroke him and Jude saw that he had another pair of gloves on, fingerless ones with little hoods he could pull over to form mittens until he needed to use his fingers for taking photos or sketching.

'No, it's fine. I was just returning your gloves.' She realised to her embarrassment that she was still wearing them.

'It doesn't look like you've finished with them yet,' said Marco. 'Keep them, Jude.'

'Are you sure?'

He lifted his hands. 'I've got these and I don't like the thought of you with cold hands.'

'I do own gloves,' said Jude sheepishly. 'I just never seem to have them with me when I need them.'

'Perhaps I should buy you a length of elastic and thread them through your coat sleeves so you never lose them.'

Jude laughed. 'I remember my mum doing that when I was little.'

'Do you want to come in for a cuppa?' Marco thumbed over his shoulder towards the door, still open and letting all the hot air out and the icy blast in.

'No,' said Jude. 'Look at the day. You might not get another chance to take snowy pictures. We can catch up another time.'

'Unless you want to come and take snowy pictures with me?'

Jude tried to read the expression on Marco's face. At one point in time, she'd thought she knew every little nuance of the way his eyes, mouth, cheeks, wrinkles, gave away how he was feeling. But since she'd turned him away once too often and he'd started dating Clara, Jude felt as though there was a lot about him that was now a mystery to her.

'Would you like the company?' she asked.

'Jude, I'd love that.' This time there was no mystery in his open smile. 'Don't judge me but I've got a flask of hot Ribena in my bag. Only one mug but you're welcome to share.'

'I'd love that too,' said Jude. She had made the decision to do whatever she needed to get back the friendship she'd held so dear before notions of romance threw a spanner in the works. Recent months had shown her that she'd rather have Marco in her life as a friend than not in it at all. And a walk in the snow, watching him capture the beauty of the season in the place she loved most in the world, seemed like a very good place to start.

Once Jude Gray made a firm decision, she tended to stick to it, and so she firmly pushed away any feelings of ardour and chose to enjoy the next hour or so with her dear friend.

* * *

Jude and Marco spent a very happy time walking through the fields and into the woods that skirted the base of the hills. He taught her where to look for the best lighting and how to use negative spaces to set up the perfect composition. They stayed out until the sun began to dip. By the time they were heading back to the farm to warm up by the Aga, Jude had learnt many things. Amongst her favourites were the fact that most artists use very little white paint when they are depicting snow, that nothing is better to warm the insides than hot Ribena, and, best of all, that she and Marco still had the capacity to be relaxed together as friends.

'Before we go in, can I just get a few shots of the animals in the paddock? I need to submit some more watercolours to the greetings card company and what's cuter than farm animals in the snow with the pink shadows of the late-afternoon sun?'

'Of course,' said Jude. 'I don't know who from the telly bunch will be around.' She peeled the sleeve of her coat back to check her watch. 'They were going to interview someone about wooden toys but that was a few hours ago now. Mind you, they must be talking about that chap somewhere over near Trumpet whose workshop looks like it should be filled with elves. That's a good twenty-minute drive in nice weather and I've no idea what Fromes Hill will be like for cars.'

Jude was hoping that the whole filming team might still be out. It would have been even better news if she got a call to say that the weather had scuppered their plans and they'd all had to book into a local inn for the night.

No such luck fell her way though and she saw Dean as soon as they were level with the campsite.

'How's that list of romantic locations coming on?' he called over when he saw her.

Jude ignored him and carried on to the paddock.

'What was that about?' Marco asked.

'He's just baiting me.' Jude opened the gate and they both went inside. 'We had a couple of run-ins earlier and he just wants to remind who he thinks is boss.'

'He seems like a bit of an arsehole,' said Marco.

'The very worst kind,' Jude agreed. 'Now let's think of nicer things like which of my animals you want to photograph. Rodney Trotter is looking rather splendid over by the ducks or what about Pancake and Gertie? They look like they're trying to be steam trains.'

Jude pointed to the edge of the paddock where the sheep and goat were nestled into each other by the trunk of a sycamore. Their warm breath was condensing in great puffs as soon as it left their bodies.

The Kerry Hill sheep that she kept in there, beautiful creatures but not show stock like the prized few in the orchard, were gathered together by the hedge near the bottom of the paddock. Something about the way they were standing made Jude's farmer's intuition prick.

'I'm just going to check on the Kerries,' she said to Marco.

Usually the shy sheep kept their distance, and most of them, true to form, scarpered when Jude got near but one ewe stayed close to the hedge, bahhing her indignation as Jude approached.

'What's up, girl?' Jude said gently as she moved steadily closer.

There was usually only one thing that got a Kerry Hill ewe's gander up in this way and that was if something was threatening her lamb. Although these animals had had their babies back in the spring, Kerry Hills were particularly fierce mothers so it was no surprise to Jude that this mum was still watching out for her little one. Sure enough, there, stuck well in the hedge that separated the paddock from the campsite, was a young Kerry.

He'd obviously pushed his way in, maybe to find shelter, and got his fleece stuck in the branches. Wiggling to get free had only served to entangle his wool even more and Jude could tell he was now well and truly ensnared.

'All right there, boy,' she said as she pulled her penknife from her coat pocket. 'We'll soon have you out.'

'Need a hand?' Marco called over.

'No, you're okay. Probably best if you steer clear so mum doesn't get too upset.'

Jude was grateful for the thick waxed sleeves of her coat as she pushed her way into the hedge so she could reach around to the fleece at the back and cut it free. It was hard going and she worked steadily, making sure she pacified both mum and youngster at the same time as she worked until eventually, with one last careful cut, he was loose and bounded away across the field with his mother at his side.

Taken aback by the sudden jerky movement, Jude tumbled sideways into the hedge and for a moment, the branches parted just enough for her to see through into the campsite on the other side.

There, in the corner of the camping field, furthest away from the entrance where the film crew had set up their caravans and trailers, someone was pushing something into a gap in the hedge. They were dressed in black and through the hedge it was impossible to see who it was but they seemed to be keen to keep themselves hidden.

'Are you okay there?' Marco held his hand out as he reached Jude.

'I am, but I'm not sure about your gloves, I'm afraid.' Jude put her hand in his and he pulled her out of the hedge.

'Don't worry about those. I'm more concerned about that cut on your face.' He took a clean handkerchief from his pocket, bent to wrap a little snow in one corner and used it to wipe Jude's cheek.

She hadn't realised that one of the hedge's twigs had caught her until she felt the sting of the cold, wet fabric against it.

'It's only a surface cut but I'd definitely pop some antiseptic on it when you get back.'

'Thanks.' Jude hoped that he couldn't see how the feeling of his fingers on her face was making her tingle. So much for her vow to kick all romantic notions into touch.

Still, she thought as she let him use the other corner of the handkerchief to dry her cheek, she was only human and it was never going to be quite as simple as flicking an off switch.

The sun was already well on its journey towards the southern hemisphere when Jude and Marco put the ducks back into their stable for the night. The film crew would be along soon to start setting up for that evening's live show.

'Do you still have time for a cuppa?' Jude asked. 'Lucy will be back from the school run with Sebbie soon. They'd love to see you.'

'Go on then,' said Marco. 'Perhaps just a quick one.'

'Do you mind if we go back through the bottom gate and up via the campsite? I just want to check something.'

Jude called the dogs to her and they all set off together. Once in the campsite, Jude headed for the corner behind the two shepherd's huts where she'd seen someone poking around in the hedge. Marco and the dogs followed and, just as they were about to duck behind the second hut, Jude was surprised to find Holly coming towards her.

'Oh!' Holly squeaked in surprise. 'Gosh, you gave me a jump.'

'Sorry,' said Jude. 'I was just going to push the snow off the solar panels. What were you doing back here?'

'Just having a nose around,' said Holly, pushing her hand into her pocket. 'Always on the lookout for interesting nooks and crannies to film in.' She looked at Marco. 'Hi, I'm Holly.'

'Marco,' he replied. 'Nice to meet you.'

'Yeah, you too.' Holly nodded enthusiastically. 'Well, I'd better be getting back to the grindstone. I need to start thinking about setting up ready for the show tonight.'

'Bye then,' said Jude.

'Who was that?' Marco asked when Holly was out of earshot.

'That is the new camera operator Dean's brought in to replace Mary.'

'Was she really round here in the pokiest part of the entire place looking for a good place to film, do you think?' Marco didn't look any more convinced than Jude felt.

'No, I don't,' she said. 'Whilst I was in the middle of that hedge there, I saw someone down here. Not Holly because I don't think I'd have missed that hair, and anyway this person was wearing darker clothes. It looked like they were putting something into the hedge which I thought was a bit odd anyway. But now that Holly's also been snooping around down here I'd say it's definitely suspicious, don't you think?'

'Do I take it we are now here on an investigative mission?'

'I just want to see if there's anything in the hedge.' Jude went to the rough place where the other person had been earlier. She parted the twigs and branches and looked inside but there was nothing there so she moved and explored other parts until she spotted something that did not belong there. It was a little plastic box and she pulled it out carefully.

'Found something?'

Jude held up the box. It was dark blue, the sort of thing that she or Lucy packed Sebbie's snacks for school in with two clips to keep the lid in place. Jude undid them and looked inside. 'It's empty,' she said.

'Why would someone hide an empty snack tub in your hedge?' Marco said. 'Are you sure there's nothing else there?'

'I couldn't see anything else,' said Jude. 'The only thing I can come up with is that there was something in there and Holly was here to collect it.'

'Like a sort of covert postal system?'

'Maybe.' Jude put the tub back where she'd found it. 'But what for, I have no idea.'

'Something that they don't want to be seen passing between each other,' Marco reasoned. 'Notes, perhaps?'

'Maybe. Although what would they be writing to each other that they couldn't put in a text, or an email, even just slip a written note to each other in passing?'

'It could be anything,' said Marco.

'I know,' agreed Jude as they started to walk back towards the house, the dogs leading the way. 'That's why I'm going to have to try and keep an eye on it. See if I can catch them leaving something and nab it before Holly gets there.'

13

Much to Sebbie's consternation, the weather warmed up a few degrees that night and the snow was starting to drop off the roof as he ate his breakfast the next morning. He was dressed in his school uniform but had added a Father Christmas hat with an enormous, fluffy bobble. Clarence, the elf, was propped against the milk bottle having been rescued from the fridge where Sebbie had discovered him under a lettuce duvet with his head on a pillow of halloumi.

'Can I go sledging before school, Aunty Judy?' he asked.

'No can do.' Jude sliced a bread roll ready to butter and fill for her nephew's packed lunch. 'I promised Mummy we'd have you at school on time.'

Lucy had been on the night shift at the care home and, with the roads too treacherous for her little hatchback, Noah and the pickup had been acting as her 4x4 taxi service, so Jude was in charge.

'But tomorrow is Saturday,' she reminded Sebbie, 'and there's always plenty of snow at the top of the hills so we can head up there nice and early with the sledges. Deal?'

'Deal.'

* * *

Once Jude had dropped Sebbie off, she headed into the main town, avoiding the steepest roads over the hills and choosing the longer route that skirted around the base. Her trusty old four-wheel drive handled the slushy remains of the snow in the lanes well and she was soon on the bigger roads which had been cleared and gritted. The sight of the Christmas lights strung across the roads and the big tree at the top of Church Street, combined with the remainder of the snow clinging to the rooftops, gave her the first rumblings of a Christmassy feeling. It had always been her favourite time of year and she was glad to find that the current situation hadn't quite managed to zap it completely from her.

Jude pulled into the car park outside the supermarket. Here, the snow had been banked up against the edges by a plough and sat in great grey piles.

Jolly Christmas tunes were playing inside and the lady on the help desk by the entrance was wearing a halo of silver tinsel in her hair. As Jude walked around, filling her trolley, she could see that every company had tried to tap into the festive loosening of purse strings with special editions of everything from crisps and chocolate biscuits to loo paper and even washing-up liquid.

As well as all the things on her shopping list, Jude also came out with a twin pack of kitchen paper printed with Father Christmas faces, tortilla chips in the shape of Christmas trees and a bottle of kitchen cleaner that would apparently make the kitchen smell of clementines and cinnamon. She knew she'd been sucked in but she felt they could all do with a few extra festive notes to keep them on track.

Once she'd paid and loaded her shopping bags into the back of the Land Rover, Jude checked her watch. It was past ten, so breakfast at Perrins House Care Home should be just about over. Granny Margot would definitely have finished and probably already be sitting somewhere, tapping her fingers as she waited patiently for Jude's promised visit.

There was a welcome blast of hot air as Jude walked through the large doors into the entrance hall a few minutes later. She felt instantly overdressed in her winter layers and shrugged them off so she could hang them on the coat rack.

'Morning, Jude,' said one of the carers who walked past as Jude was signing in. 'Come to see Margot?'

'Morning, Paula,' Jude replied. 'Yes, has she finished breakfast?'

'I think she's taken a cup of tea into the conservatory. It's group paperchain making this morning but she didn't fancy it.'

'Thanks.' Jude put the pen down and made her way through to the airy room which always made best use of whatever sunlight was on offer. That particular day there wasn't much and yet the room, stuffed with plants and rattan furniture, still seemed quite tropical.

Granny Margot was sitting on a high-backed sofa, padded by cushions decorated with exotic birds and hibiscus blooms. She was surrounded by balls of wool in an assortment of colours and was wielding a pair of fast-moving knitting needles.

'Ah, Jude!' she exclaimed in delight when she caught sight of her friend. 'I'm glad you're here. I seem to have a runaway ball.'

Granny Margot pointed to a potted lemon tree and Jude could see a line of emerald yarn stretching from the old woman's tartan slipper to the terracotta pot. Jude picked up the stray ball of wool and started to wind it back in.

'Is that the only reason you're glad to see me?' she teased. 'Just so I can rescue your wool?'

'Of course not. I'm also glad to see you because I've been bereft of any decent conversation this morning and I'm keen to talk murders and weddings.'

Jude handed Granny Margot her wool and kissed her on the cheek. 'Murders and weddings,' she said. 'We are in for a good morning.'

She pulled a chair across the tiled floor so she could sit opposite Granny Margot. 'What are you knitting?'

'I thought I'd make young Sebbie a jumper for Christmas. There's not much to show you yet.' She held up a four-inch strip of red knitting with some grey, black and the emerald green starting to build a picture of something from the bottom up. 'It's going to have a tractor on the front and I thought I'd put a sheep or two on the back, just small ones at the bottom.'

'He'll love that,' said Jude. 'You are clever.'

'It's easy to do these things when I have so many hours to do them. I can't stand being idle.'

Jude didn't need Granny Margot to tell her that. 'Talking of which, how are the plans going for Lucy's surprise party? Did you manage to persuade Gerwain to let you loose with the karaoke machine again?'

Granny Margot looked up from her knitting sagely. 'It's a work in progress,' she said.

'Perhaps if you all promised to choose from a pre-approved list of songs this time?' Jude suggested with a grin.

'Or just keep certain residents away altogether.' Granny Margot sniffed. 'Nobody wanted to hear Fred singing about strip clubs and flashing at the bartender. I don't know how that M and M chap got away with it.'

'Eminem.' Jude chuckled. 'And I gather from Lucy that you were lucky Gerwain pulled the plug when he did.'

'Yes, well, we'd all heard quite enough by then and the situation wasn't helped by the fact we had the lyrics up on the big screen so anyone who wanted to join in could. It really was very unsettling.' Granny Margot's needles clacked together with greater ferocity to show her disapproval.

'Karaoke aside, how are you getting on with the other plans?'

'I think we're just about there,' said Granny Margot. 'There have been a few hairy moments when I thought the cat was out of the bag: you know what old people are like when it comes to spilling secrets.' She rolled her eyes as though she was talking about a generation that didn't include her.

'I think you're safe,' said Jude. 'Lucy hasn't mentioned anything so I'm sure she has no idea what you're cooking up. She's going to be so touched by the whole thing, I know.'

Granny Margot stopped knitting and looked at Jude. 'Everyone wants to be a part of her special celebration even though they can't all go to the wedding itself. This is our way of letting her know how adored she is.'

'Just make sure there's a plentiful supply of tissues available,' said Jude.

'I should think we'll all be needing those.'

Granny Margot pushed her needles into the ball of red wool and then wound the other colours around it to keep everything together when she laid it down next to her.

'Now then,' she said. 'Let's talk murder. I want to know everything you can tell me about the poor camerawoman and who we think might have wanted her dead.'

Granny Margot had seen the newspaper article and had not been taken in by the subsequent statement released by the network. She sensed foul play and wasn't in the least surprised when Jude told her about the exhaust pipe that had pumped the toxic carbon monoxide into the caravan. As she spoke, Jude knew she didn't have to tell Granny Margot to keep the information to herself. Unlike many of the other residents who loved a good gossip, Granny Margot was one who used her ears more than her voice when it came to tittle tattle. She listened to everything and picked up things that most people would overlook. But she was not interested in spilling any beans for the sake of a good story, especially if they weren't her beans to spill.

'Definitely murder then,' said Granny Margot. 'Well, that's no surprise. What do we think about Annie Bird? Surely she's the most obvious suspect, seeing as the deceased woman was sleeping with her husband.'

'That's one theory,' said Jude. 'Although she seems to have been targeted herself too.'

'Because of her dramatic collapse from the peanut allergy?'

'Yes, partly. But also the fact that Mary Taper was sleeping in Annie's caravan when she was killed. They'd swapped vans just before they went to bed and we have no idea who knew of the situation.'

'That seems a very odd thing to have done.'

'This is where it gets even twistier,' said Jude. 'Annie says she wanted to swap because the noise of the generator was keeping her awake. But I think she actually wanted to be closer to Gabe.'

'I knew there was something going on between those two.'

'Still not confirmed, I should add. But I think you were on track when you picked that one up.'

'So that's two near misses for Annie in just a few days. No wonder you think she could be the real target.' Granny Margot adjusted the cushion behind her back. 'I bet she's worried. Are they going to stop filming the rest of the show now?'

Jude shook her head. 'No. Although Annie has moved into

Four Trees B&B, the director is adamant the show must go on. Do you know, it almost feels as though he's enjoying the whole thing and he's certainly trying to turn it into a "soap opera" – his words.' Jude gave finger quote marks to emphasise the term.

Granny Margot's brow creased. 'I didn't take to that man when we met and yet I still find it very hard to understand how anyone could be visibly enjoying such a situation. Let's put him very firmly near the top of our suspect list for his sheer audacity. Does he stand to gain if the show is turned into a soap opera?'

'It certainly seems that way. Or at least he thinks the soaring viewer numbers will help boost his career going forward.'

'There we are then,' said Granny Margot. 'A man with an ego and clearly no morals. He's showing no sympathy or regret for the terrible things that have happened on his own show. I'd say that all makes him sound very guilty, don't you?'

'When you put it like that, I can't see how he could be anything else.'

Two of the other residents of the care home came into the conservatory at this point, one of them clutching a set of backgammon and the other pushing a walking aid. Both had red and white Father Christmas hats sitting jauntily on their heads and loops of brightly coloured paperchains around their necks.

'Hello there, Jude,' said Ham, a man who always dressed immaculately, as if he was expecting very important guests to arrive at any moment.

'Hi, Ham.' Jude stood up to greet them. 'Janice, lovely to see you both.'

'Are you going to be long?' Granny Margot asked. 'It's just that Jude and I were rather in the middle of something.'

'Oh, don't worry about us,' said Janice. 'Ham and I won't bother you, we thought we'd sit over there by the window and have a game or two of backgammon before Yoga Carol comes for our class.'

'No, I'm afraid that's not possible.' Granny Margot spoke as though the decision was hers alone. 'Come back in twenty minutes or so if you like but Jude and I are talking in private and we haven't finished.'

'Oh,' said Ham. 'Sorry to interrupt.'

'We'll find somewhere else,' said Janice. 'It was nice to see you, Jude.'

'See you again soon,' said Jude, wondering at the power Granny Margot wielded around the glass walls of the conservatory.

'Now, where we were?' Granny Margot asked as Jude sat back down.

'We were talking about whether Mary or Annie was the actual target for murder.' Even with her winter layers stripped off, Jude still felt overly warm in the conservatory and pulled her jumper off.

'Ah, yes. That's it,' said Granny Margot. 'So far we've got Annie as a suspect if Mary was the intended victim and Simon if Annie was the one who was supposed to die.'

'Not necessarily,' said Jude. 'Simon had a row with Mary earlier that day. It was something to do with her becoming demanding, which he claims was down to a migraine. Depending on how big Mary's demands were, he could have a motive to kill either of them.'

Granny Margot nodded slowly.

'And then there is this horrid man, Dean, who might not have cared who he killed as long as he created a drama for his viewers. Am I missing anything?'

'I think if Annie had died, not even Dean could have kept the show going.' Jude hung her jumper over the back of the chair.

'Hmm, I suppose that's true.' Granny Margot cocked her head to the side. 'Although just think how popular those true-crime programmes are. Imagine the appetite for a programme about a celebrity murdered whilst filming. With all his inside information, Dean would be perfectly placed to make it, wouldn't he?'

Jude mulled this idea over. There definitely seemed to be an insatiable appetite for such programmes. Having spent time with Dean and seen the way he functioned, she realised she wouldn't put it past him to be looking at the big trends and working out a way he could tap into that market. And Granny Margot was right. If Annie Bird had been killed on location whilst making a Christmas series, Jude had no doubt that Dean would turn that to his directorial advantage in whatever way he could.

'Okay,' she said. 'I can see how either death might benefit Dean. There are three other people to consider, if we discount the wider team who came and went. Gabe the soundman, Robyn the researcher and Holly, who replaced Mary as main camera operator.'

'Well, Gabe is in a relationship with Annie Bird—'

'Possibly in a relationship with her,' Jude corrected and was rewarded with an arched eyebrow warning her to stop interrupting.

'Let's just say that they are in a relationship of some sort. And then imagine Gabe begging Annie to leave Simon so they could be a proper couple, but of course Annie denies him, perhaps even ends their affair. We would have a motive of passion on our hands, would we not?'

'Perhaps,' said Jude, unconvinced.

'Don't underestimate the power of unrequited love,' said Granny Margot. 'I told you right at the very beginning that I could tell Gabe is in love with Annie by the way he looks at her. But she is not in love with him. I'd say to her he's just a distraction, something to try and make up for the fact she knew Simon was sleeping with Mary.'

'How can you be so sure?'

'I've watched the two of them on the television, the perfect couple, so in love. But when you look carefully, it's much more one-sided than that. Haven't you ever noticed that it's always Annie who takes Simon's hand, never the other way around? She looks at him with devotion and love, whereas he looks back at her with fondness. There's a big difference.'

'You're so good at this,' said Jude.

'Years of practice,' said Granny Margot. 'I lived in an age before technology took over when we spent more time communicating with each other and watching those around us. And if I'm right and poor old Gabe is in love with someone who's just using him for sex and revenge then that might just give him a passionate motive to kill her.'

'One thing wrong with this,' said Jude. 'Annie was the one who suggested the van swap which put her next to Gabe and Mary closer to Simon.'

'Hmm, I see what you mean.' Granny Margot rested her hand against her cheek. 'That is a thinker. Maybe I'm wrong, maybe Annie is better at disguising her emotions than I gave her credit for. Either way, I wouldn't take Gabe off the suspect list just yet.'

'Which leaves Holly, the new camera operator, or Robyn, who we know blames Annie for stopping her getting her first directing role,' said Jude.

'Now, let's consider Robyn for a moment.' Granny Margot sat forward. 'If she hates Annie so much and feels so hard done by about the missed director's job, why do you suppose she's still working on the show?'

'It's a good job,' reasoned Jude.

'It can't be the only one. I gathered from my short time with the filming team that this is Dean's third series with them, which covers a full year. Robyn is a talented, experienced woman, if she wanted to leave then she could have by now. So why stay?'

Jude thought about it. Pretty much every time she'd seen Robyn she'd been stressed or grumpy, often taking her frustrations out on junior members of the team. Dean treated her poorly, she was doing her job as researcher but he also relied on her to make certain directorial decisions which he would then take credit for. It must be maddening for her, and yet she stayed put.

'She could be plotting her vengeance,' said Granny Margot. 'Not just on Annie perhaps, but on the entire show that she's given the past however many years to without getting the recognition she deserves. Perhaps she was the one who gave the story to the press for the same reason. We haven't looked at any link there yet, have we?'

'Not yet, but I'd be very interested to know who gave all that information to the newspaper.'

'Someone with an axe to grind.' Jude crossed her legs and readjusted her position in the chair. 'That could be any of them in theory.'

'Now then, we haven't talked much of Holly, who I believe gained a promotion when Mary died so that's obviously her motive.' Granny Margot might be well-advanced in years but there was absolutely nothing wrong with the sharpness of her brain.

'There's something else I think could be interesting when it comes to her,' said Jude. 'I saw someone hiding something down at the bottom of the camping field behind the shepherd's huts and then a little while later, Holly was poking around in the hedge there.'

Granny Margot sat forward a little in her seat. 'Did you see what it was?'

'It was an empty plastic snack tub.'

'Empty?'

'Yes. I can only imagine that they've been using it to deliver something to each other but I've got absolutely no idea what it could be other than a whole lot of guesswork.'

'Guesswork won't get us very far.' Granny Margot tucked one side of her bobbed hair behind an ear. 'You're going to have to monitor it.'

Jude had already thought of that. 'That's exactly what I intend to do. It might not have anything to do with Mary's death, of course.'

'But anything suspicious when there's a murder to be investigated needs keeping an eye on,' said Granny Margot. 'Especially when at least one of those involved has a motive to kill. Keep an eye on it, Jude, it would be very useful to find out who's hiding things for Holly to find, and what exactly it is.'

Granny Margot rested back against the sofa cushion and let her arms flop at her sides. 'I'd say we've got six pretty decent suspects for now: Annie, Simon, Dean, Robyn, Holly and Gabe. All of whom had the opportunity to sneak out in the night when Mary was asleep.'

'And any one of them could have taken the spare key for the caravan – it was hanging up in the production trailer which they all had access to.' Jude pulled her ponytail free and started to smooth the unruly tendrils that had escaped when she'd taken her jumper off. 'They'd have needed to get in to make sure the window catch was up so they could pull it open and poke the end of the pipe through. Also, Annie is certain she saw a carbon monoxide monitor on top of one of the cupboards which was missing when the police searched the caravan.'

Something Jude had just said obviously resonated with Granny Margot as her face had taken on that thoughtful look it did when she was processing ideas.

'We are working on the assumption that anyone could have seen Annie and Mary swap caravans, meaning that either of them could be the intended victim.' Granny Margot rubbed her bottom lip. 'And yet, if someone was setting up murder in this way, it would've had to have been done in advance.'

'You're right,' said Jude. 'Someone went in during the day to set it up, way before the van swap was made. Which means either Annie was the target all along, or someone knew in advance that it would be Mary in the van.'

'You said that Annie didn't tell anyone that she was switching vans,' said Granny Margot.

'That's what she told me, which either means she would have been the only person to have known in advance, or she lied and did tell someone else.'

'Gabe,' said Granny Margot. 'Her lover who just so happens to be in the hut next door. I think there's every chance she would have told him of her plan, don't you?'

The fact that there were two possible intended victims was starting to become somewhat confusing to Jude and she grabbed her shopping list from her handbag and turned it over so she could scribble a new list on the other side. This time a list of suspects cross-referenced to who they could have been trying to kill.

'Blimey, this is getting complicated,' she said.

'Isn't it just?' said Granny Margot. 'They all have motives and they all had the opportunity but who wanted to kill who could be any number of combinations.'

'Perhaps we'll find answers in the snack tub,' said Jude.

'Maybe,' said Granny Margot. 'I have another question for

you, Jude. Have you considered that the chocolate peanuts you found and the contaminated drink might be linked?'

'Of course,' said Jude. 'Both point to the possibility that someone was deliberately trying to give Annie an allergic reaction.'

'That's the obvious link, yes. But I meant a more direct link. Could someone have wanted to make extra sure that there was enough peanut in Annie's drink to trigger the reaction and dropped one in the other?'

Jude thought about how these pieces of the puzzle might fit together. Only a tiny trace of peanut would have been left in the machine after the coffee pods had been used. Definitely enough to trigger a reaction in someone as allergic as Annie, but still not a guarantee that the attack could be deadly. Whereas if someone managed to get a whole nut directly into the drink then the chances of a fatality would be hugely improved. Especially if the EpiPen also went missing from her bag that day.

'It could have been a very controlled way of making it happen at exactly the right time too,' Jude realised. 'A bag of peanuts open anywhere near Annie could have triggered a reaction. But coat them in chocolate and the chances would be greatly reduced.'

'Throw a peanut into the hot chocolate just before it was presented to Annie and the chocolate would melt, releasing the nut oil into the drink and causing her to collapse on live television.' Granny Margot finished the train of thought. 'Who made the hot chocolate, do you know?'

'It was a work experience boy called Chris, Dean's nephew.'

'Someone else to add to the suspect list?' Granny Margot asked.

'I don't think so. He's been questioned and cleared of any involvement in Mary's death. By then he was back home in

Lewisham and there's plenty of CCTV footage to show him having a lads' night out at a bowling alley. The friends he was with have confirmed they all went back to one boy's house afterwards to watch movies and have a sleepover. He can't have had anything to do with it.'

'So are we just dismissing the fact that he was the one who made Annie the hot chocolate that nearly killed her?' The way Granny Margot spoke showed that she thought such a thing would be a naïve omission of possible evidence.

Jude explained how Chris had been blamed for using peanut-flavoured coffee pods in the machine, proclaimed his innocence but had been sent home anyway by Dean.

'Sounds very convenient to me,' said Granny Margot. 'And I think it brings us neatly right back to Dean and his desire to turn the show into a soap opera. I can picture it all, can't you? Setting up the coffee pods and the chocolate peanuts. Hiding the EpiPen but making sure he had the spare at hand to create the drama he wanted without losing his leading lady. Using his young nephew as a scapegoat and then dismissing him quickly so that it became universally understood where the fault lay. It all seems so calculated.'

When Granny Margot laid it all out like that then it did seem to fit together as a real possibility.

'And by being the one to ultimately save her, he was hoping to divert any suspicion away from himself if the peanut in her cup was ever discovered,' Jude added.

'It might have been enough for him, but then the ratings started to boom and perhaps that was when he became even greedier. With Mary's murder, Dean is suddenly slap bang in the middle of a fascinating true-crime opportunity.'

Jude wondered if Granny Margot was getting a little carried away or if there was the possibility of something there. As she pictured Dean, peacocking his way around the farm as though he and he alone ruled everything and everyone he looked on, zero compassion for either the hospitalisation of his star presenter or the death of the camerawoman, Jude realised she wouldn't put anything past him if it meant getting ahead in a highly competitive industry.

There was the sound of heavy footsteps and Gerwain joined them in the conservatory, also sporting a festive necklace of paperchains.

'Ham said I might find you two in here,' he said with a grin. 'I gather you've claimed this as your own HQ for the morning?'

'Oh, he does overexaggerate,' said Granny Margot with a sigh. 'I just asked if Jude and I might be allowed a little peace to chat for twenty minutes or so.'

'That's what I thought it would be.' Gerwain winked at Jude. 'I've come to tell you that Carol is here and we're starting yoga in five minutes. Do you want to join in today or are you and Jude still mid-conflab?'

'I think we've got plenty to be going on with for now,' said Granny Margot. 'If someone wouldn't mind helping me up, I could do with some of Yoga Carol's magic stretches this morning.'

Gerwain put his hands out for Granny Margot to take. When she was on her feet, Jude hugged her goodbye.

'Don't forget to keep an eye on that tub,' Granny Margot said as Jude collected her jumper from the back of the chair. 'And let me know how you get on.'

'Will do,' said Jude. 'Enjoy the yoga.'

14

Re-dressed in her many layers, Jude stepped out into the cold and pulled the car key from her pocket. With it came the list of suspects that she'd written. She got into the freezing car and put the key in the ignition. Before she turned it, she looked at the list again.

It definitely seemed more and more likely that Mary had only been killed because she was in the wrong van at the wrong time. The fact that Annie had already been targeted once all but cemented this theory.

Jude stuffed the list into her handbag. The inside of the windscreen had fogged up so she used a cloth to try to clear it, managing instead to just leave smeary, wet marks in her line of vision. She pulled out the choke of the old Land Rover, which never liked starting when it was cold, and switched on the ignition. Directing the air blowers up at the screen, Jude sat for a moment and went through everything she and Granny Margot had just discussed. It really was a tangle of possibilities and she wasn't sure they'd got any nearer to finding out the truth.

The hot air cleared the windscreen and the engine had

warmed up so Jude put the car in gear and set off back towards Malvern End, all the while thinking about chocolate peanuts.

Granny Margot's idea of them being used in Annie's hot drink was an interesting one. She thought about who might have been able to slip one in. Chris, of course, although it had been Robyn who had taken the tray of drinks to the set. Dean could have intercepted the tray at some point but it would have been hard for Gabe to pull it off as he was busy with his camera the whole time.

Simon? If he had one in his pocket he could have dropped it in surreptitiously and hadn't he been the one to pass Annie her mug? If so, that would make him the only person to know which one to drop the nut into.

'Unless someone put them in all three,' Jude said aloud.

This was risky. If the nuts had been discovered then the game would be up. Except they weren't. Annie's allergic reaction came on fast and she dropped her mug, sending the remainder of the contents all over the ground. Jude tried to remember what had happened to the other mugs. Robyn had tipped them out when she'd been tidying up. Perhaps an innocent gesture but if she knew there were nuts hiding at the bottom of each one then maybe not so innocent after all.

Holly was once more out of the picture as it seemed impossible for her to have sneaked onto the busy set unseen. And what motive did she have to kill Annie anyway? Yet she was the only person Jude had seen wearing clothing made of a similar fluffy, magenta, teddy-bear fabric to the fibres stuck to the exhaust pipe.

As she drove, her mind was ping-ponging between the different players in this macabre game.

Annie, Mary, Simon, Dean, Robyn, Gabe, Holly.

Who was supposed to be dead, who had murder on their mind, and why?

Instead of driving up the drive to the farmhouse, Jude pulled off the lane into the bottom entrance of the campsite where there was an area of snow-covered gravel for guests to park on. She got out of the car and walked to the pedestrian gate that kept vehicles out of the camping area. The catch was stiff and wrestling to get it open reminded her she needed to bring down a can of WD-40. The two shepherd's huts were at the bottom of the campsite and she walked behind these to the hedge where she'd discovered the snack tub. Even in the full light of midday, the tub was tricky to spot, being dark in colour and pushed firmly into a thick patch of the evergreen dogwood.

When she did find it, it was annoyingly empty still. Jude replaced the lid and pushed it back where it had been hidden. She turned to go but the sound of a sharp rap on the door of one of the huts stopped her in her tracks.

'Hi, Annie,' said Gabe. 'Can I come in?'

Annie didn't answer but the door of the hut closed with a thud. Jude then heard both voices clearly through the little air vent that had been fitted to ensure proper ventilation.

'How are you?' Gabe asked.

Knowing that there was a real chance Annie was being targeted and that Gabe was on the list of suspects, no matter how far down it she had put him, Jude didn't feel like she wanted to leave until she knew for certain Annie was safe. She stood still and listened as the two people talked.

'I'd rather not be here,' Annie said. 'And I don't feel safe but really what choice do any of us have?'

'I won't let anything happen to you,' said Gabe.

'I know,' said Annie. 'You're the only person I feel truly safe around.'

There was a moment of quiet and Jude imagined Gabe drawing her into a comforting hug. Her active, suspicious mind then pictured him pulling out a weapon to attack whilst Annie was vulnerable and she wondered whether she could go and knock on the door to check everything was okay.

'Leave him,' said Gabe suddenly and Jude breathed a sigh of relief.

'You know I can't,' said Annie.

'I know you couldn't, but surely this changes everything?'

'I don't see why.'

'For any number of reasons.' Gabe sounded frustrated. 'Life's too short to waste any of it not being with the person you love most. Surely Mary's death has taught us that at least.'

Jude thought about Granny Margot's deduction that the person Annie still loved most was her husband and that Gabe was nothing more than a distraction.

'We should be together, Annie. You know that, it's what you want too. Let's not waste any more time.'

'Gabe, you know I love you, but—'

'No, Annie. Please, no more buts. You're in danger and I want to be able to be there to protect you.'

Annie mumbled something that Jude couldn't quite make out.

'Has Mary's death not shown you anything?' Gabe sounded exasperated. 'We both know that it was supposed to be you in the caravan, not her. You're not safe on your own and I don't see Simon rushing to look after you. Please let me do it instead.'

'Gabe, I need you to go. This is all too much for me at the moment.'

'But Annie... please.' There was desperation in his voice. 'I couldn't bear it if you ended up like Mary.'

This was the third time that he had mentioned Mary's death as a way of trying to persuade Annie to leave Simon. Jude found herself wondering whether he was capable of killing

Mary purely to make Annie feel so vulnerable she'd turn to him for protection and security. Could he also have been responsible for the peanut in the hot chocolate for the same reason?

'I can't do this right now,' said Annie. 'I know you're only trying to help and I love you for it, you know I do. But I can't breathe. I need to figure out what's best for me.'

There was silence for a short while and then Jude heard the door of the hut open.

'You know where I am,' said Gabe. 'Please think about what I said.'

This was followed by the sound of the door closing again and footsteps walking away from the hut.

Jude thought about everything she'd just heard, turning the facts over in her mind. As well as the idea that Gabe seemed so desperate for Annie to need and want him, citing Mary's death as a reason for her to be with him, there was something else. Something not so much to do with the things Jude had just heard but the fact that she'd been able to hear them so clearly in the first place.

If she'd just borne witness to an entire conversation between Annie and Gabe from where she'd been standing, then it was a real possibility that someone else could have done the same at another time. Perhaps Holly or the person who'd hidden the snack tub had been behind Gabe's hut and heard their conversation about an intended caravan swap. Or perhaps Annie had been in Mary's hut, suggesting – or demanding – that Mary would like to move into the bigger caravan. Anyone nearby would have heard every word.

And if this was the case and more people knew about the new sleeping arrangements, then this changed the suspect list Jude had constructed with Granny Margot significantly.

Holly had a motive to kill Mary. And now she possibly had the means and opportunity as well.

* * *

Since Binnie's plan to come back to work slowly and gently had come to an abrupt end with her inability to leave a murder investigation alone, Sami and she were now working together on the case as partners.

Jude had no qualms calling her that afternoon to discuss her latest theories.

They talked in detail about Annie and Gabe and how infatuated he was with her. Perhaps so much so that he was capable of disrupting her peace of mind in such a heinous way so she would turn to him for the total love and security he was offering. Binnie agreed that it was definitely a path worth exploring. She was also interested in Granny Margot's suggestion that Dean could be so driven by his hunger to be a great success that he would stop short of nothing to turn his show into must-watch television. Possibly even setting things up for something even bigger in the way of a true crime like nothing ever seen before.

'I gather viewing numbers are through the roof,' said Binnie.

'That doesn't surprise me,' said Jude. 'The public love a soap opera, and one that involves real people and real lives is even more exciting.'

'Every time I have cause to speak to Dean Dickens he gives me the creeps,' said Binnie. 'You'd think I'd be used to sexual innuendos and sleazy comments from men like him by now.'

'I know what you mean. There's something particularly nasty about him,' said Jude. 'I think it's because of the position of power he holds. It's as though he thinks he can have whatever he wants and is untouchable when it comes to consequences.'

'I have to say I'd love to be the one to knock him out of his ivory tower,' said Binnie. 'But we can't let that cloud our judgement. He is a key suspect for sure but we still have others to consider. Sami spoke to Holly about the magenta jumper you saw her wearing. She's denying she owns such a thing, so could you keep your eyes open and if you catch sight of it again, let us know so we can send someone round to get a closer look?'

'Of course,' said Jude. 'Don't you think that's interesting in itself, the fact that she is denying something that I clearly saw?'

'Maybe,' said Binnie.

'I think she's definitely up to something,' said Jude. 'And I think there's someone else involved too.'

She went on to describe the clandestine postal service using the snack tub. She also told Binnie about what she'd heard in the shepherd's hut, pointing out that this could indicate someone might have known about the caravan swap in advance.

'All interesting to know but nothing solid to go on,' said Binnie. 'Lots of people sneaking around and keeping things hidden from the rest of the team.'

'Definitely not the jolly front *Countryside Live* is famous for,' said Jude.

'Indeed not. Well, I'd better get on. Keep an eye on that tub if you can, Jude.'

* * *

That afternoon, after she'd woken from her post-night-shift sleep, Lucy received a call from the photographer she'd booked months earlier for the wedding to say that he was no longer available.

'Nice enough for him, being whisked away for a surprise Christmas in the Alps with his family, but what the hell am I supposed to do at this short notice?' Lucy asked Jude. 'I bet all the photographers within a fifty-mile radius will either be booked or not working over Christmas.'

'Calm down.' Jude directed Lucy to the kitchen table and sat her down. 'Let me fetch your laptop and then you can go through every photographer methodically until you find one. I'll go and get Sebbie from school and keep him out of your hair for a bit.'

'What if I can't get anyone though?' Lucy looked as though she was about to cry which was most unlike her, and Jude realised that this was about more than a photographer. This was about the fact that she was due to get married in three weeks and there was a lot that was out of her control. The weather, the film crew, the photographer, the fact that Frank had developed a hacking cough and she was worried he was going to pass it on to everybody else.

'Someone will be available and if not, then we will ask everyone to take loads of photos and send them to us. My favourite photo of Adam and me at our wedding wasn't by the man we paid to take pictures. It was the one you took of us in the orchard, laughing at something that I can't even remember. We'll make sure there are plenty of photos of you and Noah laughing too, I promise.'

Jude patted Lucy's shoulder and went off to retrieve her laptop.

'Thanks, Jude,' Lucy said. 'Sorry for the outburst.'

'There's a lot going on. I think you're allowed the odd bridezilla moment.'

Lucy growled at her. 'You promised never to call me that.'

Jude grinned at her sister and picked up the car keys. 'I'll go and get Sebbie. See you in a bit.'

As she drove past the film crew's caravans and trailers, she heard Robyn laying into some poor soul. Jude looked across and saw her waving her arms around angrily whilst some girl who looked close to tears was nodding her head mutely.

'Think of the money,' she told herself for the umpteenth time. 'They'll be gone before you know it.'

It was busy outside the school so Jude drove on and parked by the little row of cottages on the edge of the village. As she stepped out onto the pavement, she heard a knocking sound and looked over to see Marco waving from his front room.

She waved back before wrapping her scarf a little tighter around her neck, tucking her chin into it for extra warmth and setting off down the pavement towards school. For once, she arrived before the bell rang to signal the end of the day. When the doors did open and the teachers led their charges out to reunite them with their adults, Sebbie spotted Jude and patted Miss Elgar's arm to point his aunt out to her. His teacher waved at Jude and then gave Sebbie permission to run over and meet her. He was wearing a jolly festive hat made of thick sugar paper and decorated with cut-out images from old Christmas cards.

'I thought Mummy was coming today,' he said as he passed Jude a drawstring bag with his PE kit in.

'She had to do something on the computer so I thought I'd come and get you instead.' Jude took hold of his mittened hand. 'Love the hat, by the way.'

'I made it at the Christmas craft table,' he said proudly. 'Are we going in the tractor?'

'Not today, I'm afraid,' said Jude. 'I've got the Land Rover.'

The disappointment was evident but he didn't complain. As they walked through the village, he chattered non-stop about the weekend and how much he was looking forward to going up into the hills with his sledge. Jude couldn't get a word in edgeways but she enjoyed listening to his high little voice talking nineteen to the dozen.

'Look,' he said when they got close to the Land Rover and the row of cottages. 'It's Rex.'

Rex was a German Shepherd dog, owned by Clara, who had clearly been working from home that day and was on her way out for a walk. Aside from the Malvern Farm collies, Rex was Jude's favourite dog. When she'd first met him, he'd been untrained and a hugely intelligent but a very tricky beast. Since Clara had taken him in, she'd worked wonders with him and he was now a beautifully behaved, friendly dog.

Sebbie loved Rex and when he saw him, he dropped Jude's hand and went running up the pavement to meet him, his backpack bouncing madly as he went.

'Be careful,' Jude shouted but it was too late. Sebbie hit a particularly icy patch and his feet lost traction, sending him crashing forward onto the slushy pavement.

There was a second of silence before the scream of pain. Jude rushed over, careful not to fall herself, and bent down to check for broken bones.

'Where does it hurt?' she asked.

'My hands and knees,' Sebbie sobbed.

His school trousers were soaked through, as were the mittens, but as he stood up, it seemed as though everything was working properly.

'My hat!' he cried and Jude stooped to pick up the wet paper crown which had already lost a couple of the pictures.

'Oh, Sebbie,' said Clara as she came out of her garden with Rex on a tight lead. 'Are you okay?'

'I fell over,' Sebbie sniffled as he looked dejectedly down at his soggy knees. 'And my special Christmas hat fell in a puddle.'

'I can see that. How about you come on inside and your Aunty Jude can check you over properly whilst I find us some biscuits and a hot drink?'

Sebbie looked at her earnestly through his tears. 'Can I play with Rex for a bit too?'

Clara smiled kindly. 'Of course you can. If you've got time.' She looked at Jude.

'That would be really kind,' said Jude, holding up the PE bag. 'We've got spare clothes so it would be good to get him into something dry.'

'Well, that's settled,' said Clara. 'Rex will be delighted. You know you're his favourite boy in the world. Can you take his lead or are your hands too sore?'

'I think my hands are okay enough.' Sebbie pulled off his soggy mittens and passed them to Jude. The skin was red but he was moving both hands easily so no broken bones there.

'Here you go.' Clara passed the end of the lead to Sebbie who took it and gave Rex's ears a stroke.

'Thanks for this,' said Jude. She'd always liked Clara enormously. There was nothing not to like really, she was thoughtful, gentle, funny, great company.

She was also dating Marco.

But Jude had made a promise to put all of that well and truly behind her so, as she followed Clara into the cottage, she elbowed out thoughts of jealousy and reminded herself of all the good things about their friendship.

Jude knew Clara's cottage well. It was still owned by Granny Margot, who had been living there with her granddaughter, Sarah, when Jude had first moved to Malvern End. Since Clara had started to rent it, she had given it a bit of a facelift but for Jude the cottage was still full of bittersweet memories of the many happy times she'd spent there with Granny Margot, Sarah, Adam and their friends.

'Now then,' said Clara as they trooped down the hall to the kitchen at the back of the cottage, 'why don't you sit down at the table and check for bumps and bruises whilst I see if I've got any hot chocolate in my cupboard?'

Sebbie unclipped Rex's lead and gave his head a rub. 'Good boy,' he said. 'I'll play with you in a minute but I need to show Aunty Judy my knees first.'

As expected, Sebbie hadn't sustained any lasting damage and he was soon out of his wet things and in the dry PE kit. A bit of Rex therapy and a steaming cup of milky hot chocolate and he had forgotten all about his tumble and sore patches.

Whilst Sebbie sat on the floor and played tug-o-war with Rex and a ball attached to a piece of rope, Jude and Clara chatted over mugs of tea.

'How's everything up at the farm?' Clara asked. 'It must be awful with the film crew after what happened to that poor woman.'

'I was expecting them to stop filming, but it's still going ahead.'

'It's weird seeing them all wandering around the village. I caught a glimpse of Annie Bird this morning coming out of Four Trees.'

'Yes, she's staying there now,' said Jude.

'I thought she must be. I felt really sorry for her, she looked exhausted. It must be so difficult to put on a happy face every evening for the live show after everything that's happened this week.'

'I don't know how she does it.' Jude tucked her feet under her chair and leant forward to put her elbows on the table. 'Years of experience kicking in, I suppose.'

'Even so, first her allergy and the fact that millions of people saw her collapse live on air, and then for one of her friends to die in such a tragic accident a few days later. That's a lot for anyone to take in.'

Jude realised that Clara only knew what the general public had been told about the nature of Mary's death, which meant that Marco hadn't confided in her.

'I think she's developed a way of becoming the expected telly version of herself when the camera is on her,' said Jude, 'but as soon as it stops rolling, she drops the pretence. Like you said, she's exhausted and I think she'll be relieved when the series ends and she can take some time off.'

'With Simon?' Clara looked steadily at her.

'I, um...'

'Sorry.' Clara shook her head. 'Gosh, I sound like one of the village gossips. Please don't ever let me turn into another Janet Timms.'

Janet lived at the other end of the row of cottages, next door to Marco. She was notorious for loving nothing better than being at the centre of the village grapevine.

Jude chuckled. 'Don't worry, you've got a very long way to go before you get to that level.'

'Thank goodness,' said Clara. 'Talking about Annie Bird and the film team though, I found something in the village a couple of days ago and I was going to drop it up at the farm. Then I heard about what happened and I thought it wasn't important enough to disturb them with. Perhaps you could take it for me.'

She stood up and went out of the kitchen for a moment. When she came back in, she was carrying a piece of paper that had been folded into a small rectangle.

'Here,' she said as she passed it over to Jude. 'I'm not sure if it's important, probably not, but just in case it's needed.'

Jude unfolded the paper and found that it was actually two sheets. Both contained a printed list of times with corresponding events and places, slightly smudged as though they'd got wet and been dried out. On the top of the first was Annie's name and on the second was Gabe's.

'It looks like schedules,' said Clara.

'Where did you find them?' Jude asked. She recognised a few of the inclusions, enough to realise that the schedules were for the day Mary had been killed.

'Just by the postbox. I'd stopped to post my Christmas cards and saw it on the ground. To begin with I thought it was an envelope so I picked it up in case it had fallen out of a stack of things someone else had been posting.'

The postbox was at the opposite end of the village to Clara's cottage, closest to the entrance to Malvern Farm and the campsite. Jude looked at the way the sheets had been folded. Clara was right, they were the size of a smallish envelope. They were also a pretty close match to the size of the snack tub that had been hidden in the hedge not all that far from the post box.

In fact, if someone had been hiding things for Holly before she'd come to stay on the farm, and if Holly hadn't wanted to be seen on the campsite, then the closest place for her to park would be the layby by the postbox. It was dark soon after four in the afternoon which would have made it easier for her to walk the short distance down the lane to the bottom entrance of the camping field without being seen.

Here she could have taken the schedules, planted by someone from the crew, perhaps even heard Annie talking to Gabe about swapping caravans with Mary, and then walked back to her car, not realising she'd dropped the schedules. If she and someone else were planning to kill Annie together then knowing where she was going to be would be incredibly useful information. But why have Gabe's schedule as well? And what reason did Holly have for wanting Annie dead? Her motive so far was only for Mary.

'Thanks,' said Jude. 'I'll make sure this gets to the right people.'

She didn't add that this was not a member of the *Countryside Live* team. The right people in this instance were most definitely Sami and Binnie.

Jude and Sebbie stayed for a little while longer until they'd finished their drinks. Then they thanked Clara before heading back to the car and going home to find out how Lucy had got on with the photographers of Herefordshire, Worcestershire and Gloucestershire.

Lucy was still on the phone when Jude and Sebbie walked in but the smile on her face and the thumbs-up sign she gave them looked very promising.

Jude threw Sebbie's wet school clothes into the washing machine and then went to find a stack of old Christmas cards that she'd kept from previous years. As a child she'd always cut them up to make gift tags and the habit had stuck.

'Here,' she said to Sebbie. 'You cut out some Christmassy pictures and I'll find you some paper to make another hat you can stick them to.'

'If I have enough, I'll make hats for you, Mummy and Noah too.' Sebbie settled at the kitchen table and picked up the scissors, ready to make a start. 'Do you think Clarence the elf would like a little one?'

'I'm sure he'd love that,' said Jude. 'I've got a couple of jobs to do in the paddock but Mummy will be off the phone soon. Don't bother her until she is, okay?'

'Okay.'

It was already dark when she went to put the ducks away for the night and the paddock was buzzing with people getting things ready for that evening's live filming. Jude saw that most of the team were there so she decided it was as good a chance as any to go and have another look in the tub to see if she'd be lucky and find something in it.

She managed to make it down to the bottom of the field without much interaction with anyone. Even though she was walking through her own camping field and had every right to do so, Jude still felt jittery at the thought of being caught out. She had any number of reasons to be down here – checking the solar panels, the water pipes or the generator to name three important maintenance jobs – but it was still comforting to have the cloak of winter's darkness to hide her.

There were no lights on in either of the shepherd's huts and Jude ducked quickly behind them. She was loath to switch on her phone's torch and give herself away if anyone was watching that patch of the field. But when a blind search gave her nothing, she had no choice and swiped the icon on her screen to illuminate the stretch of hedge where she knew the tub had been.

Shining the light directly through the branches, Jude peered inside but could not see it. A thorough search of the rest of the hedge gave her nothing.

The tub was no longer there.

15

Jude was used to having the world to herself first thing in the morning. Sometimes Noah would join her briefly before he went out to do the early field rounds but often she had time to get her day moving with a quiet cup of coffee in the kitchen. Thanks to the Aga, it was always the warmest place in the house and if she only put the side lights on it was a gentle way to start the day.

That Saturday though, as soon as she left her bedroom to tiptoe downstairs, Sebbie's door flew open and he ran out fully clothed.

'Good gracious!' whispered Jude with her finger on her lips. 'Come down quietly with me so we don't wake Mummy, and then you can tell me why you're up before the sun today.'

Sebbie said nothing until they were in the kitchen and Jude had told him it was safe to talk.

'You said we could go sledging today,' he said, 'and Noah said that we should go early before everyone else went up to the hills.'

'Whilst both these things are very true, do you not think that sledging in the dark might be a bit disastrous?'

'It won't be dark for very long though. My clock already starts with a six so if we eat our breakfast and then drive up to the Beacon, the sun will be up.'

Jude loved the little boy's enthusiasm but she knew it would be nearer eight before the sun came up this close to mid-winter.

'We've got a little time first,' she said. 'I know, how about we find those Christmas cards you designed at school and we can get those written before we go? Then we can post them on the way up to the hills.'

Sebbie looked worried. 'Will we still be the first ones up there?'

'I'm almost certain of it.' Jude smiled and went to find the cards and a couple of pens.

* * *

Under Sebbie's keen leadership, with a new sun just appearing, the Land Rover was packed up with two plastic sledges, a backpack containing a flask of Jude's new favourite winter drink, hot Ribena, mugs and snacks, three collies – Noah decided old Floss was too old to enjoy a sledging expedition so they left her in her basket by the Aga – one small boy and his three adoring adults.

The snow had pretty much disappeared from the farm but as they set off up the steep gradient of Croft Bank, they found the snowline. Jude parked at the foot of one of their favourite paths up to the hills and everybody got out.

'See,' said Noah as they walked up the track. 'I told you there'd still be plenty of snow up here for you.'

Sebbie ran ahead with the dogs, trailing a stick in the deeper snow piles at the sides of the path to make patterns. He laughed when Alfie cocked his leg and melted a yellow hole in it.

'How about here?' he kept asking when he thought they were at just the right spot for the sledges.

'I keep telling you, there's not much snow left on these paths and it's a hard, gritty landing if you come off your sledge here,' said Jude. 'We're going all the way up to the saddle where the snow will be better and there's only soft grass and moss underneath it.'

As they reached a section of the hills where two paths crossed, Jude heard her name being shouted and she looked over to see Holly carrying a camera on a tripod over her shoulder and waving at her.

'Bugger it,' she mumbled under her breath. She'd thought she would have a morning at least away from anyone to do with *Countryside Live*.

'Who's that?' Lucy whispered as Holly came carefully down the side of the hill towards them.

'That's Holly, the dead woman's replacement.'

'Oh!'

'Hi, Holly,' said Jude. 'You're up early.'

'Came to capture the sunrise over the snow,' said Holly. 'It will make a magical opening shot for the show tonight. The colours up there were incredible.'

'I bet,' said Lucy. 'Oh, I recognise you. We met the other day in the village.'

'Did we?' Holly looked confused.

'Yes. You'd lost something and were looking for it on the lane by the postbox.'

'No, not me,' said Holly with a smile. 'Although it would be just like me, I'm terrible at losing things.'

'Are you sure?' asked Lucy.

'Pretty sure. Maybe I've just got one of those faces. You know?'

Although there wasn't anything particularly striking about Holly's face, Jude thought that there was no mistaking the long hair in tight curls. If Lucy said she'd seen her searching for something in the lanes then she almost certainly had. And Jude had a very good idea what that could have been.

'Probably,' said Lucy, sounding wholly unconvinced.

'Are you heading out on to the slopes?' Holly indicated the two sledges that Noah had slung over his shoulder.

'Yes,' he said. 'Promised the young 'un we'd have him out before the crowds arrive.'

'Well, you've managed that for sure.' Holly adjusted the tripod she was carrying and Jude caught sight of a furry blue cuff under her padded jacket. 'I'll join, if you don't mind. You can show me where the serious sledgers go. Might be fun to get Annie and Simon up here to talk to some of them and maybe even have a go themselves.' She looked down at Sebbie, who'd come to see what the holdup was. 'Hey, do you want to be on the telly tonight?' Holly asked.

'Yeah!' said Sebbie instantly and enthusiastically without asking her what exactly that would entail.

'Hang on a minute,' said Lucy. 'I'm not sure I'm okay with that.'

'Oh, don't worry. I'll only use a short clip. It'll be fun.'

'Aunty Judy did it,' said Sebbie. 'And Noah, and Granny Margot. Frank did it too and even Alfie and Ned with the sheep. Everyone has been on telly and I want to have my go too.'

Lucy gave Holly a furious look. 'Let's just enjoy the snow for now, hey? We can talk about the telly later.'

'Okay,' said Sebbie. 'Are we nearly at the top yet?'

'Almost there,' said Noah.

Holly seemed not to notice that her presence hadn't exactly been welcomed into the family party. She tagged along, chattering about the light and the colours that the snow was gifting them. There was no denying she really knew her stuff and Jude could see why she'd been so annoyed to have been overlooked for the main camera operator role initially.

As they breached the corner, Noah led them all up an old sheep track that went over the saddle between two hills. There wasn't a single other person up at the top and the snow was still unmarked by human footprints.

'Wow, it's incredible up here,' said Holly.

'It helps to know where you're going,' said Noah. 'Most folk like to stick to what they know.'

He took the sledges off his shoulder, separated them from each other and laid them down on the snow.

'There's a bit of a crusty ice layer,' he said. 'Perfect for sledging. Who's up first?'

'Me, me!' Sebbie bounced around in front of Noah with his hand in the air.

'Thought you might say that. Right, you get in that one and wait for me to get in mine, then Mummy and Jude can push us both off together. Okay?'

'You need to teach him to steer that thing,' said Lucy.

'No need,' said Noah. 'There's nothing for him to crash into up here and the bracken will stop him coming a cropper off the side of the hill. Are you ready?'

'Ready!' Sebbie shouted back, unable to contain his excitement.

'Give us a push then.'

Both sledges were teetering at the top of the hill and Jude stood behind Noah and gave him as big a shove as she could manage, sending him off down the slope at a rate of knots. Lucy was a little more reserved with Sebbie, who had a more sedate ride to the open patch at the bottom where the ground flattened and the sledges stopped.

Pip, Alfie and Ned went tearing down with them, barking at

the speeding plastic shells and wondering what was going on. They danced around Noah and Sebbie at the bottom, delighted that they'd kept everyone safe.

'I'd love to film them,' said Holly. 'How about just from the back? He's wearing a hat and such a big coat that nobody will recognise him. It would make such a great addition to my snowy hill montage.'

Lucy sighed. 'Fine,' she said. 'I suppose there can't be any harm in that and it'll give him his moment of fame and bragging rights in the school playground.'

'Thank you,' said Holly.

'Who's next?' Noah asked as he came back to the top of the hill, pulling both sledges behind him.

'Aunty Judy, your turn,' said Sebbie. 'Race me. And Noah, push me hard this time.'

'You got it,' said Noah.

'Come on then, you speed demon.' Jude took the rope handle of one of the sledges from Noah and positioned it at the top of the hill. She got in and watched Noah set Sebbie up.

'Ready?' Noah called.

Jude gave a thumbs up and felt Lucy's hard thrust in between her shoulder blades. The slope was fairly steep and she picked up speed quickly. Feeling the cold air rush past her cheeks and sting the moisture in her eyes made her feel like a child again and she gave a loud whoop of exhilaration. The dogs woofed their responses and before she knew it, she was at the bottom of the hill, landing at the same time as Sebbie.

'I won that time, didn't I?' Sebbie shouted.

'You sure did,' said Jude. 'That was fun. Want another go?'

Sebbie started to run back up the hill, leaving Jude to collect the sledges and pull them up by their strings.

Lucy declined the offer of taking her turn next and Holly gave her camera as an excuse, so it was back to Noah to take Sebbie down for another run, although Jude didn't think he looked upset in the least about that.

'These really do work,' said Lucy, rubbing her wrists.

Jude looked to see what she was talking about and saw that she had something bottle green and fluffy around her wrists.

'What are those?' she asked.

'Holly lent them to me. I was saying that my arms were cold even with my thick fleece and coat on and she pointed out that the gap around my wrists was letting the cold air in.'

Holly pulled back the sleeve of her own coat and showed Jude the bright blue version she was wearing herself.

'They do look really warm,' said Jude, wondering if Holly had a magenta pair as well. 'Gorgeous colours too.'

'Feel it,' said Holly. 'It's like having my wrists hugged by a teddy bear.'

Jude took her glove off and felt the fluff. Holly was right, it was just like a teddy bear.

'You don't have any more, do you?' Jude asked.

'I don't think I've got any with me,' said Holly. 'I've got several others though. It's my sister-in-law's company and she sent me one of every colour so I've got the whole rainbow somewhere. The company is called Toastie Mitts and these are Toastie Wrists, you should look them up.'

'I will,' said Jude. 'Your sister-in-law should pay you commission.'

Holly laughed. 'The amount of people I've told about these she really should. Seriously though, they are fab and they'd make excellent Christmas presents for your friends.'

'I'll have a look as soon as we get home,' said Jude. 'Toastie Mitts.'

'Dot com,' said Holly.

'Here they come,' said Lucy as Noah walked back up again with Sebbie.

'I'm going to leave you to it,' said Holly. 'I want to get more footage of people enjoying the hills in the snow and I'm expecting the rest of the crew to be up here soon so we can run some quick interviews and put a decent piece together.'

'It was nice to meet you,' said Lucy. 'Thanks for the loan of the Toastie Wrists.' She pulled them off and handed them to Holly.

'Keep hold of them for now. You can give them back to me when you've finished up here.' Holly clipped her lens cover in place, pushed the telescopic legs of her tripod in and folded them away.

'That's really kind, thanks,' said Lucy.

'No worries. Just tell all your friends about them.' Holly hauled the tripod, with the camera still attached, across her shoulder.

'Bye, Holly,' said Jude. 'I hope the filming goes well.'

'Enjoy your sledging.' Holly set off down the hill in search of the next perfect filming opportunity.

'Your turn, Jude,' said Noah, offering her the sledge.

'You go again. Lucy and I are fine chatting for a bit.'

Noah shrugged and then he and Sebbie lined up for another race down the hill.

'She was a bit full-on,' said Lucy.

'You could say that,' said Jude. 'She was lying, wasn't she? When she said it wasn't her you'd seen down in the village.'

'Definitely! That's not the sort of woman I'd forget.' Lucy pulled her hat down further over her ears. 'Am I sensing you might have an inkling why she lied?'

'More than an inkling, I'd say.' Jude explained the connections she'd made between the snack box in the hedge – the postal system being used by Holly and someone else – and the schedules Clara had found outlining where Gabe and Annie would be on the day that someone killed Mary.

'Holly lied about being at the farm,' said Jude. 'When I met her after she officially joined the main filming team she told me it was the first time she'd been there.'

'She's obviously got something to hide and you're right, it must have something to do with the schedules. Does she have any reason to want Annie dead?'

'Not that I know of,' said Jude. 'But don't forget someone else is tied up in this too. Someone who gave Holly the schedules. Dean, Simon and Robyn all have motives to want Annie dead.'

'Can we have hot Ribena now?' Sebbie came running over, his nose and cheeks pink and eyes glistening.

'Great idea.' Jude took off the backpack she was carrying.

The flask had done a better job of keeping the drink hot than she'd anticipated and a great cloud of steam swirled out when she took the lid off.

'You'd better pop a bit of snow in there to cool it down before you drink it,' she said as she passed a mug to Sebbie. 'Just make sure you choose a patch that nobody has stepped on and make sure it's not yellow.'

'Why would the snow be yellow?' Sebbie asked.

Jude pointed at Alfie. 'It might be if Alfie had already been there.'

'Eurghh!' Sebbie shrieked with laughter and went off to find a virgin patch of fresh snow to cool his drink.

Jude held her own mug close to her face and breathed in the hot, sweet blackcurrant-scented steam.

The printed schedules, the sneaking around, the lies, the snack tub in the hedge. Holly was definitely up to something, Jude just couldn't put her finger on what it was. And then there were the Toastie Wrists that she had in every colour. As soon as she got home, she would look up the company, and she would eat her bobble hat if they didn't make them in magenta.

* * *

As the sledging party made its way back down the hill, the rest of the world seemed to be making its way up it. It had been a great idea to get there early and the added bonus was that the exercise, fresh air and 6 a.m. start had tired Sebbie out so much that he was happy to be bundled into warm clothes and plonked in front of cartoons when they got home.

No hat eating was required when Jude pulled up the Toastie Mitts website on her phone. A quick search found some that looked on the screen to be a very possible match to the magenta that had been stuck to the residue on the exhaust pipe. She ordered a pair and was told that they would be with her within three to five working days. Not ideal but there was something else she could do in the meantime.

'I'd better go and drop these back at Holly's caravan before I forget,' said Lucy, picking up the green wrist warmers.

'Hang on,' said Jude. 'Before you do, can I borrow one of those for a minute?'

'What are you up to?' Lucy asked as Jude went to the oak dresser and pulled open the drawer.

'A little scientific experiment.' Jude took out a roll of heavy-duty silver tape, and rootled around in the tangled contents of the next drawer along until she found her splinter tweezers.

'Here you go.' Lucy handed her the wrist warmer. 'Are you going to elaborate at all?'

Jude peeled back a short length of tape and pushed the sticky side firmly against the fluffy green fabric. 'Someone left tiny traces of magenta fluff behind when they gassed Mary's caravan,' she said as she pulled the tape away and examined the surface for the traces of green she knew would be left behind. 'These things come in a very similar shade but the ones I just ordered will take a while to get here.'

'Very clever,' said Lucy. 'You're going to see if Binnie can get this tested instead.'

'It might be a long shot, but it's worth a try.' Jude took the tweezers and pulled a few straight strands from the teddy-like fur. She added them to the tape and passed the wrist warmer back to Lucy. 'What we really need to find though is the actual magenta pair that I'm sure I mistook for a fleece I saw Holly wearing. They may well be able to cross-match with any traces of tape residue that might be on them too.'

'That would be pretty conclusive, wouldn't it?'

'It would certainly help. Although we still have no motive for her if Annie is the real target.'

'Yet,' said Lucy. 'If she seems like the best fit though, gotta keep digging.'

Jude sighed. 'The sooner we can get the whole lot of them off the farm the better.'

'Amen to that. One week down, two more to go.'

'Talking of which, I need to go and take fresh sheets and towels down to the shepherd's huts.'

'Really?'

'Saturday is change-over day,' said Jude. 'They've paid for it and it's not for me to say when these things aren't required any longer.'

'Go on then. Get it out of the way.'

Jude collected together the things she'd need into a large laundry bag and set off for the camping field. The chillout trailer was thankfully quiet, as was the rest of the area that the filming contingent had taken over. She went on down, past all the empty wooden platforms where the canvas tents stood during the more clement months, to the two huts at the bottom of the field.

Jude knocked on the door of the first, which had been allocated to Gabe. There was no answer so she took out her key, calling out as she put it into the lock so she didn't startle anyone who might be in there.

It was empty so Jude went in, changed the sheets and swapped the old towels hanging in the tiny shower room for fresh ones. Whilst she was there, she couldn't resist taking a quick look around to see if there was anything else of interest pertaining to his relationship with Annie.

There weren't many places to squirrel things away in the small interior of the shepherd's hut but Jude thought it was worth having a look on the bookshelf above the bed and the single cupboard and drawer that were part of the tiny kitchen.

The drawer contained all the things that Jude would have expected to see, the cutlery and few utensils she'd supplied along with a lighter for the gas ring and some tea lights. In the cupboard she found all the plates, bowls and glasses had been squashed onto one shelf, leaving the other free for Gabe to store his own things. A sponge bag, some notebooks and a large roll of heavy-duty black tape.

Jude picked the tape up and looked at it, wondering why a sound engineer might need tape such as this. There could be several legitimate reasons involving his professional equipment; however, she could also think of one very obvious, more nefarious use he might have had for it.

The sudden sound of a key in the door made Jude jump and she quickly stuffed the tape into her laundry bag and shut the cupboard just as Gabe pushed the door open.

'Jude! What are you doing in here?'

Jude held up a tea towel. 'Saturday is laundry day,' she said. 'Clean sheets and towels.'

'Oh, right. Thanks.'

'No worries. Well, I'll leave you to it then.'

'Listen, we've only got two weeks left of filming so no need to come back and change the sheets again before we go.'

As Jude looked at him, she found she had the distinct impression that this was not a request to save her any time or effort. He didn't want her there, that was clear. And when his eyes flicked to the storage drawer that Marco had built into the base of the bed when he'd helped set the huts up, Jude wondered what Gabe was hiding in there.

'If you're sure.' She took a second bag out and pushed all the dirty laundry into it. 'Let me know if there's anything you need.'

Jude left the hut with a very strong feeling that there was more to find out about Gabe Crosby. He was being secretive and shifty and that made her wonder if he'd been the person she'd seen hiding things in the hedge behind his hut. She'd dismissed this up until then as he seemed so in love with Annie that she couldn't imagine him wanting her dead. But Jude knew she'd been naïve. Love that strong, when left frustrated, had triggered murderous acts of passion before.

She wanted to find out exactly what he was hiding under his bed but she would have to wait until the next time he was out on a location shoot so that she could sneak back into the hut to take a look.

16

The light was on in the other hut and Jude had a second set of clean bedding and towels to deliver so she went over and knocked on the door.

To her surprise, it was opened by Simon, carrying a tumbler of something golden.

'Oh, hi,' Jude said. 'I was just coming to make Annie's bed and drop off new towels for her.'

'She's gone back to the B&B, but come in and do what you need to do.' Simon North looked very much like a washed-out version of the bubbly television personality the country knew and loved.

Jude stepped up into the hut and put her laundry bags down on the floor.

'You must be wondering what the hell we're all still doing here after what happened.' Simon sat down in the single bamboo bucket chair and took a sip from the tumbler.

'I gather Dean has a pretty tight grasp on contracts.' Jude carefully moved Annie's possessions from the bed onto the little coffee table, next to an open bottle of brandy, so she could strip back the sheets.

'The thing about this business is that we are all only one mistake away from being cast out on to the festering heap of has-beens.' Simon rubbed a hand through his hair. 'I know that, Annie knows that, and Dean sure as hell knows that.'

Jude felt a little awkward being confined in such a small space with the morose presenter whilst she went about pulling clean pillowcases on. What was he doing in the hut anyway? He had his own large caravan to hang out in.

'Did you get any good footage up on the hills today?' she asked, trying to lighten the mood as she hurried to finish what she needed to do.

'We all went through the motions.' Simon poured himself another impressive measure of brandy and took a large gulp of it. 'Except that bloody Holly woman. She would have had us walk half the length of the hills to find the best shots if we hadn't all objected. Seriously, like it really matters that much anyway. Mary was far better at looking at things from a wider perspective rather than always trying to find the award-winning shots no matter the cost.'

He stopped and pressed his thumb into the patch just above the bridge of his nose.

'Mary was irreplaceable,' he said quietly. 'God, I miss her.' He checked himself as he looked at Jude. 'We all do.'

'It really is a horrid situation to be in. I hope Dean sees sense soon.'

Jude shook the duvet into the clean cover and rolled the used sheets into the bag with Gabe's dirty laundry. She wasn't sure whether Annie, or Simon for that matter, would be using the bed again but they'd paid for a service and so she got on with it.

'Don't hold your breath there,' said Simon.

Jude went to the shower room to gather up the towels and threw them in on top.

'I'll be off then,' she said as she gathered up her things, grateful to be able to leave Simon to his thoughts.

'Don't tell anyone I'm in here, will you?' Simon said as Jude went to open the door and she realised then just how drunk he was. 'I needed to be on my own so Annie gave me the key.'

'Are you not tempted to join her at the B&B?' Jude asked.

Simon gave a wry smile. 'I know you're not that naïve, Jude. You've seen the set-up here and you know that Annie and I are a very long way off the happily married couple that we portray on the telly. At home it's easy. We have our own parts of the house and things just work for us. There's plenty of love still there.' He shrugged lazily. 'She's still my best friend. But we can't live in the same room together or we'd drive each other round the twist.'

'You put on a very good show,' said Jude, wondering if Annie shared his take on the situation.

'We've had a lot of practice.' Simon's smile was crooked as he pointed his brandy tumbler at her. 'Oh, and if you decide you fancy making some extra cash and selling the story, I wouldn't recommend it. Others have tried in the past but it never ends well for them.'

Jude felt a shiver run through her at his words, which had landed like a warning. No – stronger. Like a threat.

'That's not something I'd do,' she said.

'No, of course not, sorry.' Simon put the empty tumbler down. 'It's been such a horrendous week and I'm not really thinking straight at the moment.' He dug his fingertips into the crown of his head and gave his scalp a harsh-looking massage. 'I suppose I'm a bit paranoid too after that article was released.'

'That's understandable.' Jude was ready to leave. 'Are you going out live this evening?'

Simon nodded pathetically. 'I'd better take a nap and then make myself a strong coffee.'

'Probably a good idea.'

She left him to sober up and went back outside to walk the big bag of dirty sheets back up to the house. When the campsite was full, she sent everything out to be laundered but it wasn't worth it just for the two huts. That meant three extra loads to put through the washing machine that weekend.

As she came close to the top of the camping field, Jude heard a strange single beep coming from somewhere near the row of caravans supplied by the network. A few steps further and there was a second one, reminding Jude of the noise her smoke alarms made when the battery needed changing.

There was a gap between each beep and to begin with Jude thought it was coming from inside one of the caravans. She set the laundry bags down on the metal seat of the old Ferguson tractor Noah had set up to entertain visiting children, and pricked her ears to the noise. Each time it sounded, she took another few steps in the direction she thought it was coming from until the trail led her to the horsebox that she'd repurposed as a shower block.

It sounded as though it was coming from beneath and, when she crouched down and tipped her head to one side in order to get a better look, the source of the noise was clearly evident. A white plastic box that looked very much like an alarm of some sort. It didn't take much brain power to work out what the alarm was likely to be and sure enough, when she retrieved the mop from the cleaning cupboard in the shower block to pull the alarm free, she saw it was a carbon monoxide detector.

Not wanting to tamper too much with the evidence but keen

to stop the person who'd tossed it there coming back and getting rid of it more permanently, Jude took a spare pillowcase from the bag of laundry and used it like a poop scoop bag to pick up the still beeping alarm.

She had so much to tell Sami and Binnie and it was a huge frustration that both of their phones went straight to voicemail. Instead she had to make do with sending them a group text so neither could complain she'd left them out or gone over their heads.

> Found missing CO monitor under the shower block. Also found roll of suspicious tape in Gabe's hut.

> Possible match to the magenta fluff – wrist warmer belonging to Holly.

> So much to talk to you about. Give me a ring or let me know if I can come for a chat and to drop everything off with you? J xx

* * *

Later that afternoon, Jude parked the Land Rover outside Binnie's house in Malvern Link and got out, armed with a bag containing all the things she needed to give her.

It was already starting to get dark, reminding Jude that they were nudging ever closer to mid-winter. At least then the days would start to get slowly longer again.

'Come in.' Binnie must have seen her through the window of her front room as the door opened before Jude was halfway up the path. 'Sami's still at work but he's coming round in a bit.'

'Before we start talking murder,' said Jude as she kissed her friend on the cheek, 'are you off because you weren't rostered on this afternoon? Or are you off because you've been overdoing it and need a break? You were very sketchy when you phoned to ask me round.'

'More the second choice if you're putting a label on it, but I'm absolutely fine. I had a bit of a headache this morning so I came home to stave it off before it turned into a full-blown migraine, that's all.'

Jude took her coat off and hung it on a row of hooks by the front door.

'Should you be talking murder cases at all then? Maybe we should do something a little less full-on.'

Binnie answered with the rise of an eyebrow before she held her hand out for the bag.

'Are these for me?'

'I was going to bring you a box of Quality Street and a bottle of eggnog but I thought you'd rather have a dying carbon monoxide monitor, a roll of industrial tape, old printouts and some bright green tufts of fluffy fabric. If I'd thought of it, I'd have put them in a Christmas stocking for you!'

'You really know how to treat me,' said Binnie with a smile. 'Thanks for these, all exciting in their own ways.'

She led the way into the front room, which was cosy and calm and beautifully decorated, a far cry from the chaos of Malvern Farm. Binnie's striped cat, Babur, was lying on the windowsill in a sunray and looked up to give them a lazy stare.

'Don't you want to wait for Sami at least?' said Jude, taking a seat on the pristine sofa which was covered in plump silk-covered scatter cushions.

'Oh, he won't mind.' Binnie sat sideways at the other end of the sofa and hooked one arm over the back so that she could scratch Babur's head. 'He can catch up when he gets here. Now why don't we start with why that bag you gave me is beeping?'

Jude curled her legs up underneath her and settled in for the long haul. 'You might want to bury that under a big pile of coats or something if you don't want it to keep you awake all night.'

'Give Sami five minutes of walking through the door and it'll probably be chucked down to the bottom of the garden!'

Jude wriggled into the comfortable caress of the sofa's soft furnishings and began to recall the details of everything she had uncovered that day. She started with the sledging trip up the hills, the chance encounter with Holly and the fact that Lucy recognised her.

'She was absolutely adamant it wasn't her but as Lucy pointed out, Holly isn't the sort of person you could get mixed up with someone else.'

'And you think she was there to use this lunchbox postal system of theirs?'

'I'm sure of it,' said Jude. 'Clara found a printed copy of Annie and Gabe's schedules next to the postbox in the lane – they're in the bag with everything else. Piecing things together, it sounds as though Clara found them not long before Lucy saw Holly sniffing around as though she'd lost something. I think Holly took them out of the snack tub, carried them back to her car which was parked in the layby next to the postbox, dropped them as she was getting out her car key or something like that and then went back to try and find them when she realised what she'd done.'

'Except Clara got there first and picked them up,' said Binnie.

'Exactly.'

'Okay, assuming you're right, what would Holly want with Annie and Gabe's schedules? I mean, clearly she wanted to keep a track of where they would be and when. But why?'

'And who gave it to her?' Jude felt that if they knew this they would be closer to finding the answer to other questions too. 'The other thing is that the schedules are for the day Mary was killed.'

'Hmm. Definitely something worth noting.'

Babur stood up and stretched before jumping down onto her lap.

'Whilst we're talking about Holly, I think I know what the magenta fluff stuck to the exhaust pipe was.'

Jude told Binnie about the Toastie Wrists and how Holly seemed to own a pair in every colour.

'The magenta fleece you told us you saw her wearing could actually have been more of these things,' said Binnie.

Jude nodded. 'I took a couple of samples of fluff from the pair she lent Lucy. They're completely the wrong colour but it might give a good enough fibre match until we can get hold of the real pair.'

'Maybe,' said Binnie. 'What we haven't yet got though is a motive. Why would Holly want to kill Annie?'

This was something that had been bothering Jude a lot. 'I don't know,' she confessed. 'If she thought Mary was still in the caravan then I could understand: we know her death gave Holly an instant career boost.'

'But that doesn't explain the snack tub or the fact that Holly might have been stalking Annie and Gabe.'

'No,' said Jude. 'It doesn't. I can only think that the answer lies in whoever has been feeding Holly the information. They're obviously working together.'

The doorbell went then. 'That'll be Sami,' said Binnie.

'You and Babur stay put.' Jude got to her feet and went to let him in.

He gave her a kiss and held out a bottle of sparkling elderflower and a large bag of crisps. 'I know the boss isn't drinking and I assumed you'd be driving so I thought this would go down better than a bottle of wine.'

'Good thinking,' said Jude. 'I'll go and get some glasses. Binnie's in the front room.'

'Have you already given her the complete lowdown or just the highlights?'

'We've only just got started. I'm sure she'll catch you up whilst I get the drinks sorted and find a bowl to put these in.'

Jude went into the kitchen and found a tray to put everything on. She took three glasses from the cupboard, tipped the crisps into one of Binnie's big copper bowls and took the brain fuel in for the two detectives.

'This Holly character is sounding a bit suspicious,' said Sami. 'Well done for snagging a sample of that wristband thing. I'll take that into the station tomorrow and get some tests done.'

'I ordered a magenta pair but they'll take a few days to get here.'

'Don't worry,' said Sami, 'I'll send someone round to see if we can't get hold of Holly's actual pair for ourselves. I can hear from the sound of it that you brought the bloody carbon monoxide alarm with you. Binnie, do you mind if I chuck the whole thing in my car for now? That beeping's going to drive me up the wall.'

Binnie laughed. 'Be my guest. It's much better than what I thought you might do with it.'

Sami went to deposit the bag of clues in his car and then returned to hear what else Jude had to say.

She told them about her run-in with Gabe, his reluctance to have her in to clean his hut and his involuntary glance at the storage in the base of his bed.

'What do you think he's hiding in there?' Sami asked.

'I have no idea,' said Jude. 'I assume you can't get a search warrant to go and have a look?'

'On what grounds?' Binnie asked.

'That's what I thought.' Jude shuffled her legs underneath her to stop the pins and needles setting in.

'We'd never recommend that you use your key to break in and have a snoop,' said Sami with a wink. 'Although technically you wouldn't be breaking and entering if you had good reason to need to gain access for some sort of maintenance check.'

'Already planned it,' said Jude. 'Although Gabe's another one with no good motive. Seeing as though I think it's highly probable Annie swapped vans to be closer to him it would make sense that she told him about the switch. In which case, if he had been the one to pipe in the exhaust fumes then he would have known it was Mary in there.'

'It seems to keep coming back down to who knew for certain about the switch,' said Binnie.

'Which is something we can't know as Annie is still claiming not to have told anyone.' Sami helped himself to a handful of crisps and sat back in his chair.

'Dean has a motive to kill either of them but so far there's little evidence to show he did it,' said Binnie. 'Annie has a motive to kill Mary and she definitely knew where she would be. What about Robyn and Simon? Any news there?'

'I saw Simon this afternoon, after I'd been in to change Gabe's towels.' Jude stretched across to put her glass down on the table as the cold drink was making her hand chilly. 'He was borrowing Annie's hut as a bit of a bolthole and it looked as though he'd sunk quite a few brandies.'

Jude told them about Simon's drunken ramblings and the threat that he seemed to make when he realised he'd said too much about the state of his marriage.

'It made me wonder what he might have done if Mary had threatened to go public about their affair,' she said. 'If he was going to kill the woman he thought enough of to risk his marriage and career then carbon monoxide somehow seems like a kind, painless option.'

'Leaving him in guilty distress, unable to perform on the telly and craving peace in his wife's hut with a bottle of brandy,' Sami noted.

'What about Robyn?' Binnie asked. 'Anything new on her?'

'Nothing concrete but I do think she's one to watch,' said Jude. 'She's got a vicious streak, we know that and she clearly resents Annie. Do you think it's plausible that she and Holly are tangled up together in some sort of murderous plot?'

Binnie lifted Babur onto the floor so she could reach forward and help herself to crisps. 'It's possible,' she said. 'But then it seems just as likely that Dean, Simon or Gabe could have given her those schedules. There are still too many gaps that need filling.'

The three friends carried on mulling over the various possibilities for a while longer until Jude noticed that Binnie was starting to slur her words ever so slightly. A sign that she was getting tired again.

'Right.' Jude got to her feet. 'Time for me to go, I'm afraid. I need to get back to the farm and see what's been going on in my absence.' She stared purposefully at Sami who took the hint.

'Me too,' he said. 'I've got loads to do this evening and I want to drop that bag off at the station first.'

Jude and Sami gathered up the glasses and crisp bowl and took them back into the kitchen to put in Binnie's dishwasher.

'Binnie looks exhausted,' Jude said in a hushed voice.

'She's overdoing it,' Sami whispered back. 'But you know what she's like. If she's not busy then she's frustrated and stressed, which is probably just as bad.'

'We'll just have to keep an eye on her,' said Jude.

'Keep an eye on who?' Binnie asked from the kitchen door.

'Annie,' said Jude quickly. 'I still think she's the real target here and I worry that someone is going to have another pop at her.'

'She's been told to take all the sensible precautions,' said Binnie. 'Let's just hope we get to the bottom of this before anything else happens.'

* * *

It was just before six in the evening when Jude dropped down the west side of the hills towards her home but it was already as dark as it was going to get that night.

As she approached the driveway up to the farm, she saw her neighbour, Mike Trout, rushing into the bottom entrance of the camping field. Wondering what was going on, she pulled up on the gravel of the parking area where she thought she could make out the sound of a fire alarm over the chugging of the Land Rover's engine.

When she switched the engine off and opened the door, the noise was far more evident.

'What's going on, Mike?' she asked as she ran after him.

'I was just putting something back in my shed when I heard the alarm go off,' he said. 'It was coming from your field so I thought I'd come and take a look, check if everything is all right.'

'Help!' It sounded like Annie and the screeching fear in her voice made Jude and Mike run a little faster to the gate. 'Help me. Please.'

Whilst Mike battled with the bolt on the small pedestrian gate, Jude vaulted the padlocked five-bar gate in the way Adam had taught her.

'Annie!' she called as she ran towards the shepherd's huts where she could see her standing on the top step of the one she was still using as a bolthole during the day. The door behind her was open and the light from the hut was illuminating her from behind, making her white-blonde hair light up like a halo. Her face was twisted in agony as she screamed again for help.

When she saw Jude, she scrambled down the steps and ran towards her.

'It's my fault,' Annie shouted as she fell into Jude's arms. 'Gabe is dead and it's all because of me.'

17

Within a few seconds of Jude arriving, they were joined first by Mike and then Simon, who rushed towards them from the other end of the camping field where he must have been in his own caravan.

The alarm had stopped sounding which indicated there was no real threat from a fire so Jude stayed with Annie.

'Calm down and tell me exactly what happened,' she said.

Annie pointed a quivering finger back towards the shepherd's hut. 'Gabe's in there,' she stuttered. 'Someone killed him and then they tried to kill me as well.'

'Who did?' Simon demanded. 'Did you see them?'

'No,' said Annie. 'I was walking up to the hut and they put something around my neck from behind and pulled it tight.'

She was wearing a blouse under a V-necked sweater and in the light coming from the hut, Jude could see a red circle around her neck, oddly studded at regular intervals with angry red welts. The fact she had no outdoor clothing on and yet she'd just said that she'd been approaching the hut confused Jude. As did the fact that it was her hut and yet Gabe was already inside it.

'Are you sure Gabe's dead?' Jude asked. 'Did you check for signs of life?'

'I couldn't, but I know what I saw.' Annie burst into tears.

'My darling. It's okay now, come here.'

Simon held out his arms and a shivering Annie looked relieved to be able to step into them.

Jude could hear Mike Trout talking to the police on the phone so she ran over to the hut and walked up the steps to see if Annie was right and there really was no chance of saving Gabe. She knew as soon as she saw the body on the floor that checking for vital signs would be fruitless. Gabe's face was turned her way, his eyes wide open and bloodshot. A trickle of blood had started to make its way from his ear down his cheek and was already drying before it finished its journey. Around his neck Jude could see similar markings to the ones on Annie's neck, although these were more pronounced, deeper and in some areas the skin had been broken.

In the sink were the burnt remains of what looked like document files. Charred pages that had been mainly destroyed but still holding their shape and with just a surviving corner to show what they might once have been.

Without disturbing the crime scene, Jude looked around to take in any other details she could. Two wine glasses stood next to the sink, both half full and one with a tiny smudge of lipstick on it. A pair of men's trainers had been tossed to one side of the hut which, taking in Gabe's socked feet, must have belonged to him.

Jude knew better than to dig around to find any hidden clues so she went out and closed the door behind her to seal the scene for the police investigation.

'I'm right, aren't I?' Annie said when Jude joined them. 'He's dead.'

'You know it is. Dean is a predator, Robyn is a bully and you and I are forced to dance to whatever tune is played for us. It's damaged our relationship and I want to get things back on track.'

Jude wondered at the irony of what Annie was saying. Wanting to fix her relationship and using her lover to do it. She felt pretty sure that Gabe had not been privy to this particular part of the plan.

'How would you leaving the show get things on track again for us?' Simon asked incredulously.

'Gabe was helping me gather evidence of the depth of the rot within the team. It's why I agreed to do this series in the first place.'

'Of course it was Gabe's idea.'

'It wasn't.' Annie took Simon's hands and looked him in the eye. 'It was all my idea, Gabe was just helping me. He's been subtly recording evidence for us to use. That was why I suggested Mary and I swapped vans so I could be closer to Gabe for us to carry on working on this together.'

Simon stood abruptly and walked over to the window where he leant and stared out. 'So you'd leave the show, and then what? I know you, Annie. You need to be in front of the camera as much as I do.'

'I have a contract with a different network.' Annie's voice was small and she had closed her eyes tightly as though trying to distance herself from what she was saying somehow. 'A documentary about what life as part of the *Countryside Live* team has really been like for me. For us. Simon, I wanted you to be a part of it too and I was going to tell you about it but then everything happened with Mary and it didn't seem appropriate.'

Jude wondered whether the inappropriateness came from Mary's affair with Annie's husband, or her death. Both seemed pretty good reasons to keep Simon in the dark about the new television project that would end the show they'd been working on as a couple for the past ten years.

'Was it you who broke the story to the papers?' Simon turned slowly to look at Annie.

'Of course it wasn't!' She looked appalled at the suggestion. 'It didn't do me any favours either, remember? I was basically accused of killing your lover.'

Simon cast his gaze downwards.

'I just want to stop enabling the likes of Dean and Robyn and to try and clean up our diseased industry.'

'But why ask Gabe for help?' Simon half whispered. 'Why not come to me?'

'Because you were otherwise engaged, and Gabe was...' Annie couldn't finish her sentence as a loud sob erupted from her.

Jude put an arm around her shoulder. 'You don't have to say anything else now,' she said. 'You've been through a terrible ordeal.'

'I should have told the police everything when Mary died,' Annie sobbed. 'Someone must have known what we were doing. They've tried to kill me twice already, I should have known they'd go for Gabe too at some point.'

She sank her head into her hands and let the sobs come freely. At this, Simon rushed back to sit by her and Jude took her arm away so that he could comfort his wife. Whatever had happened over the years, they had been a married couple for a very long time and they both clearly cared very deeply about each other.

'I've been so stupid,' croaked Annie. 'We've both been incredibly careful and then one little slip-up and now he's dead.'

Neither Jude nor Simon said anything. He hugged her tight and they let her begin to process what had happened in her own way.

stark, white and impersonal with modern everything, all of which matched perfectly but had no heart or soul. It was, however, spacious and warm, which was what they needed right then.

'What happened?' Simon asked bluntly.

'You don't have to talk until the police get here if you don't want to,' said Jude, pointedly.

Annie's face was pale and she had dark rings under her eyes. She took a large sip from the brandy glass and winced as the fiery liquid ran down her throat.

'It's all my fault,' she said as she stared into the glass. 'I should have told the police everything straight away. I just didn't think anyone knew what we were doing. And now he's dead and it's all because of me.'

Her forehead creased into deep furrows and silent tears fell from her eyes, bypassing her cheeks and landing in tiny pools on the table.

'What should you have told the police?' Simon asked. 'What's been going on?'

'I'm so sorry, Simon.' Annie directed her gaze at her husband. 'I should have confided in you right from the start. But I was angry with you. You and Mary.'

Simon blanched visibly at the mention of her name and Jude wasn't sure if it was because of his pain or his guilt.

'What are you talking about?'

'I'm planning on leaving the show.' Annie drank another swig. 'I am sick of the hypocrisy. I'm sick of pretending that we're all one happy, bubbly family at *Countryside Live* when we all know it's bullshit.'

'Is it?' Simon asked and Jude was surprised to see him looking a little shocked at the suggestion.

'Of course it is,' said Annie, clearly just as surprised as Jude.

'I'm afraid so.' Jude nodded. 'I'm so sorry, Annie.'

'What was he doing in your hut without you?' Simon asked. 'And why were you out here with no coat on?'

The very questions that Jude had been wanting to ask. She was also keen to find out why Annie had said that she was responsible for Gabe's death.

'Let's get her somewhere warm first,' said Jude.

'We can go to my caravan,' said Simon. 'It'll be nice and quiet in there.'

'I can stay here to wait for the police and make sure nobody goes into the hut,' said Mike. 'You go with Annie and Simon.'

'Thanks, Mike.' After everything that had happened, Jude didn't trust anyone and certainly didn't feel happy about Simon being alone with Annie. 'Give Noah a ring and tell him to bring the key for the padlock so he can get the big gate open for the ambulance. He'll keep you company until help arrives.'

Jude took her thick scarf off and wrapped it around Annie's neck before taking off her coat and draping it over Annie's shoulders. As they set off away from the huts, Jude's foot caught in something, almost tripping her up. She looked down and found that a string of fairy lights had been abandoned on the grass.

Of course! she thought to herself, linking the pattern of harsh indents around both Annie and Gabe's necks to the spacing between the tiny light bulbs.

'I'll catch you up,' she said to Annie and Simon. Then she ran back over and quietly pointed out the lights to Mike as the possible murder weapon so that he could show the police.

Once Jude, Annie and Simon were in the warmth of his caravan and Simon had poured out a generous measure of brandy for his wife, they sat down together at the table.

Although the caravan was at least three times the size of Jude's shepherd's huts, she knew which she preferred. This was

After a while, sirens could be heard pulling into the bottom gate of the campsite and Simon's caravan was lit with the blue flashing of the response vehicles. The sound seemed to still Annie for a while and her sobs stopped as she looked up.

'I shouldn't have left the hut,' she said. 'We should have stayed together. But he was busy compiling some of our notes and I needed to go and fetch my glasses from the chillout trailer.' She pinched the bridge of her nose. 'I knew something was wrong when I was in the campsite and heard the smoke alarm start. And then...'

Annie stopped talking and started to cry again as she gingerly touched the marks around her neck.

'Did you see who did this to you?' Simon asked.

Annie shook her head. 'They came from behind. I didn't even know they were there until I felt something around my neck. The only reason I'm alive is because of those self-defence lessons you made me take after that psycho fan attacked me. I managed to fight them off but then I must have blacked out because the next thing I knew I was on the floor and they'd gone.'

Simon hugged her tighter but Jude noticed that the look on his face seemed less one of tender sympathy and more one of fierce anger.

As she was trying to decide whether the anger was aimed at Annie's espionage or the man who attacked her, there was a knock on the door.

'I'll go.' Jude got up and went across to see who it was.

'Evening, Jude.' Sami, a uniformed officer and a paramedic were standing there with matching grim faces. 'We believe Annie Bird and Simon North are both in here?'

Jude stepped aside to let them in.

'I'll leave you to it,' she said as the caravan had reached capacity.

Sami gave her a watery smile. 'Binnie's here,' he said quietly, and Jude nodded as she left, closing the door behind her.

Outside, Jude steadied herself on the side of the caravan for a moment to gather her thoughts. Another death on the farm, and a further attempted murder. This time the marks around Annie's neck could not be explained in any other way. Whilst the peanut allergy may have been accidental, and Mary the true intended victim of her own death, someone had wrapped a set of Christmas lights around Annie's neck and tried to strangle her with them. Surely now the show would be cancelled and Annie taken away somewhere safe until the murderer had been caught?

But who was it?

Annie's revelation that she and Gabe had been building a stash of evidence to use in a documentary by a rival network highlighting the behind-the-scenes truth of *Countryside Live* was huge. Suddenly there was a whole new layer of possible motives for wanting to silence them both. It sounded as though Robyn and Dean had been the main focus of their attentions, but that didn't mean they hadn't included others in their investigations. Perhaps they'd uncovered something already. Or maybe someone had found out about them sniffing around and wanted to stop them before they dug up something dangerous.

Holly and another member of the team were up to something. The schedules that had been copied for Gabe as well as Annie suddenly seemed even more important.

Whilst Jude stood there, working her way through the facts and trying to figure out how they all fitted together, the door of the caravan opened and Simon came out looking distressed.

'Gah!' he growled and kicked out at the base of the handrail.

'Are you okay?' Jude asked, startling him as he clearly hadn't noticed her there.

'Ah, Jude.' He pushed his hands roughly through his hair.

'Sorry, it's just all so shit. And now they won't let me stay in with Annie.'

'It's just protocol after everything that's happened.'

'Apparently I've got to be interviewed again.' He looked annoyed at this which seemed an odd reaction to Jude, given the circumstances.

'They'll want to talk to everyone,' she said. 'Why don't you go and wait in the chillout trailer? Get yourself something to drink.'

For a moment, it looked as though he was going to choose to stay put but then his shoulders slouched forward and he set off towards the largest of the trailers.

Jude turned and walked in the other direction, back down towards the scene of the crime to see if she could be of any use to Binnie.

The area around the shepherd's huts was a hive of activity and Jude couldn't see her friend anywhere. She was about to leave them to it when Binnie came around the side of the hut and caught sight of her.

'Jude!' She beckoned her over.

'Here we are again,' said Jude when she reached her.

'So it appears.' Binnie took off a pair of latex gloves and folded one into the other. 'I've spoken to Mike Trout and I gather you and he were first on the scene, after Annie, of course.'

'That's right. I was driving home when I saw Mike running into the campsite which was odd so I followed him. There was a fire alarm going – you'll have already seen the burnt papers or files in the sink.'

Binnie nodded. 'Apart from Simon North, nobody else heard the fire alarm? Or at least weren't bothered enough by it to come and see what was going on.'

'No. Mind you, it's only one of those battery ones. Loud enough to wake someone in the hut but not shrill enough to carry too far, I shouldn't think. When I first pulled up and was still in the car, it was pretty quiet. It wasn't until I got out that I properly heard it. The smoke must have cleared pretty quickly with the hut door open anyway and it stopped ringing before we got there.'

'I'll get someone to test that out,' said Binnie. 'Do you know where everyone currently is?'

'Sorry, no. I've just seen Simon heading to the chillout trailer, and Annie is obviously in Simon's caravan with Sami but I haven't seen any of the others.'

'Don't worry, I've got people tracking them down. We're currently assuming that whoever strangled Gabe and Annie fled back through the campsite, judging by the fact we found the murder weapon discarded in that direction.'

'Death by fairy lights,' said Jude with a shiver. 'Annie is lucky to be alive. Thank goodness she did a self-defence course so knew how to look after herself.'

'Ah, that answers my first question,' said Binnie. 'I was wondering how she had survived an attack from a killer who'd managed to take down someone much larger than her. It could be useful too. If she can show us the moves she used to overpower her attacker, we might be able to put together an injury list we would expect to see. Certain bruising patterns to the torso. I'd also expect to see them covered in mud as I believe all self-defence techniques when attacked from behind, as I assume she was, end up on the ground.'

Jude imagined the scene. Annie wasn't exactly petite but neither was she well built. To have overcome an assailant with what must have been split-second reactions was a high endorsement for whoever had been teaching her. Without it, she would almost certainly now be dead.

'How did Simon appear to you?' Binnie asked.

'Understandably shaken,' said Jude. 'Blunt too, and a little demanding. He quizzed Annie about what she'd seen and exactly what had happened. I mean, of course he'd have had questions but it was more the way he asked them.'

'Interesting. And he's gone to the chillout trailer now?'

'That's right. He wasn't happy though, he wanted to stay with Annie whilst Sami and the paramedic were there. Binnie, I assume after what just happened, she's not going to be left alone with him until this is all sorted?'

'She'll be offered police protection which will be strongly advised,' said Binnie. 'You make it sound as though you're particularly worried about her being alone with Simon.'

'She trusts Simon and looks to him for comfort,' Jude pointed out, 'which could be very dangerous if he turned out to be the killer.'

'Good point. Talk me through your thoughts on him and the other key players,' said Binnie. 'Anything new there?'

'Sami will be finding out more from Annie now, I'm sure, but she and Gabe were gathering information about the show and the darker side of what really happens behind the scenes. Chiefly Dean's predatory behaviour and Robyn's tendency to bully. She's got a contract to take part in a documentary about it all with a rival network.'

'Bloody hell!' Binnie exclaimed. 'That's a pretty big motive for both of them. And I bet that's what the burnt files in the sink were all about.' Binnie patted her hands together in thought. 'Let's just hope that they weren't the only copies.'

'Gabe has been recording things so there must be audio files somewhere,' said Jude. 'And who only keeps important documents in paper format these days anyway?'

'You're right,' said Binnie. 'Annie has to have other evidence she can share with us. What about Simon? Did he know what she was up to?'

'If he did then he's a very good actor,' said Jude. 'He seemed pretty angry when she told him.'

'I bet he was. I wonder if there was going to be any part in her new documentary for him?'

Jude thought about everything she knew, or at least thought she knew, about Simon and Annie. They claimed to love each other still and yet he'd had an affair right under her nose. Annie had gone behind his back when it came to bringing down the show that had launched both their careers. She'd also had some sort of relationship with Gabe – although perhaps that had never been about love or even sex for her after all but more about the evidence finding.

'I can't work out exactly what the deal is between those two but if she hadn't been planning on including him in the documentary then that could mean the collapse of his career.'

A uniformed officer came over then with a plastic bag containing a piece of paper.

'Excuse me, Ma'am,' he said. 'We thought you'd want to see this. It was found inside an empty box of Christmas lights.'

Binnie took the evidence bag. 'Thanks, Jake.'

She read what was on the piece of paper and then she passed it over for Jude to look at.

My darling Annie, I know it's not easy for us to be together right now but I want you to know that you'll always be the light in my life. Gabe xxx

18

After the third possible attempt on her life, Annie accepted the offer of police protection and was taken away that evening, leaving information of her location with nobody.

Dean still refused to cancel the show and obviously had enough clout with the people at the top of the network for it to go out. Instead of the live sections, he pieced together pre-recorded pieces taken from the filming they'd done on the snowy hills that morning, and other back-up interviews that he had in his armoury. Jude didn't watch it but Lucy did and told her that it felt like there was a deliberate air of mystery over the whole thing, as though Dean was trying to maintain the drama. A voiceover note at the beginning explained how Annie and Simon were working through some personal things but planned on being back the following evening.

'He's delusional,' said Jude. She was sitting in the kitchen dressed for bed and nursing a camomile tea in the vague hope it might help her get a little sleep that night. Lucy had put carols on low and the beautiful choral voices were soothing them both into the evening, but Jude's mind refused to still. 'There have been two murders, as well as at least one – if not three – attempts at killing his leading lady, who has gone into police protection, I might add. Even he can't truly believe that the show can keep running now.'

'Like you say, he's delusional, egotistical and hard as nails. I bet he keeps waving everyone's contractual agreement under their noses.' Lucy was sorting through a laundry basket of Sebbie's clean clothes.

Jude shook her head. 'He might try but he can't have a leg to stand on. The network will pull it anyway, surely they have no choice.'

'I'd have thought so.' Lucy folded a pair of small grey trousers and added them to the pile. 'So, who do you think killed Mary and Gabe?'

'I really don't know. Dean and Robyn seem to have the most reason to want Gabe and Annie out of the way. But I don't trust Simon and I can't stop thinking about Holly and what she's been up to. And don't forget it was her wrist thingy that left fluff on the tape residue.'

'Has that been confirmed?' Lucy asked.

'Not yet, but what else could it be? It's such a vibrant colour and a specific fabric. She must have been wearing them to keep her wrists warm and they got in the way of the tape.'

'Unless she lent them to someone else,' Lucy pointed out. 'Don't forget how keen she was to promote her sister-in-law's business when she let me use a pair.'

'Of course.' Jude was cross with herself for missing such an obvious point. 'Even if we find the source of the magenta fluff, it doesn't prove who was wearing it on the night Mary died.'

Jude finished the last warm dregs of her tea and closed her eyes to enjoy John Rutter's 'Angels' Carol'. As the music washed over her, she pulled her dressing gown tighter. 'I need my bed,' she said when the carol had finished.

'Good call.' Lucy hugged her sister. 'Jude, don't take this all on yourself. Please try to remember that there is an entire investigative team working on the clues and you're not officially on the payroll.'

'I know.' Jude covered her mouth with the back of her hand as a giant yawn stretched her mouth involuntarily. 'You're right. We've got plenty of our own things to be thinking about.'

'Exactly. Now off to bed. Sleep well.'

Jude put her mug in the sink and then hauled her tired body up the wooden stairs and down the landing to the bathroom.

She crunched a toothpaste tablet between her teeth and poured water onto her toothbrush. As she scrubbed away the day's tartar, she tried to focus on family things like wedding decorations and Christmas stockings, but try as she might, she couldn't stop thinking about Annie.

She would be spending her first night under police protection with nobody she knew around to offer comfort. And, unless her killer was charged in the next couple of weeks, that's exactly where she'd be spending her Christmas.

As Jude got into bed and wriggled down into the cold sheets, trying to rub some warmth from her body into them, it wasn't Lucy's face on her wedding day or Sebbie's as he opened his presents under the tree that she thought about. It was Annie Bird and how Jude could help untangle the jumble of clues and uncover whoever was trying to kill her.

* * *

The next morning, Jude felt a pull towards the campsite and what remained of the film crew still staying there. She tried to ignore it and focus on nicer things but her inquisitive mind would not stop running through the different versions of what might have happened the night before.

She began with the facts.

Annie and Gabe had been in Annie's hut working on the evidence they'd been collating to use in the new exposure documentary.

This was mainly focused on the toxic behaviour of Dean and Robyn.

Annie had left Gabe to walk back to the chillout trailer and retrieve her glasses. She was gone for about ten minutes and when she came back she was attacked from behind by an unknown assailant who used a string of fairy lights to try and strangle her.

Annie's self-defence training kicked in and saved her life, although she passed out before she had a chance to properly see her attacker.

Whoever it was had also killed Gabe and burnt the files they'd been working on, which surely meant that the two were indisputably linked.

Simon was the only person who came down to the huts when he heard the smoke alarm and Jude did not yet know where the others had been at that time.

Jude needed more so she decided to head down that way and see who was about to chat to. There were plenty of jobs she could claim to be doing to allow her to move around and keep her ears and eyes open at the same time.

Robyn was the first person she saw. Her caravan, the smallest of them all, was parked closest to the farm and she was sitting on the steps smoking a cigarette. Jude had not known she was a smoker and wondered if this was a habit she'd reinstated because of the stresses of the week's occurrences.

'Hi,' she said as Jude approached. 'All a bit of a fuck-up, isn't it?'

'You must be exhausted.' Jude decided to go for empathy in the hope she could suck Robyn into a conversation. 'I can't imagine how hard this must be on you.'

'I've been holding this shitty show together for years and now look at what's happening to it.' Robyn used her thumb and little finger to pick a bit of tobacco from her tongue. 'I should have jumped when I had the chance.'

'Why did you stay?' Jude asked.

Robyn took a deep puff on her cigarette and blew the filthy smoke out slowly. 'That's a question I've been asking myself daily. Still, I guess it's all over now, eh?'

'What do you mean?'

'Haven't you heard? The network has pulled the rest of the series.'

Jude felt a wave of relief wash over her. It had to happen but she'd been wondering if Dean would somehow cling on to the crumbs of what was left.

'I'm sorry to hear that,' she said.

'Are you?' Robyn looked at her incredulously. 'I'm sure as hell not. I've had more than my fill of this shitshow. Dean is holding our contracts over us, making us stay put whilst he fights the network, but I reckon he'll have lost by the end of the day and we can all go home tomorrow.'

Jude had a feeling that the police would want them to stick around for a bit longer but unless they arrested anyone, the suspects would be free to leave. Although this was exactly what Jude had wanted, she had expected the mystery of the two murders to have been solved by now. If the crew left before this happened then finding the truth would become a whole lot harder.

Robyn took a last puff and then dropped the stub and ground it into the concrete with her foot. 'I hear you were there last night, when they found Gabe.'

'I heard the smoke alarm,' said Jude. 'I'm surprised you didn't.'

'I was in the chillout trailer with Holly. We were running through the schedule and heard something but we just assumed it was to do with the farm. It wasn't until the ambulance arrived we realised something bad had happened.'

'You must have seen Annie then,' said Jude. 'She went there to fetch her glasses just before the alarm went off.'

'What is this, some sort of interrogation?' Robyn stood up, looking angry. 'No, actually we didn't see Annie, just like I already told the police. She must be lying.'

Robyn opened the door of her van and disappeared inside, shutting it with a clatter.

Why would Annie lie about going to the chillout trailer for her glasses? It didn't make any sense. It was more likely that Robyn was mistaken about the timings, or she was lying herself. And, if she was lying, then where had she been instead? Jude wondered what Holly's take on the situation was and whether she'd verify Robyn's version.

The police presence was still evident when Jude let herself into the campsite. She could see the fluorescent markings of a police car down by the huts and wondered if they'd been there all night collecting evidence.

She decided to start by cleaning the toilet block. The eco-friendly compost loos that she had chosen to install needed a little more attention than regular toilets but she still felt the gain outweighed the pain. There was a cupboard inside that held a mop, bucket and other cleaning equipment as well as a fresh supply of sawdust that was used instead of water flushing.

Jude took the bucket out and squirted in a little cleaning fluid before she went outside to fill it from the external tap. Back in the loo block, she picked up the mop and soaked it in the foamy water, squeezed out the excess and used it to clean away the muddy footprints and accumulated grime. With each cubicle and then the main sink area cleaned, she rinsed the mop and put it back in the cupboard. Next she lugged out the sack of sawdust to fill up the little buckets next to each loo, and emptied the bins at the same time.

When designing the loo block, she had made best use of the space by cutting holes in the panelling that ran behind each toilet so the bins could slide inside out of the way. There was enough room above to lift the lid and drop rubbish inside so the bins could stay snugly in situ.

One of the bins looked a little out of kilter so Jude straightened it and then went to push it back into place. Having emptied them a thousand times before, she knew this one wasn't going back in as far as it should do so she pulled it out to see if anything had fallen behind it, blocking the space.

Just as she expected, there was something stopping the bin from being pushed back fully. Jude bent to pick it up.

'Bingo!' she muttered with a smile as she saw the small plastic snack tub hidden in the space behind the bin. Frustratingly it was still empty, but at least she'd found it again. The fact that it was in the female loo block narrowed down the list of people Holly could be using it to communicate with.

She put the tub back and pushed the bin into place before leaving the cubicle. Then she went to the cupboard for a fresh supply of paper towels when the main door into the block opened.

'What are you doing here?' Robyn demanded, clearly surprised to see Jude.

'Cleaning.' Jude held up the paper towels before dropping them into the dispenser. 'All yours now.'

She did not ask why Robyn had chosen to use the campsite loo when her own caravan with private facilities was just a short distance away because she was pretty sure she already knew. As Jude locked the supply cupboard, she noticed that Robyn had chosen the end cubicle, confirming her suspicion that she was there for the tub.

Jude nipped out and into the male loo block where she started to clean, all the time listening out for Robyn to leave so she could go back to investigate.

When she heard the door open, she left it a few minutes to make sure the coast was clear and then went back and headed straight for the cubicle where the tub had been hidden.

Half expecting it to have been moved again, she was delighted to see the bin was still not sitting flush against the wall. Jude locked the cubicle and pulled the bin away to retrieve the tub. This time, she could see through the dark plastic that there was something inside it, cementing the fact that Robyn was the person Holly had been dealing with.

With her heart pounding, she sat down on the closed loo seat and unclipped the lid of the tub so she could look inside. There, lying at the bottom, was a little sheaf of twenty-pound notes, unwrinkled as though they'd just been taken from a cashpoint. Jude quickly counted them. Five – so one hundred pounds. Not a huge sum but that didn't matter. The fact that Robyn had hidden it there, almost certainly for Holly to find, was far more interesting than the amount itself. What was a hundred pounds paying for? Information, a service, favours, bribe money to keep quiet about something?

Jude put the money back and took a photo with her phone before re-hiding the tub where she'd found it.

She came out of the cubicle at the same time as the main door to the loo block opened again.

'Oh! Hi, Jude,' said Holly. 'I just came in to use your facilities.' She tramped her muddy boots over Jude's freshly mopped floor. 'Saves taking my boots off to go back into my caravan.'

The completely blasé way she spoke without the hint of an apology might have been enough to persuade some people she was telling the truth, but Jude knew better. The fact that she chose the furthest cubicle where there was a pot of money hidden behind the bin was no surprise whatsoever to her.

'Carry on,' said Jude. 'There's plenty of fresh sawdust.'

Holly went in, no doubt to collect the money that Robyn had just stashed there. Whilst Jude unlocked the cupboard and took out a cloth to make herself look busy, there was the slightest scrape from inside Holly's cubicle to indicate that she'd collected the money and was replacing the bin as quietly as possible. Jude made plenty of noise to show she wasn't listening. She ran a soapy cloth around the basins and smiled in the mirror at Holly when she came out.

'I absolutely love the smell of the soap you use in here,' said Holly, rubbing a generous amount into her hands. 'It's divine.'

'Glad you like it,' said Jude as she wrung the cloth out. 'I am so sorry about what happened last night. You must be devastated.'

'Oh, gosh, yes. It's absolutely dreadful and we all feel terrible for poor Annie. She's gone into hiding, you know, and I don't blame her. Poor thing, it must be terrifying.' Holly pouted. 'Do you know, I think the strain was already starting to get to her. I mean, she says she came to the chillout trailer to fetch something yesterday but Robyn and I were there the whole time and we didn't see each other. She must have been in a real tizzy. We were in the seats right at the back of the trailer so I suppose there's a chance she might have missed us. And we were talking a lot so it's possible we didn't hear her come in.'

Holly was giving too much information that Jude hadn't asked for and that made her sound far more suspicious than if she'd just not brought it up at all.

'Anyway, I'm so glad for her that she's been taken somewhere safe now. They haven't told any of us where.' She pulled a paper towel from the newly stocked dispenser. 'Have your police friends told you?'

'Of course not,' said Jude. 'I think the whole point is that the fewer people who know, the better.'

'Sure, sure,' said Holly, pulling out a second and then third towel. 'Anyway, it was good to see you. I've got to get going. Dean is making a bunch of us take footage of the farm and the behind-the-scenes areas of the film crew. He's hoping the network will do a special programme about what happened here, like some sort of memorial or dedication to Mary and Gabe. Simon's already had a huge row with him about it. He's refusing to take part and I can't say I blame him. Between you and me, I think the whole thing is bonkers, but what do I know? I only operate the camera.'

Granny Margot had suggested Dean might be looking to make something more groundbreaking than the usual country lifestyle show. Ratings for a true-crime documentary about a very public crime that had partially played out on live television would surely be high. There seemed a very good chance that this was what he was collecting footage for, but could he have set the whole thing up for such a reason?

Holly rolled her eyes and threw her bundle of paper towels into the bin that Jude had just emptied. Then she left the loo block and Jude gave the basin another quick wipe down. She went back outside under the pretence of needing more water in her bucket but really she was scouting around to make sure that Holly had really gone.

Back in the cubicle, Jude quickly moved the bin once more and found that, exactly as she'd expected, Holly had emptied the tub.

So Holly and Robyn were definitely in cahoots about something. But where exactly did this leave them when it came to the two murders? They'd lied about their whereabouts when the smoke alarm went off and they were each other's only alibis for the time of Gabe's murder and Annie's brutal attack. Robyn had tried to cover it over by claiming Annie was the one lying whilst Holly had come up with an absurdly elaborate explanation for how Annie could have been in the trailer but not noticed Robyn or Holly there.

Jude's phone pinged as she left the loo block. She checked it and found a text from Binnie.

BINNIE
I'm heading up to the farm. Are you around this morning?

JUDE
Sure. I've got things to tell you and plenty of questions to ask too.

BINNIE
See you in an hour or so.

JUDE
See you then. Xx

* * *

When Binnie came, she had Sami with her and once again they found themselves sitting around the farmhouse kitchen table, warming their hands on mugs of tea and discussing the two murders that had happened just a stone's throw away.

Jude told them about her loo block meetings with first Robyn and then Holly and the money pot she'd found there. She also mentioned the odd explanation Holly had given as to why Annie hadn't seen her in the chillout trailer and how this clashed somewhat with Robyn's earlier accusation that Annie had either been confused or lying.

'They're definitely up to something,' said Sami. 'But I'm not sure if that's necessarily murder.'

'Did Annie remember anything else about the attack that's given you any further leads?' Jude asked.

'Unfortunately she didn't get a good look at her attacker. They came at her from behind and it seems Annie passed out from the pressure around her neck as soon as she'd fought them off.'

Sami helped himself to a lebkuchen from the packet Jude had just opened. 'She wasn't even sure if it was a man or a woman, only that they were slightly taller than her.'

'Which could be Robyn, Dean or Simon,' said Binnie. 'Holly is obviously quite a bit shorter. Annie remembers that they were wearing long black sleeves and black gloves but the really interesting thing is that she did get a clear look at the wristwatch they were wearing. It was quite unusual and might be a good lead if we can find out who owns one with silver-coloured links and a blue face with a second tiny dial set into it.'

'That's a decent amount of information,' said Jude.

'She said she used it as a focus point while she fought the attacker.'

Jude put her mug down and used her own hands to work out where they'd be in relation to the eyes of someone she was trying to strangle from behind. 'It would have been tricky for her to see the watch, surely?' she said.

'No,' Binnie replied. 'The pattern of the marks on her neck show that the attacker must have created a loop of lights, crossing them over at the back. They would then have been pulled tight with a sideways and slightly forward-reaching motion, keeping their arms locked, like this.'

She stood up and demonstrated the suggested method on Sami, using a dog lead that had been sitting on the table.

'Careful there, boss,' said Sami.

Jude could see that this would indeed mean the wrist of the attacker would have been in line with Annie's eyes.

'That could be the biggest mistake they made,' said Jude. 'If we see anyone wearing a watch that matches then we've surely found our killer.'

'We questioned everyone last night after Annie had been removed from the scene. Not one of them was wearing a watch,' said Sami.

Binnie coiled the lead up and put it back on the table before sitting down. 'It's possible they took it off when they went to get rid of their black gloves and the muddy clothes they must have been wearing when Annie threw them down on the ground.'

'Is that how she managed to overcome them?' Jude asked.

'Pretty much,' said Binnie. 'She'd been taught a technique that would work if someone was choking her from behind with an arm. It wasn't perfect as the fact she had a string of lights around her neck made it far more dangerous but she used a variation. She showed us last night. Basically it involved hooking her hands over the attacker's wrists.' Binnie curved the fingers of both hands into solid-looking hooks which she held near her neck to show what she meant. 'Then, by leaning slightly forwards, bending her knees and using her hips to thrust backwards she had the forward momentum to flip them over and bring them crashing to the ground.'

'If she'd been choked with an arm instead of a weapon, her hands would have hooked over wrist and elbow, which would have pulled them away from her throat, opening up her windpipe,' said Sami. 'But because the lights were tight around her neck, the movement actually made them pull tighter which is why she blacked out before she could see the person she'd just floored.'

'Thank God they didn't realise she was unconscious and stay to finish her off.' Jude rubbed her own neck in empathy with Annie's horrific ordeal.

'They would have been taken by complete surprise and would almost certainly have just made a run for it,' said Binnie, sitting back down at the table and picking up her mug again.

'Which takes us full circle to the who and the why,' said Jude. 'What about Simon? What if he went to see her in the hut, found Gabe there, maybe even read the love note or perhaps Gabe provoked his rival? They could have argued, maybe Gabe told him a few home truths and Simon killed in fury.'

'It's possible,' said Binnie. 'But would he have then killed Annie? And how would that fit with Mary's death or the peanut episode, both of which were well-planned and thought about in advance?'

'According to Annie, there was no affair anyway.' Sami took another lebkuchen from the packet and Jude wondered if there'd be any left by the time they'd gone through everything they wanted to talk about.

'What about the note he left her in the box of lights?' Jude asked. 'And the conversation I overheard when I was behind the huts?'

'Annie's take on the whole thing is that she knew Gabe was in love with her and she enjoyed the adoration.' Binnie rested her elbows on the table. 'She told us that he made her feel appreciated, especially given the fact Simon was making no attempt to hide his relationship with Mary from her. I think she genuinely loved Gabe but, as Granny Margot pointed out, she's still committed to her adulterous husband.'

'If we believe everything Annie told us, she and Gabe never slept together and only ever shared one illicit kiss,' said Sami. 'She said she had been clear about her intentions but he kept pursuing her nonetheless.'

'Poor guy,' said Jude. 'And Annie too, she must feel awful now. When I found her yesterday just after Gabe had been killed, the first thing she said was that she thought it was all her fault.'

'Which brings us to the evidence she was collating with Gabe and the real reason we think he was killed,' said Binnie. 'Remember that murder wasn't the only thing that happened last night. The paper evidence files were burnt. Not only that but Annie had a second phone that she only used for Gabe to send her information and so she could store it all safely. It was on the bed and it's now missing.'

'There was a second phone?' said Jude. 'Like a burner phone?'

'Kind of, but she didn't use it for calls,' said Sami. 'It was really for her to record things, take photos and store everything. She was so afraid of anyone else stumbling across what she was doing that this phone was the only place she kept all her evidence. Annoyingly nothing had been sent to the documentary team – they had a meeting booked in for the new year to go through everything then. Gabe kept a copy on an external hard drive but Annie doesn't know where it is.'

Jude remembered the reflexive glance Gabe had given the storage unit beneath his bed when he'd caught Jude cleaning in there. 'Did you check under his bed?' she asked.

'Of course, but there was nothing there of interest. Either he cleared it out himself because he was worried you'd clocked him, or someone else did it for him,' said Sami.

'So it looks like whoever killed Gabe and tried to kill Annie was trying to stop them from revealing the things they'd discovered.' To Jude this meant they were back to Dean and Robyn, possibly with the help of Holly, although Simon was still in the running if Gabe had uncovered something about him too in the course of his investigation. 'Robyn and Holly have pretty flaky alibis, what about Dean and Simon?'

Binnie ran through the alibis for Jude. Simon claimed to have been out for a walk, forgetting that the sun set so early, and was heading back to his trailer after dark when he heard the smoke alarm. He would have had just enough time to be able to kill Gabe, strangle Annie and then run back to his caravan to get changed, ready to play the anxious husband when he was needed.

Dean was on his own in his caravan listening to a podcast using his EarPods which, he said, was why he didn't hear the smoke alarm.

'He was more interested in talking about Annie's contract with the rival network than Gabe's murder,' said Binnie. 'Although he claimed he hadn't heard anything about this before, he seemed to be decidedly unruffled, certain in that cocksure way of his that she had nothing on him and that the only person who would lose out if it happened was Annie.'

'How did he work that out?' Jude asked.

'Something to do with her grasping at straws and looking like an idiot, combined with the fact that if she made one false accusation, he'd sue her for everything she had,' said Sami. 'Either way, he predicted it would be the end of her career.'

'Do you think he believed his own rubbish?' Jude tapped the stubs of her cropped fingernails against her mug.

'With someone like that, it's hard to know,' said Binnie. 'Annie seems to think she and Gabe had plenty of information that would be irrefutable...'

'Except it's all now been either stolen or burnt,' said Jude. 'Very handy for both Dean and Robyn.'

'Indeed.' Sami banged his hands on the table, making Pip and Alfie jump out of their beds to instant attention. 'Sorry, dogs, it's all just so bloody frustrating.'

'We'll get there.' Binnie rested her hand on his arm. 'We just need one really good, strong piece of evidence. Murderers nearly always make a mistake, and at some point we will find out what that is.'

'Not having much luck at the moment though, are we?' Sami sounded so despondent. 'No prints on the carbon monoxide monitor, still no sign of the magenta wrist warmer thing and the results from the lab show the green one to be inconclusive, Gabe's tape residue was tested and is a match for the one used by Mary's killer, only Gabe is now dead so we're back to the beginning there too.'

'Wait, the tape was a match?' Jude asked.

'Yes, but it's the stuff used by all the tech people for securing wires, etc. There would be loads of it about so anyone could have taken a roll,' said Binnie.

'Blast it,' said Jude. Sami was right – despite all the information and evidence they'd collected so far, it still felt as though they were a long way from finding the truth. In the meantime, there'd been another murder and Annie's life was still in danger. But Jude knew that Binnie was also right. It would just take one piece of luck, one piece of evidence and they'd be back on track again.

19

After Binnie and Sami had gone, Jude felt itchy and tense. She couldn't sit around waiting for that important piece of evidence to just fall into her lap, she had to go and look for it. Her coat was hanging by the Aga to keep it warm and she picked it up, putting it on as she headed towards the door, which opened before she got there.

'You're not going out, are you?' Lucy asked as she came into the house carrying a basket full of pinecones and other things, Sebbie next to her holding a bundle of fir tree branches. 'Sebbie and I were hoping you'd help us mock up some napkin rings and centrepieces for the wedding to see which ones we like the best.'

'We've been foraging,' Sebbie said proudly as he deposited the branches on the table.

'There's something I need to do,' said Jude. 'Later, maybe?'

Lucy's face fell as she put the basket down on the table. 'Not to worry. Sebbie and I can get on with these and perhaps you'll have solved the mystery before we come to make the real ones.'

Jude looked at her sister unloading tiny cones from the larch trees, sprigs of various evergreen plants and the thin bendy twigs of the silver birch. Lucy was getting married at the end of the month and Jude was so busy inserting herself into the middle of the murder investigation that she'd not really been giving her the time she'd promised her.

'Sorry,' she said, taking her coat back off and hanging it up. 'Of course I'll help.'

'Hooray!' Sebbie cheered. 'Mummy said we can do it in the sitting room and put *The Grinch* on.'

'*The Grinch*, hey?' Jude scooped Sebbie into her arms and began to tickle him. 'Are you sure you're brave enough? He's pretty scary, you know.'

'No, Aunty Judy!' Sebbie giggled. 'He's not scary. He's just mean and green.'

The dogs started bouncing around, joining in with the fun and Jude let Sebbie go. She was smiling and realised that a bit of family time was exactly what she needed. Picking up the branches, Jude led the way into the sitting room where Sebbie flicked on the lights of the Christmas tree and dug around in the sofa cushions to find the remote control for the telly.

Lucy came in with the box of her wintery foraging rewards and Jude gave her a warm smile which she instantly returned.

'Come on,' said Jude. 'Let's find the Grinch.'

* * *

Twisting birch twigs together to make little loops and trying out various different methods of sticking on the embellishments took the rest of the morning. *The Grinch* had been followed by *The Snowman* and then its sequel whilst Lucy, Jude and Sebbie were busy with their crafting. Noah came back from his field rounds and rustled up some soup for lunch so it was well into the afternoon by the time Jude finally made it back out to have a snoop around.

Her first port of call was the loo block where she checked the snack tub, only to find it was empty.

As she opened the main door to leave, she bumped into Robyn heading her way.

'Hi,' Jude said as she held the door for her.

Robyn didn't say anything, just gave a curt nod as she passed Jude.

Jude switched her phone to silent and walked around the side of the loo block so she was hidden from view. There she waited until she heard Robyn leaving. Peering around the corner, she watched Robyn walk off towards the farmyard and then Jude broke cover and went quickly back in to see what Robyn had left this time. More money perhaps, or something else.

She knew that the tub had gone even before she moved the bin as it was now sitting flush against the back wall.

Robyn had to have taken it, which meant she was probably now off to find a new hiding place. If Jude was quick, she might be able to find out where exactly that was. She'd seen Robyn head towards the yard and so she followed as quickly as she could without raising suspicion should anyone be watching. She kept to the trees as she skirted the pond and hid behind a giant oak on the edge of the yard.

Initially she couldn't see Robyn and it felt like some sort of stealth combat game as she tried to remain hidden.

She moved as silently as possible from the tree to the feed silo and then on to a pile of old wooden pallets that had been stacked high next to the big storage barn. This stood beside the largest of the farm's barns which was split in two and mainly used during the lambing season. From there, Jude could hear footsteps which sounded like they were approaching from the other end. She slowly side-stepped and found a gap that she could look through, giving her a clear view of the back end of the barns whilst remaining hidden.

Robyn walked slowly past the big back doors of the lambing shed and when she got to the gap between that and the storage barn, she slipped in. Jude knew there was only just enough space to walk between them and a drain had been sunk into the concrete along the full length to divert any water away. There was currently a large pile of hurdles stacked up at the other end that had been cleared out of the lambing shed to make space for the wedding preparations. This meant that whilst she was in the gap, Robyn was perfectly hidden from anyone unless they happened to be walking on the concrete behind the sheds, or in the fields beyond. But she'd have a much better view of them than they would of her, so it was the perfect hiding spot.

Jude waited. It took a little while but eventually Robyn's head peered around the side of the barn. She checked both ways and then stepped out, turning, to Jude's horror, not to return the way she'd come, but the opposite way – directly towards Jude.

It would only take a few steps for Robyn to reach the pallets and find Jude watching her. Jude could make a run for it but she wouldn't be able to get anywhere worth hiding quick enough without making noises that would give her away. She couldn't let Robyn know that she'd seen her or the snack tub would be moved again and Jude might not find it next time.

Thinking quickly, Jude realised her only chance was to be the opposite of sneaky. She had every right to be where she was, carrying out jobs on her own farm. She turned around and saw the silo just a couple of steps behind her with a pile of feed sacks underneath.

Jude grabbed one of the sacks and thrust it under the feed chute, pulling the chain to release a rush of sheep food down the metal slide with a loud rattle. When it was half full she let go of the chain to stop the flow and put the sack down on the ground. There was a wheelbarrow with a few inches of rainwater in it, which she tipped over, grumbling loudly about people not leaving it propped up to stop the rain getting in. She knew it was almost certainly her who'd done this but she thought it added to the authenticity of her little performance.

Lugging the sack of feed into the barrow, she hoped she'd done enough to persuade Robyn that she was there to do a job and had no idea there was a television researcher lurking around the corner.

Jude forced herself not to look in the direction of the pallets as she started pushing the barrow away from the sheds. Committed to the role, she took it all the way down to the paddock and into the tack room. The metal feed bin had needed topping up anyway so at least that was a good job done.

With the sack now empty, she returned it to the barrow and went back to the silo to drop both off. It was so tempting to go straight round to the space between the sheds and see if she could see the snack tub, but she didn't want to risk it in case Robyn was being ultra cautious and was still there.

Instead, she went around to the front of the barns and then on to the first section of the lambing shed where she slipped inside. Jude walked as quietly as she could to the side wall that bordered the passage where she felt sure Robyn had hidden the snack tub. There she strained her ears for any sign of movement but all was silent so she decided to risk it and go out of the back door to take a look.

The door rattled as she slid it sideways but there was no way of stopping that. Although she kept reminding herself that she wasn't doing anything wrong and that this was her land, she still felt as though she was trespassing somehow as she stepped out onto the concrete slab.

Jude walked the few steps until she reached the entrance to the alleyway. It was dark in there but that didn't stop her from being able to make out the figure of Holly standing near the back end.

'Are you all right in there?' Jude called, feigning innocence to lure her out.

'Yes, thank you so much for asking. I was just...' She tailed off, clearly realising that even she couldn't pretend that the thin, dark gap between two barns was a good spot to do some filming.

Holly walked forwards and Jude could see that she had the tub in her hand and that there was something silhouetted inside it.

'You found what you came for then?' Jude decided that the time had come to brazen it out.

'This?' Holly looked down at the tub in her hands. 'It's just... nothing, really.'

She went to put it in her pocket but Jude stood barring her escape and held her hand out.

'The police have been looking for that, actually. I told them where I'd seen Robyn hiding it and they're heading over now to take it. Perhaps I can look after it until they get here?'

Jude wasn't immune to telling the odd white lie when necessary but when she did she was always so anxious that it was as obvious as if someone had stuck an enormous name-badge on her saying LIAR.

She half expected Holly to charge past her and try to make a run for it but she didn't. To Jude's immense surprise, she dropped her shoulders, sighed and handed the tub straight over.

'Thank God for that,' Holly said. 'I've had enough of this

whole espionage thing but I wasn't really sure how to wriggle my way out of it, to be honest.'

Jude took the tub and lifted the lid. Inside was a black external hard drive.

'Gabe's, I assume,' she said.

'Gosh, you really are more clued up than I took you for,' said Holly. 'Yes, that's Gabe's.'

Jude zipped the hard drive securely in her coat pocket and took out her phone.

'Were you putting it there for Robyn, or did she leave it for you?'

'I'm just the drop-off girl.' Holly raised both her hands and Jude saw the flash of a magenta Toastie Wrist. 'Robyn's little bitch, paid to do whatever she wants me to do. To begin with I didn't mind. I needed the extra cash and Robyn can be quite... persuasive.'

'What was she paying you to do?' Jude was desperate to call Binnie and get her and Sami over but seeing as she'd already told Holly they were on the way she was in a tricky position.

'Mainly stalk Annie to gather evidence about her affair with Gabe. Robyn has this idea that if we can get hold of photographic, indisputable proof that they were sleeping together she could sell the story and bring not only Annie down but also the show. Can you imagine? The darling of daytime telly being outed as a scarlet woman? Scandalous!'

'Was she having an affair?' Jude asked.

'Of course she was,' Holly scoffed. 'Did we get solid proof? Now that's a different matter altogether. Look, I don't want to be difficult but could we find somewhere a bit warmer to sit while we wait for the police?'

Jude had the hard drive in her possession and Holly didn't seem to be ready to stage an escape so Jude nodded and led the way into the lambing shed where she gestured for Holly to sit in one of the old chairs there.

'I'd better just call DS Abadi to tell him where we are,' she said as she flicked on the electric heater.

Sami answered quickly when Jude rang.

'Hi, Jude.'

'Hello. I'm just phoning to say we've moved into the lambing shed. It's warmer in there, but Holly is still with me and she's given up the tub with the hard drive in it. Turns out the whole espionage thing was pretty much all Robyn, and Holly is very happy to tell you everything when you get here.' She knew Sami well enough to know that he'd take all the information he needed from her message and not ask questions until he arrived.

'Gotcha,' said Sami. 'Well done, Jude. I'm at the station but I'll head over now. Can you keep her there for fifteen minutes or so?'

'Ah, I see, that's why it's taking you so long. Yes, shouldn't be a problem. See you soon.'

Jude put the phone down.

'There was a crash somewhere on West Malvern Road,' she fibbed. 'He's had to take a detour but he's on his way. He said to just stay put for now. I can make tea if you like?'

She indicated the kettle that had seen better days and the odd assortment of chipped mugs that sat next to a tin of tea bags. During the busy lambing season, this was Jude's manky little oasis. Holly, though, wasn't quite as easy to please.

'You're sweet but I'm okay, thanks.'

'You were telling me about what you and Robyn found out.' Jude perched on the edge of the table.

'I was, wasn't I? It's actually such a relief to be talking about all of this. Before Mary died, I quite enjoyed sneaking around looking for juicy bits of backstage gossip. I found out more about Mary and Simon than I did about Annie and Gabe though.'

A thought occurred to Jude. 'It was you who went to the papers, wasn't it?'

'No comment,' said Holly pointedly, which told Jude everything she needed to know.

Holly had an axe to grind with Mary and Simon as she felt she'd been back-benched for the better job because of their affair and the strings that had been pulled. She could imagine Holly wanting to pay them back by taking their story to the paper, but to include Mary's death was on a very different level. She'd probably been paid handsomely for the insider information. Did murder attract a greater fee than proof of a celebrity affair?

'Don't look at me like that, Jude. I was always the better photographer and yet I was the one stuck in features earning way less than Mary. I needed to make up the shortfall somehow.' Holly's face had become sulky and defensive. 'I wasn't lying when I said I wanted to stop. I tried to tell Robyn I was finished but she said she'd tell the network that it was me who'd gone to the papers. If she did that then I'd never work in telly again.'

'And now?' Jude asked.

'Now I think Robyn has done enough to discredit herself so much that nobody will believe a word she says.' Holly crossed her arms and stretched her legs out in front of her. 'I have all the proof I need to show that she was the one leading the witch hunt as far as Annie Bird goes. She was the one who set up the link to the newspaper, not me. Although I was the courier of information, the connection is all hers and I will plead coercion and blackmail. And not just that, when the police finally get here I will tell them the truth about the night Gabe and Annie were attacked.'

'What do you mean?' Jude felt a tingle run through her, wondering if this was the key piece of evidence that they had been looking for.

'I mean that I wasn't in the chillout trailer with Robyn the entire time,' said Holly. 'I went back to my caravan for a nap, something I often do if I've been up early filming and I've got a late live broadcast.'

'When would you say this was?' Jude remembered it was just before six when she saw Mike Trout running into the bottom entrance of the campsite, alerted by the smoke alarm.

'I suppose it would have been around five thirty. I remember I set my alarm for six fifteen to give me enough time to prepare for the evening show.'

If Holly was telling the truth, and at that moment Jude wasn't sure what she believed, then this would explain why Annie hadn't seen her when she'd gone back to the chillout trailer for her glasses, but it would also mean that Robyn had no alibi for the time Gabe and Annie had been attacked.

Jude heard a car pull up outside in the yard, followed by the slamming of two car doors.

'That'll be DS Abadi.' Jude wondered if Binnie was with him but when Sami came into the barn, he was with a uniformed officer she knew called Nige Johnston. It had been a long day for Binnie, a long week in fact, and Jude hoped this meant she'd gone back home to rest.

'Sorry it took us a while to get here,' said Sami, walking over to Holly with his hand outstretched.

'Jude and I have been chatting.' Holly shook his hand but didn't get up.

'I gather you have a hard drive we might be interested in.' Sami pulled another chair over so he was facing Holly, and Nige did the same. He was carrying an electronic tablet with him to make notes and Jude knew that his body cam was almost certainly recording everything too.

Jude stood up and delved in her pocket to retrieve the hard

drive which she handed over to Sami before resuming her perch on the table.

'Thanks.' Sami slipped it into an evidence bag. 'Where did you get this?'

'From Gabe's hut,' said Holly. 'I went to see him yesterday morning to ask him something about a feature we were supposed to be filming together. He didn't answer when I knocked but I knew he was in there so I moved the step over to the window to climb up and look in.'

Jude looked at Sami, both surprised at the blasé way in which she was owning up to such brazen snooping. Holly opened her eyes wide and shrugged her shoulders to excuse this invasion of privacy.

'What?' she said. 'With all the weird stuff that's been happening, I just wanted to check he was okay.'

'And was he?' Sami asked.

'Yes. He was doing something on his laptop with some photos of Robyn. I couldn't see exactly what but I did notice the hard drive plugged in. I'd already caught him snooping around before and I'd got the feeling that he was trying to get dirt on Robyn. Crazy, isn't it? Robyn using me to try to get the gossip on Annie and all the time Gabe was doing the same to her.'

Jude had already made this connection, realising that half the filming crew had been involved in trying to find ways of flinging mud at each other for various reasons.

'So you'd discovered the existence of this hard drive and you decided you want to get your hands on it.'

'I wanted to get Robyn off my case once and for all,' said Holly. 'I thought that if I managed to get hold of it, I could use it as a bargaining tool. I knew Gabe kept the key to his hut in his kit bag so when he was having lunch in the chillout trailer, I took it. I'd seen him put the hard drive in a green first-aid box so I knew what to look for. There aren't that many places to hide things in the hut so it didn't take me long.'

'Under the bed?' Jude guessed.

Holly looked over at her. 'You seem to know an awful lot about this.'

Jude shrugged. 'You and Robyn aren't the only ones interested in what's been happening around here.'

'You said you took it at lunchtime,' said Sami. 'What did you do with it then?'

'I looked to see what was on it, which proved very interesting.' Holly sat forwards and tucked her feet under the chair. 'Gabe had put together a whole heap of videos and photos of Robyn bullying members of the team. Detailed records of everything she'd done with dates, times and the names of the individuals. Similar things for Dean, only with him it was more the alpha male tendencies. You must know what I'm talking about, Jude.'

She looked at Jude again, who nodded. 'You mean his predatory nature and the way he is with females who work for him.'

'Work for him, want to work for him, are interviewed by him, who just bring him a sodding cup of tea. He has very few boundaries and it looks like Gabe was going to bring it all out into the spotlight. I must admit, it made me see Gabe in a whole new light.' Holly sounded impressed and Jude realised that she didn't seem to be aware Annie had also been involved in the investigation. 'And it gave me everything I needed to make sure Robyn left me alone.'

'Has Robyn seen the content yet?' Sami asked.

'No. But she knows what's on it. I have to say, I took great delight in bringing that to her attention but I wasn't about to give it over to her until I'd been properly paid.'

'And have you?'

'She paid up this morning. We have a delivery system that I

think Jude is already very well aware of. Robyn left the money in the loo block but I had a text to say she was changing the hiding place. I was just making the drop when Jude found me.'

'When will Robyn be coming to collect the hard drive?' Sami was sitting further forward in his chair.

'When I send her a funny GIF.' She rolled her eyes. 'It's the signal we give each other, her idea and it's totally ridiculous if you ask me. She's gone full secret agent. Everything has to be so cloak and dagger. She doesn't like to text so when she does it's all in code. A funny GIF to indicate we've made a drop. Three ticks to say there's been a change of hiding place with a photo or two to show the new location, which I then have to delete. I don't know why we can't just meet up in her caravan and be done with it.'

Jude had been wondering the same thing and could only imagine that Robyn was desperate to distance herself from Holly and not be seen too often solely in her company so that questions wouldn't be asked.

'Go and put the tub back in its hiding place and then send her the GIF,' said Sami. 'We'll wait in here and then nab her when she comes to collect it.'

Holly grinned broadly, showing how much she was enjoying turning the tables on Robyn. Jude wondered if she realised how much trouble she was in herself. She was the one who'd got hold of the hard drive, she'd sold stories to the press including details of Mary's death, and she had just lost her alibi for the time of Gabe's murder. At the very least she'd surely be charged with perverting the course of justice.

She'd also been extremely quick to spill everything she knew to land Robyn in deep water, perhaps hoping it would mean saving her own skin.

'There was one other thing on the hard drive that you'll no doubt find as interesting as I did,' said Holly. 'Gabe discovered that Mary had been pregnant before starting work on this series but that she miscarried. I think he was trying to find out who the father was but we all know the answer to that.'

'Are you sure?' Jude asked.

'I'm only telling you what you'll see in his files anyway. But Gabe seemed sure enough.'

That one little piece of information threw up a whole sandstorm of new questions.

Was the baby Simon's? That was certainly what Holly was insinuating but it was by no means a given. If it was Simon's then this would surely be something that he would have wanted to keep secret, and if it wasn't his but he knew about it then there was a sizeable chance he would have been furious with Mary. Were either of these reasons to kill?

Had Annie known? Surely Gabe would have been very keen to hammer this nail into the coffin of Annie and Simon's marriage. Which begged the next question: if he hadn't, then why not?

'Thank you,' said Sami. 'We'll be looking into the content of all the files in detail. One more thing before you put that tub back.' He took another evidence bag out and opened it up. 'Please could you drop those wrist warmers you're wearing in here.'

Holly's smile dropped. 'Whatever for?'

'Just following all lines of enquiry.' Sami shook the empty bag. 'If you'd be so kind.'

Holly looked shaken but she had no choice. She took the Toastie Wrists off and dropped them into the bag. Then she went out to lay the trap to catch Robyn.

20

Both Robyn and Holly were taken back to the police station for questioning and neither one was happy about the situation. Robyn had been furious when she realised she'd been set up and Holly had obviously thought she'd done enough to dodge further suspicion.

Dean was also taken in to discuss the evidence found on the hard drive.

That evening, Sunday's *Countryside Live* was replaced by an old episode of *Antiques Roadshow*. There was a televised message explaining that the rest of the series had been unavoidably cancelled. This time there was no mention of the deaths that had caused the abrupt halting of the show and Jude wondered how long it would be before the entire story came out – or at least a version of it.

'What do you think's happening down at the station?' Lucy turned the television volume down. 'Do you reckon anyone has broken and given themselves away as the murderer yet?'

'If we're lucky,' said Jude. 'I really want this all to be over.'

She wasn't sure it was going to be quite that simple though. Everything seemed to be pointing towards Robyn and Holly working together somehow and yet there were still too many unanswered questions for Jude.

'I reckon Annie Bird will be too.' Noah was lying back on the sofa with his hands resting on his stomach and his socked feet stretched towards the log burner.

'I can't imagine what it must be like for her, knowing that someone wants to kill her.' Lucy rested her head on Noah's shoulder and he took her hand.

Seeing the two of them like that made Jude think of Marco. For a moment she imagined what it would be like if he was sitting next to her right then, taking her hand in a simple act of togetherness. What it might be like to go to bed that night and feel his warmth and presence next to her. Wake up without that familiar sense of being on her own.

She shook the thoughts away. She was lucky in so many ways. Lucy, Noah, Sebbie, Granny Margot, Frank: they were her family. She had good friends, her farming network and nobody was trying to kill her.

Annie Bird flew into her mind's eye. Everything came down to her and who wanted her dead. Jude thought of the four suspects again. Robyn and Holly, of course. Sami, Binnie and the team would have twenty-four hours to find out what they could from the pair of them before they had to charge them with something or let them go. So far all they knew was that the two women had been watching Gabe and had got hold of his hard drive. There was still a way to go before this was turned into something solid enough to hang two counts of murder on plus several attempts at Annie's life.

Who had the biggest reason to want her dead?

Robyn, the career-stunted would-be director, who had been denied her big break when Annie had backed Dean's appointment over her, had been looking for revenge. Holly had confirmed that. She'd also known that Gabe and Annie were gathering evidence of her bullying tactics to use in a documentary that would be aired on a large network. If that went out and Robyn was identified then she would never work in television again. She had motive, she also had the means and opportunity so perhaps this case was almost closed.

But if it proved not to be her or Holly, then who?

Simon, the husband who had cheated on her with someone who had miscarried his baby. Annie had told Jude that she and Simon had never wanted children. Had he really felt that way or had he wanted to be a father after all and decided to start afresh with Mary? If so, then Annie could have made things very difficult for him and his career, if she wasn't disposed of first, that was.

If it was Simon who had tried to kill his wife to be with his mistress then the terrible twist of fate that meant it was Mary who had died instead would surely be nigh on impossible for him to deal with. Had it driven him to the point of further murderous intentions? Or had he killed Gabe because of the things he'd discovered? His possible motives were definitely starting to mount up.

Dean Dickens potentially had even more to lose from the findings of Annie and Gabe's investigations. They were digging into the sexually predatory nature of his personality. According to Annie, they had video footage of his indecent behaviour and this could not just end his career but also see criminal charges brought against him.

Both Robyn and Dean stood to benefit greatly if Gabe and

Annie had died and the files containing all the evidence against them were destroyed or taken. No network would produce a slanderous, sensational documentary without solid proof. But Annie hadn't died, she'd lived to tell the tale, and the evidence hadn't all been destroyed. Although Annie's phone had not been found, Gabe's hard drive had. Depending on exactly what was on it, Dean and Robyn could both already be in a heap of trouble.

The hard drive was the key piece of evidence and the fact that it was Holly who'd found it couldn't be brushed aside. The camera operator who'd had an instant career boost when the first murder opened up a prime position for her. Whose magenta wrist warmers had quite possibly been present when the fatal exhaust fumes were channelled through the caravan window. Although Holly had nothing to gain from Gabe's death on the face of it, if she had killed Mary then it was a very handy way of deflecting attention away from herself. She had given up the hard drive with a sense of relief, incriminating Robyn without a hint of remorse. Although she was too short to have attacked Annie, she had the information she needed to encourage someone else to do it. Someone who had a very real reason to want her and Gabe out of the way. Had she taken the news of what she'd seen on the hard drive to Dean and planted the idea of murder in his head? Or maybe it was Robyn who'd needed nothing more than a bit of a nudge? Both Dean and Robyn had shown a tendency for aggression. Both had motive and neither had a decent alibi.

All four suspects were more than capable of playing their part in murder but Jude would have to wait until the next day to find out more.

* * *

When Jude went down to let the ducks out and feed the animals in the morning, everything seemed eerily quiet after the constant noise and movement that the filming crew had brought with them.

Jude couldn't wait for Binnie or Sami to get in touch so she put a note on the group chat.

> Any news?

Binnie's reply came back before Jude and her dogs had walked down to the stable block.

> We're holding them on charges of perverting the course of justice, awaiting bail, could be out soon. Nothing to pin murder on either of them. Have filed for search warrants to go through Dean's and Robyn's caravans. Will be up there later on. Have asked all to stay on site and not go home. Sorry.

'Damn it,' Jude mumbled.

The second message that came through from Binnie was also frustrating.

> Just had results from Holly's wrist warmer. No match.

The magenta fibres were one of the only solid pieces of evidence for Mary's murder that they had to go on and now this had led to another dead end. No scrap of anything that could prove any one of them had been there the night Mary died. Nothing other than Annie's description of the watch and the rough height of her attacker to point the finger at Gabe's murderer.

There had been mention of the strangulations being crimes of chance rather than the more calculated organisation of Mary's murder and the peanut-tainted hot chocolate. But as Jude thought more about it, she realised that it couldn't have been. Someone went down to the shepherd's hut with the intention of killing; why else would they wear all black, including gloves? There was no doubt in her mind that they knew about both the paper and electronic files in advance and they needed to get rid of them. But they chose to go when Gabe was there. The timing was spot on. They were able to kill Gabe when he was on his own and then wait for Annie to return.

As Jude filled the hay bags and broke the ice on the water trough, her muscles were working on their own whilst her brain was busy trying to pull together some threads that were bothering her.

'The Christmas lights,' she whispered to the sheep as she tipped pellets into their feeding station. 'Why choose those as a murder weapon?'

Judging by the note that had been found in the box, they'd been a gift from Gabe to Annie. The murderer had not brought them to the scene but they had either known they'd be there or had taken the opportunity when they saw them. But if the murder was planned, as the black clothes and perfect timing suggested, surely the killer would have thought about their weapon in advance, and taken it with them.

It didn't make sense. There was something really obvious that Jude was missing. The more she tried to find it amongst the tangle of threads, the more it seemed to wriggle away from her.

By the time the animals had been dealt with and Jude was locking up the tack room, another message came through the group chat. This time from Sami.

> Found connection between Annie's contact at the rival network and Dean Dickens. They used to work together and according to his PA they still go out drinking. Feel he may have told Dean what Annie was planning. Will talk to him later today. Jude, please let us know if anyone looks like they're planning on leaving the farm.

Jude answered with a thumbs-up emoji and put her phone back in her pocket.

So, Dean might also have known what Annie and Gabe were up to. With any luck, the search warrants would be signed off swiftly and something of interest would be discovered in one of the caravans that would help move the investigation along somewhat.

Jude gave everything in the paddock a last check and called the dogs to her before heading back towards the yard. The Christmas lights were still bothering her. It was almost as though there was something symbolic about their use. A love token from Gabe to Annie, used to kill one and try to kill the other.

She was so lost in her own thoughts that she wasn't aware of anything other than the ground in front of her feet as she walked up to the gate. Her bare hands were so cold that she fumbled with the baling twine, unable to catch it over the gate post on the first attempt.

'Bollocks!' she cursed as the twine slipped and cut into her hand. It took another couple of attempts and then, with the gate finally secure, she carried on her way, examining the ripped skin of her fingers. Jude didn't notice the gate of the campsite being opened so when she looked up, she was caught unawares by Simon North coming towards her with his head bent low.

Alfie chose that moment to run in front of her and Jude was

knocked off balance, suddenly finding herself arse-down on the frozen mud.

'Are you okay?'

Jude looked up and saw Simon, unkempt with a chin covered in stubble and huge bags beneath his eyes. He was holding out a hand, clad in a banana-yellow glove, and Jude took it to allow him to help her back to her feet.

'Thanks,' said Jude.

As his arm strained to pull her up, the sleeve of his coat pulled back slightly to reveal the cuff of the glove, lined with a warm layer of magenta-coloured fur. She gasped as she realised what this could mean and turned it into a grunt of exertion as she regained her footing. The fur of the lining spilled out of the cuff of the glove. Were these gloves responsible for the fibres left at the first murder scene?

'I could do with a pair of those.' She tried to maintain composure as she let go of Simon's hand.

'What?'

'Your gloves,' she said. 'My hands are freezing from breaking the ice on the animals' water. I couldn't even close the gate just now they were so cold.'

Simon looked distractedly at his hands.

'Oh, right, yeah.'

'They look waterproof,' Jude went on. 'Are they?'

'I don't know.' Simon did not look in the mood to talk but Jude wanted to see if she could persuade him to part with a glove, just for a moment. All she needed was to hold one of them long enough to try to pinch out a bit of the fluff. 'I think so. Some ski-wear company sent them to me for a bit of free advertising.'

'Do you mind if I take a look?' Jude asked. 'I've been looking for a warm waterproof pair I can wear on the farm.'

Simon reluctantly pushed the sleeve of his coat back to see if there was a label on them and Jude saw the hint of a fluffy magenta lining peeking out from the cuff again. He didn't hand them over though.

'Doesn't say the brand,' said Simon. 'Sorry.'

He started to move away from her and Jude felt as though she should be doing something to stop him. Sami had asked her to make sure everyone stayed on site if she could and now here she was confronted by Simon North heading away from the farm. Not just that but he was wearing a pair of gloves that might just be the missing piece of the puzzle.

If the lights had been chosen as a murder weapon because of their significance as a love token then Simon was the obvious person to have used them.

'Where are you heading?' she asked, nodding at his warm coat and walking boots.

'I need a break from this place,' said Simon. 'I'm going for a walk to clear my head and then I'm going to pack.'

'Pack? Are you allowed to leave?'

Simon gave a low growl of something that fell between despair, annoyance and frustration. 'I don't really care. I've got a car coming to take me home this afternoon.'

'You must be going out of your mind with worry for Annie,' said Jude.

'I'll be glad to be back home with her so I can make sure she's safe.'

Jude was surprised by this declaration. 'Surely she's going to stay in police protection until whoever tried to kill her has been caught.'

'We'll see,' said Simon.

He'd clearly had enough of the conversation as he carried on his previous course over the stile that led to the footpath without saying goodbye.

Jude took her phone out straight away and sent a message asking Sami if he could extend the search warrant to cover Simon's caravan as well.

SAMI
> Why? What have you found?

JUDE
> He's wearing gloves lined with magenta fur. He's booked a car to take him home this afternoon and he seems to think Annie will be meeting him there.

SAMI
> WTF? Where is he now?

JUDE
> Gone for a walk.

SAMI
> Need more than gloves to get a search warrant. Don't suppose you saw a watch as well?

JUDE
> Fraid not.

SAMI
> Okay. Will see what I can do. Thanks.

Jude knew she didn't have time to think too carefully about the options. Simon would be gone for perhaps an hour or so and then he'd be back to pack his things up ready for the car to take him home. Whilst the police would then be able to go in and search the caravan without a warrant, anything of interest would almost certainly have gone with Simon. Sami might be able to get the warrant before Simon left but his doubt did not give Jude hope. If there was anything to find in that caravan then it would be down to her to do so.

There was one easy way to get into Simon's caravan but only if the production van where the spare keys were kept was open. That would depend on someone being inside it and seeing as the series had been canned, there seemed very little chance of that. Jude went over to check and, sure enough, with a rattle of the door, she found it was locked up.

'Everything okay, Jude?'

She turned to see Bav, the junior runner who Robyn had been so vile to, coming towards her.

'Oh, hi,' said Jude. 'I was hoping someone might be around. I think I might have dropped something in there yesterday but I guess Dean has the only key.'

'Is it urgent?' asked Bav.

Jude thought quickly. 'It is really. It's the key to my car. I had it in my pocket when I went to talk to Dean and that was the last time I saw it. Annoyingly the second key was lost years ago so without this one we're a bit scuppered.'

'Oh, no.' Bav glanced around tentatively. 'Look, it's totally against policy but I think everything's already gone down the pan so I can't see the harm.' He took a key from his pocket. 'Robyn told me to fetch some stuff for her yesterday and then she, you know, left before I could give her key back.'

Perhaps somebody else who'd been treated the way Bav had by Robyn would gloat a little at her downfall but he looked resolutely sombre as he fitted the key into the lock.

'You're a life saver,' said Jude. 'Thank you so much, Bav.'

The two of them walked up the metal steps into the production trailer which was now dark with all of the equipment turned off.

'Who else would have had a key?' Jude asked as Bav flicked the light on and shut the door.

She knew that anyone who had a key to the production van would also have access to all the other trailers and caravans, including the one Mary was in when she died.

'Robyn, Gabe, Mary and a couple of others, I guess,' Bav said. 'The main production team.' He started to look around at the floor. 'Where were you when you think you dropped it?'

'Over by that chair.' Jude put her hand in her pocket and felt around for the Land Rover key she knew she had in there.

Whilst Bav was distracted looking beneath the chair, Jude went over to the row of keys and took the one for Simon's caravan. Bav looked up and Jude folded the key into the palm of her hand. Then she flashed the key to her Land Rover. 'Here it is,' she said. 'Someone must have found it and put it on the hook for safekeeping.'

She slipped both keys back into her pocket. 'Thank goodness for that.'

'Yeah, that *was* lucky.' Bav didn't look wholly convinced but didn't say anything else. Jude might just have got away with it.

'Thanks for your help,' she said as she climbed back out of the van.

'No worries,' said Bav. 'Just do me a favour and don't tell anyone where you got the key from.'

Jude wasn't sure if he was referring to the Land Rover key, the key Bav had used to let her into the production van, or the key to Simon's caravan which had now left a gap on the hooks if anyone was being particularly observant.

'Of course not,' said Jude. 'I appreciate it.'

'See you later, Jude.'

Jude watched Bav go for a moment before heading over to Simon's caravan. She felt exposed as she went straight to the front door with the key in her hand, but she had no choice. She couldn't wait and risk Simon coming back.

Speed was more important than stealth if she was going to find something incriminating. She needed to prove the increasing suspicion she had that Simon and his magenta-lined, expensive ski gloves were somehow right at the heart of everything that had happened.

21

Jude's heart was racing as she let herself into the enormous caravan that had been Simon's home for the past week or so and closed the door behind her.

Time was not on her side and, unlike the shepherd's huts which were pocket-sized in comparison, there was a lot of caravan to search. She started in the kitchenette, pulling out drawers and rifling through cupboards, but there was nothing worth noting. The shower room was similarly fruitless.

Simon's bedroom was compact but still luxurious with a decent-sized bed and plenty of overhead storage. Almost identical to the one where Mary had died.

Jude lifted the mattress and looked underneath but found nothing. Then she went through the little bedside cabinet and wardrobe.

Nothing.

Turning her attention to the cupboards mounted on the wall above the bed, Jude pulled out piles of neatly folded clothes and ran her hand along the back of the cupboards. Still she found nothing.

There was one last cupboard to check, directly above the head of the bed. When Jude knelt on the pillow to reach it, a pain shot through her kneecap as it connected with something hard and unexpected. Jude sat back and lifted the pillow, shaking it so that whatever was hiding in the pillowcase would fall to the duvet without her touching it.

'Gotcha,' she said with a grin when she saw what it was.

A watch lay face down on the thick white cotton of the cover. The silver-coloured links matched the description of the watch Annie had said her attacker had been wearing.

And Jude could see something engraved on the back.

She took two tissues from the box next to the bed and used them to pick the watch up so she could take a closer look.

Simon, it's time for us now. I love you. Mary xxx

Jude knew before she turned it over that the face would be blue with a tiny dial set into it, just as Annie had described.

More than that, snagged in the links was a white-blonde hair. The same colour as Annie Bird's. It must have got caught when Simon had sneaked up behind her and thrown a loop of Christmas lights around her neck.

Jude took the watch into the main sitting area of the caravan where she perched on the arm of the big L-shaped sofa to call Sami. The phone went straight to voicemail so she left a short message to let him know she'd tried him first but as there was no answer she'd call Binnie.

Binnie picked up straight away.

'Hi, Jude, how can I help?'

'It's more how I can help you,' said Jude. 'Don't get mad but I've found the watch in Simon North's caravan.'

'Let's just gloss over the why and how you got into Simon

North's caravan for a moment and come back to that later.' Jude could picture the exasperated look on Binnie's face. 'Tell me about the watch.'

'It was hidden in his pillow. Don't worry, I used tissues to handle it.'

'And it matches the description Annie gave us?'

'Blue face, mini dial set in it, silver links. But I can add two other points of interest.' Jude used the tissue to turn the watch over again. 'A hair caught in the strap that looks very much like it could be Annie's, and an inscription that reads: *Simon, it's time for us now. I love you. Mary*, followed by three kisses.'

'Yes!' Binnie was clearly as excited by this find as Jude was. 'Where are you and the watch now?'

'Still in the caravan. Simon's gone for a walk but he'll be coming back to pack at some point, he says he's going home.' As she spoke, Jude's eyes had been wandering, automatically searching the space for anything else of interest. 'I got the impression he thinks Annie is going to meet him there.'

Binnie let out an audible breath. 'She's been naïve and stupid. We told her to leave her phone off so it couldn't be tracked and the attending officer put it safely out of the way. Only it turns out you were right and she still trusted Simon completely, despite everything. I've literally just found out she's been sending him text messages.'

'Bugger it,' said Jude. 'Do you think he knows where she is?'

'Possibly. She definitely mentioned that she wanted to go home with him.'

Jude's gaze fell on the cushion of the sofa and she saw that there was a slight gap between it and the base as though something was underneath, stopping it from lying flush. She stood up and went over to lift the cushion, finding beneath it a nest of hidden treasures that made her gasp.

'Sami said there's a team coming up with search warrants for Dean and Robyn's vans.'

'They should be almost with you,' Binnie confirmed.

'Binnie, you have to get them to come into Simon's van first,' she said. 'If the watch isn't enough to get him for Gabe's murder and Annie's attempted murder then this should do it. I've just found some gold pods that look just like the peanut ones used to taint the coffee machine, and there's also an EpiPen. Both hidden under the sofa cushions.'

'Bloody hell, Jude.'

'I know. It must be him who's been trying to kill Annie, which means it stands to reason he also killed Gabe and probably Mary too, although I think that might have been a mistake, wouldn't you say?'

He had clearly been in love with Mary, perhaps wanting to make a fresh start with her and try again for another baby. Had he killed her in error, the row they'd had that day meaning she hadn't told him she was switching vans with Annie? Jude could picture the scene clearly now, Simon in his yellow gloves with their magenta lining. Not only protecting his hands from the cold but also from the heat of the exhaust pipe. Hoping to get his wife out of the way to give him the freedom to be with Mary.

He'd already tried once, tainting the coffee machine and adding a chocolate peanut to Annie's drink to be sure she'd go into anaphylactic shock. Hiding her EpiPen in the hope it would be too late by the time the spare one had been located and brought to her.

Perhaps he had gone to Annie's hut to try again, although by that time his key motive had gone. Mary was already dead, as was his hope of setting up a new life with her. It was possible he'd only gone down to the hut that night to talk to Annie. Only when he got there it wasn't Annie he found but Gabe, perhaps stringing the lights up for her as a surprise. Had this been enough to make him flip? Seeing Gabe and Annie apparently happy when he was in such deep turmoil after killing the woman he wanted to start a new life with must have been a stab through the heart and a kick in the guts for him.

It would surely all come out once the police had him in for questioning.

'He won't be able to wriggle out of this,' said Jude. 'Not with so much evidence stacked against him.'

'You need to get out of there,' said Binnie.

'I don't want him to hide the evidence,' said Jude.

'I said, get out of there.' Binnie's voice had morphed into something sharp and frantic and Jude realised that she was thinking about the last time Jude had dabbled in a bit of undercover investigating. That had not ended well and now Binnie was afraid for Jude's safety.

'Okay,' said Jude calmly. 'I'll go. What do you want me to do with the watch and the other evidence?'

'Just leave it,' said Binnie. 'The team will be with you in a few minutes and I'll make sure they know to go to Simon's van first.'

Jude heard a sound outside the door of the caravan. She looked out of the window and saw Simon North running away.

'Shit,' she said, heading for the door. 'Simon was outside. He must have heard at least some of what I said and he's on the run.'

Jude left the door open as she ran outside and followed Simon out of the campsite.

'Jude, leave him!'

'He can't do anything to me out here. I just want to see where he's heading.' She ran on past the pond and into the yard.

Noah's pickup was standing there with the engine running but no sign of the driver. Jude knew he wouldn't be far away; he often did this in the winter to defrost the windscreen and warm the cab up. She couldn't see him though and Simon was nearly there.

'Bugger it,' Jude said. 'He's going to take Noah's pickup.'

She dug in her pocket for the key to her Land Rover, grateful she'd parked it in the barn overnight so it was frost free. As Simon opened the door to the pickup and jumped inside, Jude sent a silent prayer to her old car, pleading with it to start quickly despite the cold. She clicked the phone to speaker mode and when she was in the driving seat, flung it into the coin tray and thrust the key into the ignition.

'You beautiful thing!' she cheered as the engine roared into life.

'What are you doing?' Binnie's voice crackled through the speaker.

'I'm following him,' said Jude. 'Stay on the phone and I'll tell you where he's heading.'

'Just leave it, Jude. I'll send squad cars over and put an urgent alert out for anyone in the area to head that way.'

Jude sped out of the yard and down the drive, catching sight of the tail end of Noah's pickup as it disappeared around the corner. She didn't answer Binnie but concentrated on the twists and potholes of the drive.

Simon was travelling at a fair lick and she had to focus to keep up with him.

'Jude, I said leave it.' Binnie was shouting now.

'We'll lose him,' said Jude. 'What if he's heading to find Annie?'

'There are people there to protect her. For God's sake, Jude.'

Jude sighed and started to slow. She could see the pickup nearing the mouth of the driveway. Binnie was right – to follow him out onto the lanes would be dangerous and he was already jeopardising the safety of anyone else already out there.

'I'm backing off,' she said. 'He's turning right out of the farm towards the—'

Jude's words caught in her mouth as she watched the pickup take the turn with far too much speed. There was ice still on the corner where the sun couldn't reach past the shadow of an old oak tree and the pickup's high centre of gravity made it unstable.

'Holy shit!' she exclaimed as the pickup skidded out across the tarmac, spinning 180 degrees before hitting the banked edge with such velocity that it flipped right over onto the roof.

Jude unclipped her seatbelt and switched her engine off. She threw the door open with one hand whilst grabbing the phone with the other. 'Binnie, he's crashed. Send an ambulance, it looks pretty bad. I'm going to check on him.'

She switched the phone off and ran to where the pickup was lying, wheels still spinning in the air.

'Simon?' she shouted as she approached the cab, phone still in hand.

The roof had buckled but not badly, leaving the inside of the cab dented but relatively unscathed. If Simon had taken a second to secure his seatbelt he might have been able to have walked away from the crash with no more than cuts, bruises and perhaps whiplash or concussion.

Without this though, he had been flung out of his seat and was lying in a crumpled heap in the bowl of the dented roof.

22

Jude tested the door handle. Thankfully the crash had released the central locking and she was able to get in.

'Simon. Simon, can you hear me?'

There was no answer and Jude saw the back of his head was wet with blood. She could see the rhythmic, steady rise and fall of his chest, however, telling her that he was still alive.

She took hold of his hand, which was floppy and unresponsive.

'I've called for help,' she said. 'An ambulance is on the way. Can you squeeze my hand?'

For a fleeting moment, as she tried her best to open his airway in the cramped conditions of the inverted pickup cab, Jude thought of the preposterous situation she was now in. Here was a man who had committed murder. Two people were dead, almost certainly because of his actions, and he'd intended on killing a third. Yet there she was, doing her utmost to save his life.

She shook the thought away. It was not up to her to decide who lived and who didn't. Besides, if she allowed him to die then he would never be held accountable for his actions.

'Simon, stay with me,' she said as she watched his chest to make sure the lungs were still pulling air into his body. 'We'll get you to hospital in no time. Hang in there.'

Her phone rang and she saw it was Binnie so she clicked to answer, not waiting for her to begin the conversation.

'Binnie, he's alive but unconscious,' Jude said. 'How's that ambulance coming on?'

'It's on its way. Are you okay?'

'I'm absolutely fine. Just making sure Simon lives to answer your questions.'

* * *

Simon did live, partly thanks to Jude. He was taken to Hereford County Hospital where he was stabilised but remained in a coma.

Meanwhile, his caravan was searched and enough evidence gained for Binnie and Sami to agree that they had almost certainly got their murderer.

'The consultant seems pretty sure he'll be out of the coma before too long,' said Binnie when she went to see Jude on the farm that afternoon. 'We'll arrest him as soon as he's fit and well enough. It seems your meddling paid off this time, Jude.'

'What about the others?' Jude asked. 'Dean, Robyn and Holly? Did they really have nothing to do with any of it?'

'It appears not, although we're still going through statements and all the evidence to make sure we haven't missed anything.'

'How's Annie?' Jude wondered at the impact this would have on her. The man she'd loved, had built a life around and carved out a career with had wanted to kill her. He'd tried not once, but three times, leaving two deaths as collateral damage.

'She's completely crushed by all accounts,' said Binnie. 'She's also keen to come back here to collect her things and say goodbye to the team.'

'Wow,' Jude exclaimed. 'I'm not sure that's something I'd want to do in the situation.'

Binnie shrugged. 'I think she wants to find a little closure when it comes to *Countryside Live*. Then who knows? Perhaps she'll take time to start building a new life out of the public eye.'

This was something that Jude could understand and she hoped Annie would, in time, be able to get what she needed away from the falsehood of her celebrity status.

'When is she coming?' Jude asked.

'Tomorrow. She said she'd like to talk to you but she doesn't want to visit the farm.'

'That's understandable,' said Jude. 'So much happened here that I'm sure she'll spend the rest of her life trying to process. Do you know what she wants to talk to me about?'

'You solved the mystery,' said Binnie. 'Perhaps she wants to thank you, or maybe she has questions. Are you happy for me to set it up?'

'Sure.' Jude realised that she wanted to see Annie Bird one last time too. 'Where will she be?'

'Four Trees,' said Binnie. 'She still has a lot of stuff in her room at the B&B she wants to collect and Paddy has said she can use the sitting room there to bring the full team together so she can say her goodbyes to them.'

'That's got to have taken some guts,' said Jude.

'I think she's used to living out her life in front of an audience so this feels natural to her. And when it's done, she can move on.'

Perhaps Binnie was right. Although this was the last thing Jude would've wanted to have done given the situation, her life had been completely different from Annie's. Annie Bird had really broken into the world of television thanks to the enormous success of *Countryside Live*. She had worked on it for over a decade, making friends and enemies along the way. To her it was more than a job, it was a way of life and that was something Jude could definitely relate to.

She couldn't overlook the fact that Annie herself had been plotting to bring the whole thing crashing down with the new documentary she and Gabe had been working on. But that was something she had held the reins of. What had happened instead had been something she'd had no control over and she had paid a heavy price. Not only that but her husband had been at the centre of it all.

Perhaps calling everyone together one last time was her way of clawing back a little of that control so she could leave with a greater chance of, as Binnie called it, closure.

* * *

That night, Jude did not sleep well. Something was bothering her and she couldn't put her finger on it.

The murders had been solved and Simon North would be arrested as soon as he woke from his coma. She'd found the evidence to show he had tried to kill his wife by using peanut coffee in the machine and taking the lifesaving EpiPen from her bag. The watch that Annie had described had been discovered in his possession, inscribed by his lover and with one of his wife's hairs snagged in the links. He had solid motives to want Annie and Gabe dead and he had been enormously affected by the death of Mary, whom he had almost certainly killed by mistake whilst wearing the magenta-lined winter gloves.

Then there was his sudden departure. Surely he'd have only fled if he was guilty.

It all added up. And yet there was something clawing at the

back of her mind, telling her that there was still a missing piece of the puzzle.

Robyn and Holly were now out on bail; was that what was making Jude feel so uncomfortable?

By the time she got out of bed and went into the kitchen to make the first coffee of the day, Jude was exhausted. She'd slept fitfully and not for more than an hour or two at a time.

Lucy had set up Clarence the elf the night before so that it looked as though he'd been pilfering biscuits. She'd positioned his hat to be caught in the lid of the biscuit tin and had arranged a scattering of crumbs around where he'd been propped next to Sebbie's lunchbox. A little smear of chocolate on his top lip finished the effect and it made Jude smile. Despite it all, Christmas was still heading their way and perhaps now that the investigation was drawing to a close and the filming had finished she'd be able to throw herself into the fun with a bit more verve.

Binnie had liaised with Annie, who was expecting Jude at Four Trees B&B later that morning. Whilst she went about her daily chores, she wondered how it was going for the poor woman. She had arranged for the *Countryside Live* team to meet and Jude imagined them all sitting together in the big, airy communal room at Four Trees.

Had Annie managed to keep herself together as she spoke to the people she'd worked with for so long? Which of them had turned up and what reception had they given her? Jude hoped that it would have been a supportive one in the main. It had always seemed that the extended crew members liked her. Not Robyn and Dean though, especially now they knew the extent of her investigations into the way they conducted themselves during production of the series. Although the documentary would now almost certainly not be made, neither of them were out of the woods as far as the evidence Gabe and Annie had gathered went. Jude knew there would be things on the hard drive that would ask big questions of them both. Was this the loose end that was irritating Jude?

Although nobody had come to say goodbye to Jude, she knew that the film crew were leaving because of the amount of traffic flowing through the farmyard. She watched the production trailer disappear off down the drive and several of the caravans, although she imagined the police had identified the ones they wanted to be left until they'd finished searching them for evidence.

Eventually it was time for her to make her way down into the village to meet Annie for the last time.

'She's up in her room,' said Paddy, the owner of Four Trees B&B. 'She told me to send you up when you arrived.' Paddy looked sombre, a mood that reflected Jude's own. 'Terrible business this whole thing has been for her. Poor love. Let's just hope she can find a bit of peace now it's all over.'

Paddy's words sent a quiver of doubt through Jude. There it was again, the niggling feeling that it wasn't all over yet: that she'd missed something important. It didn't matter that all signs were lit up with neon and pointed directly at the man currently lying in a hospital bed. Jude was not satisfied with the outcome. There was nothing whatsoever for her to hang her doubts on and yet they would not leave her alone.

'Who's there?' Annie called through the closed door when Jude knocked on it.

'It's me. Jude.'

The sound of a key being turned in the lock was followed by the door being opened. Annie smiled when she saw Jude, although it did little to hide the mask of exhaustion and grief she was wearing.

'Thank you for coming to see me,' she said. 'I know you're busy and we've all caused you enough problems already.'

'Don't be daft.' Jude walked into the bedroom suite and waited for Annie to close the door before they both sat down on wicker chairs that had been set up in the bay window.

'I gather I have you to thank for getting to the bottom of what happened.'

'I was just one person in a wider investigation,' said Jude.

'Well, I wanted to thank you in person. Without you I might have been waiting for a long time to discover the truth. I feel so naïve and foolish.' Annie put her hand to her chin and looked out of the window.

'I don't think you were either of those things,' Jude said gently.

'Oh, I was. I trusted the man I loved and overlooked him completely when trying to work out who was trying to hurt me.' Her forehead creased deeply. 'I still can't believe it. I knew our marriage wasn't perfect and that he had looked outside of it for certain comforts, but I truly thought we still loved each other in our own ways. How wrong I was.'

Jude thought back to the times she'd seen them together and knew she agreed with that sentiment. It really had seemed as though he loved her still. It had been an odd, flawed love but it had seemed so genuine.

'If you hadn't found so much proof that everything was down to him then I wouldn't believe it.' Annie turned to look at Jude. 'But there's no doubt, is there?' There was a desperation in her voice and Jude longed to give her some sort of hope, but she couldn't.

'The evidence was all there,' she said.

Doubt bubbled up once more as Jude said the words. The evidence had all been there, it was true. Clarence the naughty

Christmas elf suddenly made himself known in Jude's mind. The crumbs Lucy had laid, the smudge of chocolate and the hat that had been carefully positioned to signpost his guilt. When Sebbie had come into the kitchen, he had put all the clues together and jumped to the conclusion that Lucy had intended. He was the biscuit thief, no doubt about it.

Was it the same with the coffee pods and the EpiPen? Had they been too easy to find, as though someone had planted them as a signpost to Simon's guilt? But what of the watch? Was it possible that someone had also taken that in order to frame him, knowing that this would be the only thing Annie would see when she was being strangled? It was certainly very handy that one of her hairs had been caught in the strap.

It would have taken some planning, but it was not impossible.

Simon had run, though. He had taken off so quickly, crashing the stolen pickup in his rush to escape. These were not the actions of an innocent man.

Unless...

If he had overheard Jude's phone conversation with Binnie then he knew the evidence was stacked against him regardless of whether he had put it there himself or someone else had done it for him. He had no alibis and he had strong motives. Had he panicked, realising that it would be very hard for him to explain his way out of the situation?

It was definitely possible and if it was true and someone had framed him, then that meant the killer was still out there. If that was the case then Annie was still not safe.

23

Jude had not seen any police presence when she came into the B&B and she wasn't sure if Annie was still being guarded for her own safety now that Simon was out of the way. She wasn't sure how to bring this up with Annie without either worrying her or giving her false hopes that Simon may not be the killer after all.

Instead, whilst Annie gazed out of the window up towards the hills, Jude took her phone out and sent a quick message on the group chat to Binnie and Sami.

> Have nagging doubt. Might not be Simon. No proof or facts but think Annie not safe yet. At 4 Trees with her now. Will stay here till police arrive.

'What will you do now?' Jude asked as she put her phone away.

'What?' Annie turned to her. 'Sorry. I was just thinking about Simon. What did you ask me?'

'I was just wondering what your plans are going forward,'

said Jude. 'I hope you've got people to help you through the next stage.'

'I'm going to have the documentary to keep me busy.'

Jude was surprised by this, having assumed it would be canned after everything that had happened.

'Are you sure that's what you want to do?'

'Of course it is,' said Annie. 'More than ever now. I want to honour Gabe's memory and I need this whole story out in the open, it's what he deserves. I've been told that Gabe's hard drive was found so I'm hoping to be able to access the files from that once the police have finished with it. Or maybe my phone will turn up in Simon's caravan. Who knows what else is lurking under those sofa cushions.'

Jude felt a new thread dangle at the mention of the sofa cushions. How had Annie known where the things had been discovered in Simon's caravan? It was possible the police had told her but it seemed an unlikely, specific piece of information to pass on. Jude knew that in these situations, people tended to be given only the facts that they needed.

'As far as I know, it was only your EpiPen and the coffee pods there.' Jude was alert now, listening out for any small thing that Annie might say to further fuel the spark of something developing in Jude's mind.

'I still can't believe he went to such lengths to try and kill me.' Annie blew out a long sigh. 'It's bad enough that he deliberately tainted the coffee machine, but to steal my EpiPen?'

Was she acting? It was hard to tell.

'And then to put a peanut directly into my hot chocolate. It was all just so calculated.' She dropped her head into her hands. 'I loved him so much. I was even willing to forgive his indiscretions.'

Annie knew about the coffee pods and the missing EpiPen.

She may even have been told that both had been found in Simon's caravan. But Jude was almost certain that the idea someone had dropped a chocolate-covered peanut directly into Annie's drink had not been widely circulated. It was something that could never be proven and so it was a useless piece of supposition.

What did this mean? Had Annie deliberately given herself an anaphylactic reaction live on television and then set it up as a deliberate attack on her life? It would have been a very risky game to play. She'd have had to rely on the fact that enough people knew where the back-up EpiPen was kept. Gabe had known, Jude could remember him running to fetch it, and it had been Dean who'd brought it out, which meant he'd also known.

It was a ridiculous idea though, surely. Annie had been strangled with a set of Christmas lights. Was it even possible she'd have been able to do this to herself?

And why? What would she stand to gain? Perhaps it had something to do with the documentary she was collating information for. Attempted murder live on air was pretty sensational and would make a fabulous PR angle. Granny Margot had suggested that Dean had been laying the foundations for an extraordinary true-crime programme; perhaps there was a chance Annie had been reaching for the same goal.

She was still planning on making the documentary, only now she had the extra weight of three attempts on her life supposedly made by her husband. This way, she got all the fame, adulation, public sympathy and money whilst her philandering husband lost his freedom and his reputation.

'I'm slightly anxious that the director will want to take what happened and use it in the documentary. What do you think?'

Annie was looking at her, wide-eyed with innocence, but Jude felt she could see a steely resolution behind the facade. *Had it always been there?* she wondered.

'You must do whatever feels right for you,' said Jude.

Here was a woman who had apparently been on the receiving end of a string of murder attempts, dished out by the husband she professed she still loved. She had discovered the body of a man she'd been working closely with, and the person who had strangled him had turned the weapon on her. Most people would surely crumple in these circumstances, unsure what to do next or how to carry on with the general day to day of living.

Yet there Annie Bird was, discussing the details of her next television project and how much of her ordeal she should share with a global audience.

Jude knew that Annie could have brought about her own anaphylaxis, she could also easily have been the one to fit the exhaust pipe into the trailer where she knew Mary was asleep. If Simon had been given a pair of yellow ski gloves with magenta fur lining as a marketing ploy then it stood to reason the company would have sent a pair for Annie too.

Annie could also have strangled Gabe, perhaps because he threatened her plan somehow. The strength and skills she'd gained from regular self-defence lessons would have given her the means and her alibi had been perfect. By making herself into a victim, she had removed any thoughts that she was in fact the murderer.

But she must've been desperate to have wrapped a string of lights around her own neck and pulled them tight enough to leave the deep red marks they had. Jude thought about the demonstration Binnie had given in the farm kitchen using a dog lead. The pattern of marks showed that there had been degree of forward motion in the pull of the lights. Was that because the person tightening them had not come from behind as suggested, but was actually using them on herself?

It would explain why Robyn hadn't seen Annie when she claimed she'd gone to the chillout trailer to fetch her glasses. Jude had assumed it was Robyn who'd lied. Once again, playing the victim would have meant Annie was the one who would be believed, something that Robyn would have been all too aware of when she'd asked Holly to back her up with a fib of her own.

'It's all been so difficult.' Annie gave another deep sigh and her eyes filled with tears. 'I suppose I just want the world to hear things from my point of view. To give a clear message that the industry I love is corrupt and flawed but that some of us are willing to put their lives on the line to expose the rot.'

Jude could see then why Annie had invited her round to the B&B. It wasn't so she could thank her and say goodbye. It was because she loved an audience. That was why she'd gathered the *Countryside Live* crew together as well. Annie needed the limelight and this documentary that would highlight her as both victim and saviour would give her exactly what she craved.

Jude needed to get out of there. She needed to talk to Binnie and Sami and tell them everything she now suspected.

'I think you're doing an incredible thing,' said Jude. 'It's so brave of you.'

Annie leant forward and clasped Jude's hands. 'Thank you, Jude. It's going to be a long and difficult project but I know it's the right thing to do.'

'I'll definitely be watching out for it to air.' Jude stood up. 'I'd better get going now though, there's a lot to do back at the farm before Christmas.'

'Of course.' Annie stood too. 'And you've got the wedding to get ready for as well, haven't you?'

'Just a couple of weeks to go now.'

Annie walked to Jude and gave her a hug. 'Thank you again for everything, Jude. I hope you have a happy Christmas with your family and that the wedding goes wonderfully.'

'Thank you,' said Jude, pulling away from Annie.

As she went to leave, an idea came to her that might help to prove her theory.

'Oh, before I go, I hope you don't mind me asking but Simon had a pair of gloves that he said were the warmest things but also thin enough not to be cumbersome. It's exactly what I need for when I'm out in the fields trying to cut the twine from haybales and things like that. I wondered if you'd been sent a pair as well and knew the make?'

A brief look of confusion crossed Annie's face before she went over to a chest of drawers and opened it. 'I think these are the ones you're talking about.' She pulled out a pair of gloves exactly the same as the ones Jude had seen Simon wearing. 'We both got sent a pair from some ski-gear company in the hope we'd endorse them. Perk of the job.'

'Brilliant!' Jude said. 'Those are the ones. Do you mind if I have a look?'

Annie handed them over with their palms together and Jude pulled them apart. They both saw the sooty black mark on one of the thumbs at the same time which was all Jude needed to know that this was the pair that had been used to handle the exhaust pipe of the petrol generator that had killed Mary Taper.

Jude felt her features freeze for a second before arranging them back into friendly order.

'That's great,' she said. 'Thank you, I'll see if I can get Lucy to get me a pair for Christmas.'

Jude moved towards the door but Annie stepped into her path to block the exit.

'I'd love a bit more of a chat, before you go,' she said.

'I really do need to get home,' said Jude, her heart hammering.

'Maybe I'm over sensitive at the moment but it feels like there's something more to my gloves than just you wanting to keep your hands warm.'

'No.' Jude knew she was giving herself away but was completely unsure of how to play it any differently. 'I just need some new gloves and I knew Simon had the perfect pair.'

Annie looked at her quizzically, the same way one of Jude's collies might look at her in the field if it was trying to work out what her next move might be.

'I told the police I didn't need their protection now that Simon's been named as my would-be killer. You were the one who led them to him, Jude. Are you having any doubts now?'

Jude felt a part of her wither under Annie's stare, certain that she could tell exactly what Jude was thinking and trying desperately to hide it.

'There's too much evidence against him.' Jude needed Annie to believe that she had no reason to have changed her mind. 'And he fled the scene, stealing a pickup in the process. I'm sorry, Annie, I wish I could tell you otherwise but there seems no doubt as to his guilt.'

Annie stared at her again, trying to read her face for the truth.

'I'd offer to give you those gloves, you know,' Annie said. 'Only they seem to have been stained by something.'

'Have they?' Jude said.

This was a mistake. She had made a knee-jerk comment in an attempt to gloss over what could well be a vital clue in linking the gloves to the exhaust pipe. Only as soon as she'd said it, she realised that what she'd actually done was highlight her suspicion of the sooty mark. It had been obvious and they both knew she'd seen it so why pretend she hadn't? Unless she knew what it represented.

'You have put me in a bit of a tricky situation,' said Annie. She went to her coat which was hanging from a hook on the back of the door and dug in the pocket, not once taking her eyes off Jude. When she pulled her hand out, Jude could see that it contained what looked like a chunky toy pistol.

'Don't worry,' said Annie. 'It's just a Taser. Simon bought it after the psycho fan attacked me. It's illegal, sadly, but it does make me feel safer. I told him I couldn't use it and he thought I'd handed it in to the police anonymously, but I'm not that stupid.'

'Very sensible,' said Jude. Her mind was whirring, thinking how she could get herself out of this scrape. The Taser wouldn't kill her, but she didn't fancy finding out just how incapacitating it would be if Annie pulled the trigger.

'I don't want to use it, Jude. But I need a bit of time to think.'

'Think about what?' Jude asked, still trying desperately to retain the act of innocence.

'About what to do with you.' Her eyes had lost all their vulnerability, a wildness taking over that Jude had not seen in them before. 'You know the truth. I know you do. I mean, who goes to see someone who's just discovered her husband has tried to kill her three times and asks about gloves?'

Jude could have kicked herself. She'd pushed too far, showing her hand instead of leaving when she had the chance and letting the police deal with it.

'I really did just want a new pair of gloves,' she said.

'Perhaps I might have believed that if I hadn't seen your reaction when you saw the mark from the exhaust pipe. You knew exactly what you were looking at. And now you've put me in an extremely tricky position.'

She tapped the side of the yellow and black plastic gun

against the palm of her hand. 'Think, think, think.' Every word punched out like a fist in the air made Annie seem a little more unhinged, a little more dangerous.

'It must have been so difficult for you,' Jude ventured. 'Living with such a toxic work atmosphere. I can see why this documentary is so important to you.'

'It was Dean and Robyn who started this whole thing.' Annie had taken the bait. Jude needed to keep her talking until someone came to see what was going on. If she was talking then she wasn't plotting a way of making sure Jude kept her mouth shut. Going by her track record, Jude didn't think anything was off limits and with a Taser in her hand, Annie was clearly the one in charge.

'I can't believe how much those two got away with over the years,' said Jude. 'Hopefully your evidence will be enough to give them what they deserve.'

'Oh, I'll make sure of it. I want as many people to see my programme as possible. I want them all to see how badly I've been used. They'll see what Simon North was capable of and they'll admire Annie Bird for carrying on regardless.' She had moved so smoothly from Robyn and Dean on to Simon that the switch was seamless. 'He was going to leave me for Mary. Simon, who always said he never wanted children with me, suddenly decided that a family with her was worth throwing away everything we had worked for.' She spat the words out as though they tasted every bit as bitter as they sounded.

Jude said nothing but waited for her to carry on.

'He didn't have the guts to tell me himself, of course. It was poor, sweet, stupid Gabe who heard them talking together. He thought that if he told me what my husband was planning then it would make me leave Simon and start a relationship with Gabe instead.'

Annie let out a single loud guffaw.

'He really thought the only reason I wasn't with him was because of Simon. Do you know when Simon was planning on telling me he was leaving me for her?'

Annie looked at Jude as though she was personally to blame for Simon's choices. Jude shook her head.

'After the last show of the series,' Annie continued. 'Christmas Eve. Jesus, of all the shitty things to do to someone who's been at your side for almost twenty years. I couldn't use that in the documentary as that would be my legacy, the wife who was cast aside and bitter.'

'Whereas if you used a peanut in your hot chocolate to give yourself a live allergic reaction...' Jude chanced.

'Oh, so you did figure that out then. I knew I'd made a mistake when I mentioned it to you earlier. Yes, I thought he'd see sense and come back to me. I really wanted him to be a part of the next chapter away from *Countryside* fecking *Live* with me.'

'Only he didn't want that, did he?'

'No. It turns out he didn't.'

'So you staged a second attempt on your life, which meant not only was your role as victim strengthened but you also got Mary out of the way. You became the heroine of your own story.'

Annie's arms stiffened visibly as she prodded the Taser in Jude's direction. 'When did you realise? Was it the gloves?'

Jude didn't answer. 'Annie, you won't be able to get away with this.'

'I will!' Annie screeched. 'I almost have. If a pair of gloves is all you've got on me then I can get rid of those. I just need to think of what to do with you.'

'I'm on your side.' Jude tried to pacify her and keep her talking. Surely someone would arrive soon and they'd be able to overpower her together. 'I know how badly you've been treated. You just did what you had to do.'

Annie's fingers tapped against the Taser again. 'Gabe worked out what I'd done too. He said he wouldn't tell anyone but I didn't believe him so don't think I'll be taken in by your tactics, Jude.'

Jude knew exactly what Annie was capable of when she was pushed into a corner. Gabe must have told her what he knew the night she'd killed him. The note in the fairy lights box was a token of love. She felt sure that he'd been sincere if he'd sworn to Annie that he'd keep her secret, but she'd killed him anyway. Jude had to admit that her dedication to the cover-up had been second to none. Burning the files and getting rid of her mobile phone to make it look as though the killer's motive had been to expunge all traces of their investigation. Half strangling herself to take away any suspicion that she was involved. She must have already planted the coffee pods and EpiPen by then, hoping to frame Simon for the first crime, and assumed that this would then make him the key suspect for Holly's murder as well.

How fortunate that the gloves she'd used that night had shed a few fibres that would match the pair Simon also owned. Jude had assumed that Annie hadn't known about the magenta fluff being left on the tape residue but perhaps she'd found out about it after all. She and Gabe certainly had their ways of getting important information.

'I get it,' said Jude. 'I really do, but from here, surely your only way out is to work with me.'

'Do not be mistaken in thinking I'm stupid.' Annie's voice had dropped dangerously low and Jude watched as her finger played with the trigger of the Taser gun. 'In case you haven't already figured it out, I have a way of turning opportunities to my advantage. I plant seeds, I grow new versions of events and I make people believe them. I take what's gifted to me and I find a way to use it. Simon's watch from that little whore, for example. I felt it snag my hair when he tried to comfort me after Gabe was killed. He thought I didn't know about the nauseating message on the inside but I did. Fate gave me the chance to use it against him and I didn't waste it. A great addition to the things I'd already planted in his caravan. I knew Simon would never find those himself because he is a creature of habit and always chooses the same seat. I did think someone else would get there sooner, but no matter.' She lifted one hand to tap her temple. 'You see, Jude? I'm clever. I've been ahead of the game all the way so far. I just need to work out how to stay ahead now.'

'I've never doubted your cleverness. I knew it was all you from the moment I found a bag of chocolate peanuts in the chillout trailer. It made me wonder, why chocolate-coated peanuts, why not just regular ones?' Jude had to feed her ego, keep her mind away from plotting. 'Then I realised. They had to be covered in chocolate to keep the peanut away from direct skin contact. You needed to wait until the right time, then you could drop one in your drink, let the heat of the cocoa melt the chocolate and release the peanut oil.' Jude clasped her hands together and tried to look as though she really admired Annie's strategy which was horrific and yet undoubtedly very clever. 'That's why the packet had been resealed so carefully, it was to stop any of them escaping when you weren't expecting it. You've lived with your allergy a long time so you know what level of contact you can cope with before you're in danger. It was still risky but you thought it was worth it. Especially as you made sure everyone knew where your second EpiPen was kept.'

Annie cocked her head and stared harder at Jude.

'I don't believe you knew back then.'

'Maybe not completely, but I had my hunches. I admire you, Annie.'

Annie raised an eyebrow. 'That, I definitely don't believe.'

A loud knock at the door triggered two things. Jude opened her mouth to shout for help from whoever was on the other side, but before she could utter a single word, she felt her entire body ignite with the bites from a thousand fire ants. She fell to the ground, her brain unable to pick apart what was happening to her as she convulsed on the floor.

She was aware of an angry voice filling the room but she was powerless to do anything to alert them of her predicament.

'Annie, I know you're in there,' Robyn shouted. 'I've got something I think you'll want to discuss. A way we can both win from all of this shite. Annie?'

Through watering eyes, Jude could make out the shape of the door as it burst open, knocking into an unsuspecting Annie who clearly hadn't bothered to lock it. There was instant relief as the Taser fell from her hands and the connection was severed.

Jude was wobbly but unhurt as she shook herself into life and launched herself at the nation's favourite television presenter, catching her off guard and pushing her to the floor.

'What the hell?' Robyn was clearly taken aback.

'She's the killer,' Jude yelled as she grappled with Annie. 'Help me!'

Robyn didn't need any further coaxing. She ran forward and sat heavily on Annie's thrashing legs whilst Jude pinned her arms back behind her.

'No,' shouted Annie as she fought to free herself. 'No, this is not how it ends. I will not let it. Not after everything I've done.'

Jude used all her power to stop Annie from pulling her arms free. All the years of wrestling ewes during lambing and pinning them against the wall or floor of the shed had paid off and she was still holding tight when two police officers arrived on the scene.

To her utter dismay, when they rushed forwards, Jude realised they didn't have Annie Bird in their sights. One of the officers grabbed hold of Robyn and heaved her off whilst the other came for Jude.

Annie scrambled to her feet. 'Oh, thank goodness you arrived,' she said. 'They just went for me.'

Jude wriggled against the man holding her, realising that the message she'd sent to Binnie and Sami was that Annie could be in danger. A message that had clearly been passed on to the attending officers who had put two and two together on arrival at the scene and assumed Annie was the one in trouble.

'Let go,' Jude shouted as Annie manoeuvred herself towards the door. 'You've got it wrong. She's the killer.'

'Don't let her escape, you idiots.' Robyn was fighting just as hard as Jude was to be released.

The two police officers looked at each other in confusion as Annie took her opportunity and tore out of the door, slamming it shut behind her. Jude heard the turn of a key and realised that Annie had managed to deftly swipe it from the lock on the way out.

The officer closest to the door let Jude go and tested the handle. 'Bugger it.'

'You let her get away.' Robyn was furious as she shook off the other officer.

Jude's temporary captor spoke into the crackling walkie-talkie attached to the chest section of his vest.

'Borthwick and I have been locked in Annie Bird's room with two women who claim Annie is the killer.'

'Is one of them Jude Gray?' Sami's voice came through the airwaves.

The officers looked at Robyn and Jude.

'Yes! Sami, it's me.' Jude ran to the window and looked out.

'Annie killed Gabe and Mary. Long story but she's now on the run. I can see her out of the window of Four Trees, heading down the road in the direction of the pub.'

'Gotcha,' said Sami. 'We're almost with you. Sit tight.'

'There's not much else we can do.' Jude stared pointedly at the two officers, although the sheepish looks on their faces told her they didn't need any further reasons to feel daft.

Jude watched helplessly as Annie ran on past the pub. In a moment, she'd turn the corner and Jude would lose sight of her. But then she stopped in her tracks and turned to run back the way she'd just come. To begin with, Jude couldn't understand what she was doing but then she heard the distant sound of approaching sirens and Jude realised she was looking for a better escape route. As she neared the pub again, directly opposite the B&B, Marco came out of the house next door with Spud Simons. Spud was a casual labourer on the farm and built like a tank.

'Stop her,' Jude shouted at the pair of them.

Marco and Spud looked up.

'Jude?' Marco called.

'She's the killer,' Jude shouted back.

Annie had already run past but Marco and Spud were fast. They were on her within a couple of seconds, grabbing one arm each and holding tight until the unmarked police car arrived and screeched to a halt on the gravel of the pub's car park. Sami jumped out with a pair of handcuffs ready to lock into place.

Jude stared down at Annie, who stared right back at her.

'You win,' Annie shouted. 'Congratulations, Jude Gray. You beat me.'

Jude shook her head sadly. 'It was never a game,' she whispered.

24

The final production trailer leaving Malvern Farm had been a real relief for Jude. With Christmas just over a week away and the wedding a few days after that, it was time to get on with the celebrations.

Sebbie's starring role as a rugby shorts-wearing snowman in the school play had been a triumph and he was now shattered and ready for the term to end.

Presents that had arrived were wrapped and squirrelled away for the big day, the turkey had been ordered and the cards sent. Temporary flooring had been laid in the lambing shed for Lucy and Noah's big day and gas-fuelled patio heaters were set up ready with full canisters.

The day Simon North woke from his coma to find out his wife had been arrested for two murders and was currently sitting in prison awaiting trial, Binnie, Jude and Sami decided to go for a drink at The Lamb.

'Game of dominoes?' Sami asked as they settled around a table by the fire.

'Why not?' Jude took a sip of her mulled wine.

Sami went over to the games table to fetch the wooden dominoes box.

'Any news on Annie's trial date?' Jude asked.

'Not yet,' said Binnie. 'Not that it'll make much difference to her. She won't be coming out of prison any time soon.'

Sami returned and tipped the dominoes out onto the table. They all set about flipping them over and shuffling them around before each person chose their starting seven.

'Room for two more?'

Jude looked up to see Clara and Marco heading their way with Rex on his lead.

'Of course,' said Binnie. 'Grab another chair.'

'You sit there by Jude and I'll take a stool so I can have Rex in this corner,' said Clara.

Whilst she went to the other side of the bar area to fetch a stool to sit on, Marco did as he was told and sat down on the bench next to Jude. His knee bumped hers and for a moment she wanted to push against it and savour the connection. Then sense took over and she pulled away.

'Shuffle again,' Jude said. 'If we've got five playing then we should only take five pieces each.'

Clara came back and positioned her stool at the head of the table. 'Deal me in,' she said.

Jude tried to allow herself to relax in Marco and Clara's company but feeling his warmth so close to her made it impossible to concentrate. She'd tried her hardest to embrace the friendship that was on offer from both of them. It had worked when she was with one of them at a time but not when they were bunched up together like this.

She rested her hand on the table, gripping her mulled wine glass. When Marco played his next piece, his fingers brushed against her, triggering every nerve ending under the surface of her skin. She jerked her hand away and a little of the sticky wine slopped over the side of the glass.

'Oh, Jude, I'm so sorry.' He took a clean blue-spotted handkerchief from his pocket and dabbed her hand with it.

Jude was powerless to do anything other than stare at his face. The features she loved so much still despite all her efforts not to let that happen.

'Did it scald you?' Marco asked, his eyes finding hers.

'No,' she said.

'Are you sure?' he asked and Jude noted the odd huskiness of his voice as she detected his pupils dilate just a fraction.

'It's fine.' She coughed to break the spell and pulled her hand away.

'Your turn, I think, Clara,' said Binnie.

Jude turned her attention to her friend at the end of the table. Clara was watching her with interest and Jude felt herself blush.

She went to bed that night and for the first time in the longest time, Jude Gray wept. Quietly and with no great histrionics, she cried for the husband who had died so young, for the second chance of love that she'd lost, for the home that would no doubt be emptied soon once the newlyweds found a place of their own to move into. She allowed herself the rare indulgence of self-pity, imagining a world where she lived alone and grew old in the company of her dogs.

The next morning, she awoke early, drank a large mug of coffee and waited for the day to begin so she could walk her fields and tend to her animals as the sun rose.

25

Christmas Day itself was perfect in many ways. It started early with an over-excited Sebbie diving into the treats and surprises in his stocking. Frank and Jude did the field rounds whilst Lucy and Noah put together an enormous breakfast.

Presents were opened, guests arrived, games played and a late lunch was eaten until everyone's belts and buttons had to be loosened.

When the last person left and it was just the four residents of Malvern Farmhouse remaining, Noah took Sebbie upstairs for his bath, leaving Jude and Lucy to put their feet up in front of the log burner.

They'd poured themselves tots of warming Amaretto and Jude felt her body relax as she sank into the saggy old sofa.

'How are you feeling?' she asked.

'Happy.' Lucy rested her head on her sister's shoulder. 'You?'

'The same.' Jude turned to kiss Lucy's forehead. 'Only three sleeps to go until you become Mrs Harrow.'

'I know, and yet look how remarkably relaxed I am about it

all.' Lucy held her hand out flat in front of her to show how steady it was.

'That's because you know everything will be absolutely perfect.'

'I love you, Jude.' Lucy snuggled further into her sister's embrace.

'I love you too, Lou-Lou.'

* * *

The day of the wedding arrived clear and crisp. Jude looked out of the kitchen window and sighed deeply as she watched the early colours of the dawning sky shift and change. The apricot and candy-floss pastels gave way to lilac and then icy blue as she went about her daily jobs, making sure the animals were fed and watered.

As she came back into the yard, she heard music from the lambing shed and went over to see what was going on. Noah and Lucy were in there with a man who had come nice and early to set up his music system and run some sound checks. The lambing shed looked beautiful, with chairs set out ready to accommodate the guests who would be arriving at three for the ceremony.

Folded onto each chair was a cosy hand-knitted blanket, courtesy of Granny Margot's stitch and bitch club at the care home. Needles had been clacking for months and copious balls of chunky yarn had been turned into squares for the guests to cover their knees or drape around their shoulders whilst they sat.

The swags of holly, ivy and fir that Lucy and Jude had hung from the walls of the shed had been accompanied by flower arrangements that had been delivered the day before. In the second shed, tables had been arranged for the wedding supper, with the foraged centrepieces looking lovely on the white linen cloths.

Everything was in place and Jude's prediction of perfection looked as though it had been spot on.

***

As the day progressed, Noah was banished to the pink cottage with his father to get ready. He took Sebbie with him, gifting Lucy and Jude some time to prepare themselves in peace.

The hairdresser that Lucy had booked called a couple of hours before he was supposed to arrive to say he'd fallen on a patch of ice and was currently sitting in his partner's car on his way to the accident and emergency department in Worcester with a suspected broken wrist.

Jude braced herself for the panicked fallout when Lucy put the phone down but miraculously it didn't come. Lucy merely closed her eyes for a few seconds and then turned to her sister.

'One less person to disturb us,' she said.

'Really?' Jude said incredulously. 'You don't want me to see if I can find someone else?'

Lucy shook her head. 'No,' she said. 'You do it for me.'

'Me?' Jude felt sick at the thought. 'I don't know anything about hair.'

'Yes, you do,' said Lucy. 'When we were little, you always did my hair for me.'

'You want French plaits? Because that's about my limit.'

Lucy laughed. 'I don't think they'd go with my veil. No, I just want you to brush my hair for me like you used to. We can use the straighteners to make it shiny and I've got the clip I bought so just push it in one side like this.' She used her hand to sweep the hair off her face.

'Beautiful,' said Jude. She looked at her sister and felt her heart grow. 'I'm incredibly proud of you, Lou-Lou. And in case I haven't told you enough, I'm so grateful you chose to come and live here. I know things will change now, they're bound to, and that's absolutely the way it should be. But I'll always cherish the years we had in this house together.'

Lucy hugged her tight and they stayed like that for a short while before they pulled away to find the first tissues of the day.

* * *

'Ready?' Jude asked.

She was standing with Lucy and Sebbie in the farmhouse kitchen.

Lucy looked absolutely stunning in the vintage fifties wedding dress she'd found online. It was full skirted and nipped in at the waist, decorated with lace and pearls. Her understated make-up matched the simple hairstyle Jude had helped her create and a simple veil hung down her back.

Sebbie had been scrubbed until he shone and was dressed in a clean pair of trousers and a shirt he'd chosen himself, made from a fabric covered in printed dinosaurs. Jude could see the ring box he was gripping tightly, hugely proud of himself for being tasked with such an important job.

Jude herself was in a full-length velvet dress of sage green with a thick navy-blue shawl to cover her shoulders and arms. She passed a matching one to Lucy, only hers was ivory in colour.

Lucy picked up the two bouquets from the kitchen counter and passed the smaller one to Jude.

She bent to pat the dogs who had congregated around them to wish her well and then she stood up and took a deep breath.

'Ready,' she said.

The lambing shed was full of smiling faces, which all turned to the door as an enormously talented string duet began to play Vivaldi's 'Winter', and Lucy, Jude and Sebbie walked in.

The fast, rousing music and the sheer beauty of her usually mucky but functional shed made every hair on Jude's arms stand to attention. The last time it had looked like this had been for her own wedding and for a moment, as she walked her sister down the aisle to where Noah was waiting with a look of pure happiness on his face, it felt as though Adam was with her.

Jude gave Lucy one small kiss and took her bouquet from her. Then she ushered Sebbie into the waiting chair on the front row and sat herself down next to Granny Margot. Gerwain was sitting at the end of the row with his iPad which was set up with a Zoom call to stream the ceremony onto the big screen back at the care home. The residents and staff had given Lucy the most wonderful party the week before. Ideas of karaoke had been ditched and a professional DJ hired instead for those who wanted to dance. Granny Margot had reported that some of the women had got a little over-excited when a rumour was started that a stripper was going to be there. It didn't take much imagination to work out who had been behind that particular joke.

The love and effort that had been poured into the party had meant an awful lot to Lucy, who looked straight into the iPad and blew a kiss to those watching from Perrins House.

'You both look beautiful.' Granny Margot squeezed Jude's hand and she could see that she was already dabbing her eyes with the edge of a white cotton hanky.

* * *

After the service, the guests were invited to mingle whilst a group of teenagers from the village who'd been hired to see to the smooth running of the wedding moved all the chairs into the second part of the shed where the supper tables were waiting.

A steady stream of people came over to talk to Jude as she stood with a glass of champagne in her hand. Frank, Binnie and Sami were there of course, Mrs James from the post office, Ted and Barbara from The Lamb, Paddy from Four Trees, Mike and Val Trout who lived next door. Friends from the village, some from Lucy's previous life in the Thames Valley and plenty from the farming community.

The notable absence was Jude and Lucy's father, who had decided not to come and who, in truth, wasn't missed at all.

'How are you feeling?' Jude asked when Binnie came over. 'Taking things a little easier now that Annie's behind bars?'

'I'm being sensible. Sami is making sure of it, which I have to say is starting to get a little irritating.'

Jude chuckled. Both her detective friends were such strong characters and she could imagine the inevitable clashes as one tried to look after the other.

'I'm so glad we got to the bottom of everything before Christmas,' said Jude. 'Have you heard anything more about Simon?'

'Not since he was sent home from hospital. He's got two options now, I suppose. He can either slink off and stay as far away from the limelight as possible, waiting for all of this to die down.'

'Yes,' Jude agreed, 'or he can do what Annie was planning and milk it loudly and publicly for all it's worth.'

She couldn't say for sure but Jude had the sneaking suspicion that, unlike his wife, he'd opt for a quiet life from now on.

Binnie went off to sit for a while with Granny Margot and Jude did the dutiful mingling that she felt was expected of her. As she chatted to the guests, she kept catching sight of Marco and Clara, sometimes together and sometimes talking to different people. She hadn't seen either of them since the domino game at The Lamb and she knew that she'd have to talk to them at some point. She was glad though that Frank's sharp shepherd's whistle cut through the chatter to call everyone into the dining area.

Jude was positioned between Noah and Frank on a table they shared with Lucy, Granny Margot, Gerwain, Binnie and Sami. Sebbie was happy to be on the children's table with some of his friends from school whose parents had also been invited.

Lucy had asked Jude to give a speech and she was glad to get that out of the way before the food was served. She kept it short, added a few jokes and sat down afterwards with a sense that she could now relax and enjoy the rest of the day.

The food was delicious, the wine free flowing, and everything went without a hitch.

Whilst they were eating, the part of the shed that had been used for the ceremony was being prepared for the evening. By the time the cake had been cut, the coffee and tea cups cleared away and the formalities all taken care of, the sun had well and truly gone to bed for the night. The darkness outside made the disco ball and the colourful lighting above the dance floor even more exciting and Jude felt a thrill as she stepped inside to watch Lucy and Noah take to the floor for their first dance.

Gradually the guests began to join them and the party zinged with the energy of people having a good time.

Jude spun Sebbie around to several songs before her feet began to ache and she took herself to the side to kick her shoes off under a chair.

For the first time that day, she suddenly found herself in the company of Clara.

'Hi, Jude. What a gorgeous wedding that was, Lucy looks so happy.'

'She really does,' Jude agreed. 'It's good to see you. How was your Christmas?'

'I went back to my parents' for a couple of nights,' said Clara. 'My brother was there with his wife and baby so it was a really lovely family one.'

Jude tried not to think of Marco being there, fitting in with someone else's family and getting to know his potential in-laws.

'It sounds perfect,' she said.

'It wasn't what I planned but it was exactly what I needed in the end.'

'Oh?'

'I don't know if you heard but Marco and I broke up on Christmas Eve.'

Jude felt her heart leap into her throat as though it was trying to escape through her open mouth.

'No,' she managed to stutter. 'No, I hadn't. I'm sorry to hear that.'

'Thanks, but you shouldn't be. It was never really destined to last. We decided we were far more suited as friends.' Clara smiled and wrinkled her nose a little. 'I think it had been that way from the start, really. Certainly with Marco anyway, but I always knew it too, deep down.'

'You did?'

'Jude, I'm not blind. I could tell from the very beginning that I was only Marco's second choice. Perhaps I thought things might change, given a bit of time. But when I saw you together at the pub the other night I knew it was time to admit defeat.'

Jude's mouth had gone dry, hardly daring to believe what Clara was saying and feeling horrendously guilty at the same time that she clearly hadn't done a better job of masking her feelings for Marco.

'Clara, I'm so sorry,' she said. 'I really never meant to—'

'Don't.' Clara shook her head and smiled again. 'You've done nothing wrong. I knew he loved you when I asked him out. To be clear, I didn't think you loved him back. But it's obvious now that you do and I don't want to be the spare wheel in anybody's story. I deserve more than that.'

'You really do,' said Jude.

'My turn will come, I'm sure of it, but right now it's yours.'

Clara nodded over Jude's shoulder and she turned to see Marco watching them from across the lambing shed. His face was dancing with the pulsing colours of the disco lights and even from a distance Jude could see that Clara was right. All the feelings she'd tried to deny, ignore and squash to protect herself flooded through her as the shackles were thrown to one side.

'Thank you,' she said to Clara without taking her eyes off Marco.

Then she walked towards the man she'd known she belonged with ever since he'd turned up on Malvern Farm to ask if he could stay in one of her shepherd's huts more than two years ago.

'Hello,' he said.

Jude stared into his eyes for a moment, wanting to make sure that Clara hadn't been mistaken. What she saw there told her everything and she pulled him to her, closed her eyes and kissed him with all the intensity that waiting so long had built.

When the kiss was over, their arms were still wrapped around each other and Jude noticed that the bouncy disco music had been replaced by a slower tune designed for couples.

'Shall we dance?' Marco asked.

Jude rested her cheek against his and they started to sway gently to the rhythm. Noah and Lucy were dancing together close by and the two sisters caught each other's eyes and shared a moment of pure happiness for themselves and for each other. Jude noticed Granny Margot sitting on one of the chairs nearest the dance floor with an exhausted Sebbie on her knee, not quite asleep but snuggled into her generous arms.

Binnie and Sami were sitting close by, heads together, talking earnestly about something and laughing over the remains of a bottle of Westons perry.

'Penny for your thoughts?' Marco whispered into her ear.

Jude felt her heart swell as she knew that what she had was worth infinitely more than a penny. She squeezed Marco a little tighter. 'I was wondering about the ewes up in the top field and when we need to get them moved over to the stubble turnips.'

Marco pulled away and looked straight into her eyes. 'Please tell me you weren't.'

'Of course I wasn't.' Jude laughed. 'Although I am now!'

'I'm always going to have to share you with the farm, aren't I?'

'We come as a package,' said Jude. 'But if you think you can handle that then I would love to give us a try.'

Marco's smile crinkled the corners of his eyes and made dimples pop where his mouth met his cheeks. 'I would very much love that too.'

As they kissed again, Jude's mind cleared itself of the farm, her animals and the early start she couldn't avoid the next morning. And for a glorious moment, the only thing that was important in the world was that she was with Marco and that it felt wonderfully and completely right.

* * *

MORE FROM KATE WELLS

Another book from Kate Wells, *Killer at the County Show*, is available to order now here:
https://mybook.to/KillerCountyBackAd

ACKNOWLEDGEMENTS

As always, my ongoing and enormous thanks to the whole Malvern Farm team.

To Emily, Amanda and everyone at Boldwood Books for making the series everything it is.

Christmas is my favourite time of the year and I have felt very blessed to be able to bring it to Malvern Farm. A Christmas special was a real dream for me and here it is!

To my dear friend, Fiona Barker, who first gave me the idea of sending a film crew to Malvern Farm. Thank you, Fi – I'm truly lucky to have you.

For me, Christmas isn't Christmas without music and in particular the annual carol service. I have had the utter pleasure of being a part of the choir of St Andrew's Church in Caversham for the past seven years. Last year was my very last carol service with this incredible group of singers, as my family and I are moving back to Malvern.

So, this book is for you. For Frances, who leads us so patiently (and who has been such a support of this series). And for Rosie, Alison, Lynda, Shelley, Nick, Robin, Joanna and Roy, who have shared the choir stalls with me throughout the years. Also for Paul, whose incredible talent on the organ brings us all to life in a wonderful way.

I will miss you all and want to thank you for the music, the joy and the friendship.

To my treasured three, Will, Lily and Mima. We are about to

start the next chapter of our own story and it comes with huge excitement but also lots of uncertainties and anxieties as we up sticks and you leave behind the worlds you've built. Thank you for making it all so easy with your endless positivity and love. Always stronger together and I'm glad that I'm together with you.

Facebook: @KateWells/Poels
Instagram: @KatePoelsWrites

ABOUT THE AUTHOR

Kate Wells is the author of a number of well-reviewed books for children, and is now writing cosy crime set in the Malvern hills, inspired by the farm where she grew up.

Sign up to Kate Wells' mailing list for news, competitions and updates on future books.

Visit Kate's website: www.katepoels.co.uk

Follow Kate on social media:

ALSO BY KATE WELLS

Murder on the Farm

Stranger in the Village

A Body by the Henhouse

Death in the Hills

Killer at the County Show

A Very Merry Murder

POISON & pens

POISON & PENS IS THE HOME OF COZY MYSTERIES SO POUR YOURSELF A CUP OF TEA & GET SLEUTHING!

DISCOVER PAGE-TURNING NOVELS FROM YOUR FAVOURITE AUTHORS & MEET NEW FRIENDS

JOIN OUR FACEBOOK GROUP

BIT.LYPOISONANDPENSFB

SIGN UP TO OUR NEWSLETTER

BIT.LY/POISONANDPENSNEWS

Boldwood

Boldwood Books is an award-winning fiction publishing company seeking out the best stories from around the world.

Find out more at www.boldwoodbooks.com

Join our reader community for brilliant books, competitions and offers!

Follow us
@BoldwoodBooks
@TheBoldBookClub

Sign up to our weekly deals newsletter

https://bit.ly/BoldwoodBNewsletter